220 DEAD—28 SURVIVORS

Lauren stared at the newspaper. Black headlines screamed at her: DEATH COUNT MOUNTS IN AIRPLANE CRASH. A cold sweat broke out all over her body as she kept reading . . . *list of those who died taken from the manifest . . . some unidentifiable . . . plane broken in half on impact . . . survivors taken to area hospital . . .*

She lay back on the pillow, stunned, barely able to comprehend the reality of her own good fortune.

Finally she picked up the paper again. As her eye traveled down the page, she was suddenly arrested by the sight of her own name.

She couldn't take her eyes from the shocking words: "Alexander Compton, international financier, mourns the death of his wife, Lauren Townsend Compton, who was killed Wednesday in the crash of Flight 333 en route to Chicago."

Lauren's hand was shaking as she put the newspaper down. She had Diane Roberts' purse . . . her identification. The world thought she was Diane Roberts.

She could now *be* Diane Roberts.

THE OTHER SIDE OF THE MIRROR

JUDITH MARSHALL

PINNACLE BOOKS
WINDSOR PUBLISHING CORP.

Special thanks to the personnel at the Ritz Carlton Hotel, Chicago; the William Findlay Fine Arts Galleries, Chicago; Estelle Shwiff, Florence Arts Gallery, Dallas; Jackie Parr; Glenna Rogers; Reverend Terrell Pearson; Jacque Boyd; Dr. Frank Cardenas, Jr., M.D.; Agent Peter Miller for placing this work; Editor Ann La Farge for believing in this book; and to Bill Scantlin and Dr. Jack Dworin, M.D. for their steadfast support.

PINNACLE BOOKS

are published by

Windsor Publishing Corp.
475 Park Avenue South
New York, NY 10016

Copyright © 1991 by Irene Dworin and Bea Scantlin

First printing: July, 1991

Printed in the United States of America

Chapter One

Lauren froze in terror as she stared at her apartment door. It stood slightly ajar. Alex had found her. He would kill her this time. Trembling, she propped her bag of groceries against the wall, ready to run or scream at the slightest sound. Every nerve in her body tensed as she stood in the hallway and listened for an endless time. Silence. The waiting was unbearable, but it was useless to run. He would only find her again. Better to face him now. Maybe she could stall him. Maybe he would listen, give her a divorce. At least she still had the tape.

Perspiration trickled between her breasts as she took a deep breath and pushed the door open wider. If Alex were there, she would face him. She had no alternative. Her eyes widened in disbelief at the sight that greeted her—not Alex, but utter chaos. Everything she owned had been slashed and mutilated or pulled out of drawers, tossed on the floor, and smashed to pieces. Someone had done Alex's dirty work for him. The apartment was filled with a deserted silence, yet there remained the faint smell of a spicy, familiar fragrance. Whose? She couldn't think, could barely breathe. A chill ran down her spine.

Her fear turned to red-hot fury. She rushed inside, running through the rooms, slamming at everything that hadn't already been smashed. "Damn you, Alex! You—you bastard!" Her clothes had been ripped from the closet and tossed about like rags, dishes emptied from kitchen cabinets, broken and shattered, contents of every drawer in the apartment dumped on the floor, all of it littering every square inch of the three small rooms.

Angry tears filled her green eyes and threatened to stream down her face as she glared at the sight and wondered how on earth she could escape the powerful arm that had reached across a whole continent to find her. She had fled from her Long Island home just over a month ago, arriving in Los Angeles, thinking he would never find her here. What a fool she had been!

"Hey, Lauren, I found this bag in the hall. Buying groceries for the neighbors these days?"

"No, I'm not. But excuse the mess. It's the maid's day off." Lauren felt relief at the sight of Trudy, her new neighbor. She watched her wade through the trash, looking for a clear spot to put the bag of groceries. Trudy lived in the same building only a few doors down and had moved in just three days ago. The two young women had met at the pool and immediately struck up a conversation. Pert and slender, with shoulder-length brown hair and a warm smile, Trudy was in her midthirties, several years older than Lauren. At last Lauren felt she had found someone who could help take the edge off her loneliness.

"My God, have you been robbed? I was headed home and noticed your groceries out in the hall and then saw your open door. Oh, you poor thing, you're shaking all over." Trudy bent to put her arm around Lauren, who was sitting on the floor, her dark hair spilling over her face. "What a rotten mess! This is

6

awful, but thank goodness you're not hurt."

"I've got to get away from here right now." Lauren picked up the broken pieces of a bowl and absently tried to fit them together. She felt totally undone. Everything in the apartment was in ruins, much like her life. She choked back a sob.

"Leave? You can't be serious. Things like this happen every day. We'll put it all back together and find out what's missing. Forget leaving, for God's sake . . . But have you called the police?"

These things might happen every day, Lauren thought, but not for the same reason. She couldn't tell Trudy about Alex or involve her by confiding in her at all. Yet she was bursting to scream Alex's name over and over again as she stood and began to pace the room, fighting back tears of anger and frustration.

"No, I can't call the police, and please don't ask me why." The local police would have a field day if she did call them. She could see the headlines now: *Notorious Underworld Boss Trashes Wife's Apartment in Search of Incriminating Tape.* Too long for a headline, she decided, feeling on the edge of hysteria. There would have to be an involved story, one that told of how Alexander Compton, a man twice her age, had dazzled a young, innocent girl, fresh out of college, with his money and his self-assurance. He had charmed her into thinking that he was right for her, and she had been greedy. She had been willing to marry for security because she feared being alone. And after five years of living with Alex Compton, she was still alone.

"Why can't you tell me? What's going on? What the hell are you doing with that broken clock? Put it down right now and try to relax."

Lauren dropped the clock. She had no idea she'd even had it in her hand. She knew she had to do some serious thinking, make plans, get moving, and she'd better do it fast, but she felt too numb. Maybe it was time to go to Senator Kingsley. She had called him soon after she left the estate in Oyster Bay. She knew that he headed the committee investigating her husband's alleged criminal enterprises, and now she realized all the allegations were true. She had had Alex's private library professionally bugged in hopes of finding proof of his affairs with other women and hopefully force him into agreeing to a divorce. What she had discovered was so shocking that if a tape were admissible in a court of law, Alex, along with a few of his international buddies, would spend a long time behind bars.

Senator Kingsley had tried to persuade her to bring the tape to him, had offered to send someone to pick it up. Lauren had assured him that she had no idea of the extent of Alex's involvements until she listened to the tape. He seemed to be the head of a worldwide syndicate that operated many legitimate businesses, but also those that dealt in stolen heavy-duty equipment, arms, railroad cars, even hijacking, loan sharking, and extortion. It was a huge empire. She had assured the senator of her cooperation in the event of a trial, but insisted that she could not part with the tape since it was the only leverage she had.

"My husband did all this." Lauren felt she had to give Trudy some reason for not reporting the mess. She went into the bedroom, with Trudy following right behind.

"Your husband! He must be a real s.o.b. You never mentioned being married."

"It's something I've been trying to get out of and would just as soon forget." Lauren finally found a suitcase and started picking up pieces of clothing, ready to toss anything wearable inside. She was flat on the floor, reaching under the bed for a missing black shoe. "Ah, there it is." As she tossed it into the suitcase, a heel caught on the torn lining. "Damn! What stupid fool would think I'd hide a tape in—" She bit her lip. She had said too much.

"Tape? He was looking for a tape?"

"Yes, but forget I said that. I don't want to involve you. These people play for keeps."

"Hey, you sound like you need a friend, and I'm not afraid. No one knows we're even acquainted. Really, I want to help. What's on the tape?"

"The point is, he's not even sure I have a tape. Right now, all he knows is that someone bugged his library, and if he were sure I did it, I'd be dead."

"You've got to be kidding."

"No, he plays rough. I've had samples in the past, and that's one reason I want a divorce, but he absolutely refuses to give me one. When I had his library bugged, I found a real snake pit. And that's all I'm going to tell you, so go home and forget you ever knew me. Believe me, I'm poison to anyone who helps me."

"What about your family? Isn't there someone you can turn to?"

Lauren took a deep breath. "No, I have no family." Where would she start if she were to talk of family? Once she had a mother whom she could barely remember. Now and then she felt the faint sense of a special fragrance that reminded her of her mother. This was part of the lovely vision her dad so often spoke of after her mother died. All the memories of her mother had been gathered from him. Lauren adored him, and they shared a bond of love so strong that when it was broken by his fatal heart attack when she was fourteen, she almost died, too. But survive she did, taken in by a maiden aunt who had no interest in anything but the insurance money. Only because it was stipulated in the will did she later send Lauren to Radcliffe.

"Do you still have the tape?" Trudy asked.

Lauren shook the cobwebs from her head. "Yes."

"Then he didn't find it. No wonder he tore this place apart. I hope you have it hidden in a safety-deposit box or in a locker somewhere."

"No, nowhere like that."

"Well then, where? Do you have it with you? I want to help. That creep would never get it from me."

Lauren smiled for the first time since coming home. Trudy really wanted to help. She'd miss her. Was it always going to be this way, forever being parted from anyone who could matter to her? "You're really an angel, but I'd never part with the tape, believe me. I keep it with me every second."

"If it's all that important, I hope you had a copy made, just in case."

"No, that never entered my mind. You can tell I'm a novice at this cloak-and-dagger stuff."

"I didn't mean to worry you. For all I know, you're making all the right moves." She looked at Lauren in bewilderment. "Now what are you doing?"

Lauren was tossing broken glass into a wastebasket. She stopped, realizing she could never make any headway at the rate she was going. She didn't have time. She had to move as far away from Los Angeles as she could. "I can't stop to clean up this mess. I've got to get out of here." In despair, she ran her fingers through her dark hair, not knowing where to start. "Funny thing is, I landed my first job today in a little boutique. I thought it was kind of a turning point, a sign that things would be better. Boy, was I wrong!"

"Your first job? You've never worked for a living?"

"Don't act so impressed. I married right out of college, so my résumé is a blank sheet of paper. That's the reason I couldn't find anyone to talk to me, let

10

alone hire me."

"If I had your looks, I would have knocked on a few doors in Hollywood. With that face and figure and that luscious dark hair, they'd have grabbed you."

"Thanks for the try at ego boosting, but nothing can help me right now except a plan for getting out of here without being followed."

"I wasn't flattering you. Damn, next to you, I feel like a real dog."

"Don't be ridiculous. You're a darling."

"Yeah, someone the boys pass up but the mothers love. Well, back to you and this charming mess. If you're really planning to run off, leave everything as it is. I'll square things with the manager, clean up some, whatever needs to be done. That should be the least of your worries. Where will you go?"

"I've had Chicago as a backup from the beginning, just in case. I've been on both coasts, so now I guess it's time to try the Midwest. God, I hate to pull up stakes again!" Tears welled up in Lauren's green eyes once more. "It's almost two o'clock, and I've got to call the airlines and pack some of these clothes that aren't ruined, get myself going."

"What can I do to help? I know, I can make your plane reservations. That always takes so long over the phone. Why, your phone may even be bugged, so I'll use mine." Trudy laughed. "Now you've got me thinking like a conspirator."

"Good idea. Would you? And by the way, I'll give you the money to settle things here for me. And I want you to take anything you can use that isn't broken or torn. Some of these clothes are really nice." For a moment Lauren looked longingly at her lovely things. She would empty the suitcase and start over again, pack only a few clothes. To hell with Alex and his expensive gifts!

11

"Really? Thanks. You do want the earliest flight to Chicago, don't you?"

"The sooner the better. Just give me time to get to the airport."

As Trudy hurried out the door, Lauren dumped everything from the suitcase with the torn lining and started over again. This time, she felt as though she had her head on a little straighter. Everything she picked up was either wrinkled or torn. "Damn you, Alex!" she muttered to herself. "And damn *me* for being so stupid!" Just imagine, she thought, if she had kept her nose out of Alex's business she'd still be the naive mistress of a beautiful Long Island mansion, fearing her husband and hating herself more each day. Thank God she'd finally gotten the nerve to do something. And she didn't regret for one minute that she'd found out about his business dealings. Somehow, some way, she would make him pay for all the rotten schemes he was involved in, all the people he had ruined or killed, including his own child.

She found out all too soon that she was little more than a possession to Alex, a trophy wife whom he could introduce to his friends. With Alex demanding to know every move she made she had little freedom. She had to get out of the farce they called a marriage. And now it was useless to try to get away from him again. One of his men would be behind her all the way. No matter where she chose to hide, Alex or his spies would ferret it out. She sank to her knees and hot tears sprang up in her eyes. *Oh, God, I've got to get hold of myself and figure this out.* She had so little time and so much to do, and it could all be for nothing. She forced herself to stand up and gave an angry swipe at her tears, determined to finish packing.

She picked up a black Chanel suit that was still in good shape and began to fold it for packing. But before she placed it in the bag, a plan began to form in her head, and a ray of hope shone in her mind like a beacon dispelling the fear that she'd felt only moments before. It just might work. If she could talk Trudy into helping her, she could slip by the tail and be two thousand miles from here in a matter of hours. She was an amateur, going up against professionals, but it was worth a try. Her adrenalin began to surge as excitement built inside her. Maybe this time she could get away from Alex for good, and just thinking about it brought a sparkle to eyes that had long been dulled by fear.

She finished her hasty job of packing and was still rehearsing what she must do as she dressed herself in the well-tailored black suit and high-heeled pumps, then put on a wide-brimmed black hat that covered part of her face and much of her dark hair. She was closing the suitcase when Trudy knocked at the door.

"My, don't you look glamorous!" Trudy said. "Leaving this world in style, huh?"

"Might as well," Lauren said. "Come in."

"You're all set," said Trudy as she walked into the living room. "You have a seat on American Flight 333 departing at four-thirty. That should give you plenty of time."

"That's perfect. Thanks."

"Can I help you with anything else?"

"I have a big favor to ask, and I realize we hardly know each other, but . . ."

"Try me."

"Please say no if I'm asking too much."

Trudy smiled. "You have to tell me first."

"Well, to begin with, you'll take a cab and meet me at Henri's—it's a dress shop in a shopping center just four or five blocks west of here."

"Okay, we'll go to Henri's, then what?"

"I'll buy a new dress, and you'll put on this suit, walk

13

out of the shop, and drive away in my car. Have I thoroughly confused you?"

"I think I have it straight. In other words, I'll be a decoy."

"Exactly. I feel sure Alex will have me followed, and maybe we can throw his man off the trail. Think we can pull it off?"

"It's worth a try."

"Then you'll do it?"

Trudy frowned. "Of course I will, but there's one small problem."

"Oh, no, what have I forgotten?"

"I'll never look as good as you do in that suit."

"You don't give yourself enough credit. You had me scared for a minute."

"I do have a legitimate question though," Trudy said. "What about your suitcase? How will you manage that?"

"I haven't worked that out yet. Guess I'll just take it into the shop with me."

"But if you're actually being followed, won't it look suspicious when I walk out without one?"

"I hadn't thought of that."

"I have an idea," Trudy said. "I'll bring the bag in since I'm not the one being watched."

"Of course! That's much better." She gave Trudy a hug. "What would I have done if you hadn't come along?"

Half an hour later, Lauren was in Henri's, just a few blocks away. She had hastily bought and changed into a beige dress with a matching silk scarf and shoes. She had just finished paying for the new outfit when Trudy walked in, lugging the suitcase.

She followed Trudy to the dressing room and

14

whispered, "We were right about the tail. A man followed me all the way here, and now he's parked across the street." Her hands shook as she handed Trudy her suit, hat, and shoes.

"Settle down," Trudy said as she closed the door. "I'll only be a minute, and somehow I think this might work."

Lauren paced the floor, then walked to the window and looked outside. The blue sedan was still there. She got a good look at the driver, a swarthy-looking character, about fifty, with thinning black hair. She noticed that he was wearing wire-rimmed glasses and had on a brown turtleneck shirt. He seemed to be waiting patiently, yet looked bored with the whole thing. She gave him a sly little smile.

After a few minutes, Trudy stepped out of the dressing room. She looked stunning in Lauren's year-old designer suit. Her hair was a little lighter than Lauren's, but the black hat covered most of it, making her role as a decoy hardly noticeable, especially from across the street.

"You look beautiful," Lauren said, smiling.

"Well, I'm amazed that I can walk in this skirt. It's a little tight in places."

"It doesn't show, and I'm glad it's yours now."

"Mine? Thanks!"

"Here are my car keys. Maybe someday I can pick up the car. Time's growing short, so you'd better leave." Lauren embraced her new friend. "What can I say but thanks."

"Send me your new address."

"I will."

Lauren walked to the door with Trudy and watched her get into the VW and drive away. The blue sedan pulled from the curb and accelerated quickly into the late-afternoon traffic to follow. Trudy had come through and it was all going to be all right. She could feel it.

Trudy rounded the corner and stopped at the curb. The blue sedan pulled up beside her and paused for a second. She gave Bertinelli a signal, and with a wave, he grinned and quickly sped away. It had all worked out so easily. Of course, it would have been even better if Lauren had cooperated.

Damn, she'd tried for three days to get Lauren to talk. Alex Compton had doubted all along that his wife had the guts to put the bugs in his library, but he was determined to locate her and find out for sure. She had tried every trick she knew to get Lauren to admit it, but deep down she hadn't believed that the spoiled little bitch had actually carried it out. Ransacking her apartment was a last resort to try to uncover what she believed to be a nonexistent tape. But Lauren had done it after all. At least the search had paid off in the long run. It forced her to panic and need a confidante. It had been fun throwing Lauren's things around, but hell, she wished she'd been a little more careful with those expensive clothes, now that they were hers. At least she got a nice Chanel suit out of the deal.

When she'd called Alex at his office in New York less than an hour ago, he was furious when she told him that Lauren had actually been responsible for the bugging. She had wanted to take her out right then, but killing her would not have produced the tape, and Alex was frantic to learn its contents, or at least make sure it was destroyed. All she could do was follow orders, and hope that his next move would take care of both his wife and the tape. Time would tell. At least Alex's stupid wife was out of her hair.

Trudy climbed out of the VW, walked to the pay

phone on the corner, and dropped in a coin before dialing Alex's private number in New York.

"She's on her way to the airport . . ." Trudy began.

"Is Bertinelli on the job?"

"Right behind her. I got him a seat on the same plane."

"Good girl." She heard Alex draw on his pipe. "Still no tape?"

"Sorry. I still haven't had a chance to go through her purse, but she has the tape with her, and it has to be there. She never lets that purse out of her sight."

"What about the plastic explosive?"

"It's in her luggage, just like you said, and set to go off just before they land. God, I'm glad to get that thing out of my apartment."

"Too bad it couldn't have been a bigger one," Alex said, "but we couldn't take the risk. Nowadays they can spot a larger device. Oh, well, we'll see what happens."

"But about Bertinelli? He'll be on the plane, too."

"No more than he deserves. Now you know what happens when money's skimmed off the top."

"I see. Is that all, Mr. Compton?"

"For now. Just sit tight, and I'll give you a call."

Chapter Two

Anticipation and hope quickened in Lauren as she watched Alex's man drive away. Her plan had worked. She hurried out of the store and hailed a cab to take her to the airport.

Lauren kept a careful watch out the back window for several minutes, and, finally satisfied that no one was following, she checked her handbag to make sure the envelope containing the remainder of her cash, a little over two thousand dollars, was still intact. She felt foolish that she'd kept the money hidden in her purse all this time, since Alex had found her anyway, but she thought opening a bank account was much too risky. With Alex's connections in the financial world, she had been afraid to leave such an obvious clue behind. She looked inside her bag again and noted that the special compact, with the tape concealed in the false bottom, was safely tucked within a zippered compartment. As long as she had it, Alex would let her live. He'd never risk letting it fall into the wrong hands. She turned again and scanned the other cars in the rear window. Thank God the blue car was still nowhere in sight. Realizing how drained she felt, she lay back on the seat, eyes closed.

The ride to the airport took over an hour in the rush-hour traffic. Once there, Lauren made a dash for the counter, where she paid for a tourist-class ticket to Chicago, checked her suitcase, and picked up her boarding pass. The loudspeaker announced the last boarding call, so she went directly to the plane.

Fifteen minutes later, congratulating herself and chuckling at what a fool she had made of Alex, she was high in the sky above Los Angeles, headed east. To celebrate, she ordered a drink. It was hard to believe that she had actually pulled it off. She would be forever indebted to Trudy; she would never had made it without her help.

Lauren sat in an aisle seat, about ten rows from the back of the jumbo jet. She regretted that her seat was over the wing. Somehow, every pocket of turbulence seemed magnified in this section of the plane, but still she felt grateful that she had gotten a seat at all with such short notice. She finished her drink and tried to nap. Falling asleep in airplanes, trains, and cars had always been easy for Lauren, but now, when she felt so keyed up with nervous energy, it was impossible. She flipped through all the in-flight publications, read a few articles in an old magazine that she found in the seat pocket, and picked at the dinner served about an hour into the flight. She envied the man in the seat beside her, snoring shamelessly, apparently enjoying his slumber. At least she didn't have a chatty seatmate.

A sick feeling came over her when she thought of Alex and the reasons she had married him. At the time, she had told herself she loved him, but now she realized that it hadn't been love at all, but mindless infatuation. She had married a father image without realizing it. And yes, Alex's wealth had played a large part. It took years to admit it, but all during the time at Radcliffe, she had envied the girls from wealthy families, their lovely clothes and cars, their homes and social standings. Alex offered her a chance to be a part of all that.

She had met him at Southampton the summer after graduation while visiting Amy Porter, one of her friends from school. Alex was there on business with Amy's father, and he took an immediate fancy to her. She thought him remarkably distinguished-looking and handsome, with his thick silver hair, dark eyebrows, and intense gray eyes. Strength and power emanated from his tall, broad-shouldered frame, and to a twenty-two-year-old girl, he represented a world of excitement reserved for the fortunate few. He had made a fortune in his fifty-one years and owned controlling interests in enterprises throughout the world. She was aware of rumors of his connections to the underworld, but she was too dazzled by his homes in Palm Springs, Long Island, and Costa del Sol—plus the diamonds he showered on her—to pay much attention.

She knew that Alex had been married once before and was the father of a grown daughter, but beyond that, she knew very little about his shadowy past. He never spoke of his ex-wife, and as far as she knew, he never visited his daughter. At the time, she was too flattered by his attentiveness and the way he doted on her every whim to be bothered by his lack of concern for his only child. No one had paid any special attention to her since she was fourteen years old, and she was carried away in the bliss of love. Or what she thought was love.

The first three years of their life together went well enough, filled with travel, expensive jewelry, cars, and clothes, but it didn't take long to figure out that there were certain areas of his life that she had to close her eyes to—the foreign-looking men who came to their homes, his business dealings, his ties to political circles.

She learned early on to ignore his activities or else live in constant fear of his wrath. He supplied her with unlimited use of his credit cards and all his great wealth could provide, but material things soon lost their allure. She longed for something enduring between them—a child of their own.

When she first brought up the subject, Alex flew into a rage. A child would only tie her down, he insisted, and he was much too old to consider starting another family. She was to forget such foolishness here and now and never bring up the subject again.

His attitude toward her changed after that, and they had sexual relations only once during the next two months. He made love to her after a long night of drinking, and she wondered if he even had any recollection of it afterward. But once was all it took, and she was wild with excitement when she discovered that she was pregnant. She couldn't wait to tell him the good news. She knew Alex well enough to realize that a son would be a symbol to him, an alter ego, and the hope of having a baby boy would excite him. But Alex proved her wrong. As soon as the words were out of her mouth, he exploded in fury. He had hit her before, but this time it was a beating.

He slapped her to the floor. "You bitch! So you've found yourself a young, horny boyfriend!"

"No, Alex, stop! Please . . . it's not what you think . . . It's your child! You've got to believe me."

"The hell you say." He jerked her to her feet and hit her across the face with his fist, a sharp pain shooting through her eye. "So you figured old Alex would believe anything, didn't you? Well, I'll be damned if I'm senile yet!" He knocked her down with the back of his hand and kicked her in the stomach.

"Please, Alex . . . don't!" she begged. "Please . . . you've got to believe me. It's your—"

She never finished trying to make him listen. He kicked her again and again, and for a few frantic minutes she thought she would die. When the bleeding became uncontrollable, he finally took her to the hospital, telling the attendants she had fallen down the stairs.

When she awoke after surgery, she knew without being told that she had lost the baby. Her marriage was lost, too, and when Alex came to visit, she asked for a divorce.

"Nobody leaves me," he said in a low, controlled voice. "I do the leaving, and only when I'm ready."

She was too afraid of him after that to mention divorce again. From that moment on, he had her every move watched. She felt cornered, trapped, desperately needing her freedom. She knew he had his women, and she hit on the idea of bugging his library to gain some leverage to help her get the divorce. Little did she know at the time what she was getting into.

Another hour dragged by, and Lauren's legs ached from sitting still so long. She decided to leave her seat for a while and go to the rear of the plane to the lavatory. Picking up her handbag, she made her way down the aisle and stopped dead-still about three rows from the back. To her right sat the man who had followed her to Henri's! She was sure of it. He was wearing the same brown turtleneck shirt, the same wire-rimmed glasses, and had the same swarthy look. The blood suddenly drained from her face as she stared at him, fear clutching her heart like a metal vise. "Oh, my God!" she whispered under her breath. The man stared back at her, but when their eyes met, he looked away quickly and pretended to be engrossed in his newspaper. Lauren felt paralyzed with panic, her legs began to buckle, her heart pounded, and she didn't know what to do. There was no place to run, no place to hide, and the walls of the plane seemed to close in around her. Somehow she managed to move her legs and clutched her purse close to her body like a shield of protection. She ran headlong down the aisle, opened the door to the lavatory, and stumbled inside.

Leaning against the closed door, she regained her balance. How on earth had this happened? It wasn't possible, yet it was true. He had stopped Trudy and made her talk! Maybe he had harmed her, God forbid. She should never have asked her friend to take such a risk. But there hadn't been time for him to confront Trudy, make it to the airport, and buy a ticket. She had barely made it to the plane herself. *Oh, damn you, Alex! There's no way I can win!* She caught sight of her reflection in the mirror of the tiny cubicle, and her glazed, frightened eyes were too much for her. She suddenly burst into tears and covered her face with her hands, her whole body shaking with sobs. *What am I going to do? I might as well give up.*

She raised her head and looked at her reflection again. The mask of fear was still there. *No, damn it, I won't give up!* She filled a paper cup with water and gulped it down, then blotted her face with a handful of tissues and did what she could to patch up her makeup. She couldn't hide in the lavatory for another hour and weep like a frightened, defenseless child. Alexander Compton had not won yet. Somehow she would make her way down the aisle again, sit down, and plan another escape.

As she stepped out the door, Lauren bumped headlong into a young woman waiting outside. "Oh, I'm sorry, I wasn't watching where I was going. I hope you're not hurt."

"No, I'm fine." The other woman looked at Lauren intently, apparently taking in her pale face and her shaking hands. "Is something wrong?"

"No, I'm okay."

"You don't look well at all."

"I—I guess I'm just a little airsick from all the turbulence back here."

"You're sitting near the rear?"

"A few rows up, but I'll be fine."

"Say, I have an idea. I'm sitting near the front, just behind first class, and there's an empty seat beside me. I'm sure it would be okay if you'd like to change seats. There's a whole hour or so left to go. How about it?"

Lauren considered the offer for a few seconds. It would put more distance between herself and Alex's man. At least she would be out of his sight and wouldn't feel him breathing down her neck. "That's a good idea. Thanks."

"Terrific. Give me a minute to run in here, and we'll go together. I'd planned to freshen my makeup, but I won't take the time now. I can do that later."

The wait seemed like an eternity as Lauren stood outside the door, but minutes later, the woman reappeared. As they walked up the aisle, Lauren kept her eyes straight ahead, but she cringed when she felt the man's eyes boring into her back. They stopped at her assigned seat and she picked up her makeup case, then followed the young woman to the front of the plane, where Lauren stored her case in the compartment overhead.

The other woman took her seat next to the window and picked up her purse, a paperback novel, a light jacket, and an attaché case from the vacant seat by the aisle. As Lauren slipped into the seat, her new companion said, "It's a shame I've been taking up two seats when you've been uncomfortable back there." She shoved the attaché case and jacket beside the small box under the seat in front of her. "I brought so much on board there's no room for my purse."

"Here," Lauren said, "I'll put your bag with mine. There's plenty of room."

"Well, I see you have the real thing . . . a real Louis Vuitton. Mine's just a cheap imitation."

Lauren held the two handbags together. "They're so much alike it's hard to tell them apart." She placed them under the other seat. "Now we're all set."

The woman extended her hand. "I'm Diane Roberts."

"I'm Lauren Compton." She immediately regretted giving the stranger her name. She felt physically ill from her encounter with Alex's man just minutes ago. For all she knew, this woman could very well be one of his spies, too. She realized how easily she trusted people, always ready to take them at face value. She would be careful this time. She could tell that Diane was eager to strike up a conversation, and she was in no mood to have to guard her every word when she could barely think with her mind churning so.

"So you're headed for Chicago, too. Relatives there?"

"No, no relatives. In fact, I don't have much family at all."

"Neither do I." Diane's face became pensive. "My father died two years ago, and now I'm alone in the world. All I have now is my work, thank God. I'm a reporter."

"For a newspaper?"

"Free lance, actually. I like to do investigative work. In fact, I've just been offered a dream job."

"That's nice . . ." Lauren could already tell that she would have little time to figure a way out of this mess. Diane seemed bent on telling her life history, and she didn't want to be rude. All she could think of was the man at the rear of the plane and what lay ahead of her once they landed. She still couldn't figure out how on earth he had managed to get on the plane in time. But then Alex was capable of anything.

"Have you ever heard of Lucrezia?" Diane asked.

"What? I'm sorry, I guess I wasn't listening."

"Lucrezia—the famous artist."

"Of course." She and Alex owned one of her paintings, and Lauren had admired Lucrezia's work for years.

"Well, I'm going to work for her."

"Do you paint?"

Diane laughed. "No, I hardly qualify as an artist."

"A model?" Lauren took a good look at Diane. She wasn't very attractive, and she appeared to be at least thirty years old, too old to begin such a career. Still she was tall and slender, and with the right makeup, she could be rather pretty.

"I'm an investigative reporter, remember?"

"Oh, that's right. Forgive me. I've got lots of things on my mind." Lauren realized she couldn't concentrate long enough to carry on a decent conversation. She so desperately needed some time alone. If this woman didn't stop talking soon, she thought she might scream.

"It seems that Lucrezia Saunders is ill, nephritis, I've been told, a kidney disease. Besides my other work, I'll be sort of a companion to her, too."

"I'm sorry to hear that. Did you say Saunders? I thought she was Italian."

"She is, but she married an Englishman when she was very young. She's a widow now, poor thing, and getting old, but she's still able to travel quite a bit. What's so wonderful about my job is that I'll go with her to her galleries—London, New York. I can't believe I'm so lucky."

"That's nice." Would this woman ever stop talking! Lauren folded her arms across her middle to ease the hard knot in her stomach and try to stop her insides from shaking. Maybe sitting near the front gave her an advantage. Maybe she could get out quickly and be on

27

the other side of the airport before Alex's man got off the plane.

"I've never met Lucrezia," Diane went on, "but she sounds so lively on the phone. She insists that her illness be kept secret from Cole Saunders—he's her nephew and also her lawyer. I've spoken to him several times on the phone, making arrangements for this trip. If he's half as good-looking as he sounds, I don't know how much investigating I'll get done, but this will be some story if I can get to the bottom of it. And I'll owe it all to Dr. Carnot, my dad's doctor. He recommended me for this job after I did some investigative work at the hospital. Did you read about the trouble at the American Hospital in San Franciso? Well, I wrote that story."

"I'm sorry, what did you say?"

"Oh, my, I'm talking too much and you're not feeling well."

"That's all right," Lauren said. "I'm afraid I'm not very good company, but it was so good of you to bring me up here."

"Just glad I could help." Diane reached under the seat and pulled out her book. "I'll read and be quiet a while, give you a chance to relax." She switched on her overhead light and settled back.

Relieved, Lauren leaned back on the seat and closed her eyes. She felt too drained at this point to think of another scheme, and, besides, it seemed so pointless. However, landing in a large airport did have its advantages. She could fade into the crowd and not wait for her luggage. But what if Alex had someone else waiting for her at the airport? She forced the thought from her mind.

Right now she had to figure out how on earth Alex's man had managed to get on the same plane and be seated just a few rows from her. No one but Trudy had

28

known her plans, so there was no way the man could have known, unless he waylaid Trudy somehow and forced her to talk. Yet she had already decided there wouldn't have been time. But who could have told him? She felt the color drain from her face, and she sat bolt upright. Oh, my God! Trudy! She felt suddenly cold all over. What if she were working for Alex? Oh, no, not Trudy. How could she even think such a thing? She had acted like such a good friend and had been willing to do anything she could to help. But then again, Lauren realized, Trudy had moved into the apartment complex just recently and had immediately found a way to get acquainted. It all began to make sense. Lauren realized how little she knew about this woman. She hadn't thought much about the fact that Trudy had no job; she had explained that her income came from alimony from her ex-husband. But now it seemed a possiblity that Alex had provided her with a job and money all this time. Surely she was letting her imagination run wild, yet this seemed to be the only solution. And then she thought of something else. The smell in the apartment when she first went in, a spicy fragrance that she couldn't quite put her finger on. It was Trudy's perfume. That was it! Oh, God, it had been Trudy, and now Alex knew her plans.

What had she told Trudy about Alex? She couldn't think of much she had said except that he was her husband. She tried to remember the conversation, and a wave of panic suddenly swept over her. *The tape! Oh, Lord, the tape!* She had admitted that she had bugged Alex's library, and now he knew about that. And Trudy had tried so hard to get her hands on the tape. It all fit. Damn, she was always so gullible! She had played right into Alex's hands, and he had found out what he wanted to know. Now if he found *her,* she would be dead.

Another half hour went by, with Lauren still frozen with fear. Diane, who had been so quiet all this time, startled her suddenly and tapped her on the shoulder.

"Would you mind handing me my purse? We'll be landing before long, and I want to do something with my face before I meet Cole Saunders." She gave Lauren a wink. "I'm going back to the lavatory."

Lauren reached for the handbag and gave it to Diane.

"I won't be long."

After Diane walked away, Lauren rubbed her eyes and tried to clear her thinking. It might not be a bad idea to follow Diane and wash her own face, make herself more alert when they landed. She was about to stand up when the plane jolted abruptly, almost as though it had hit a huge bump in the sky. The FASTEN SEAT BELT sign flashed on at that moment, and before Lauren could locate the belt, she felt the plane jolt again, followed this time by a shiver that seemed to ripple through the cabin. Cries of alarm went up all around her, and she could hear the passengers in the rear echoing their fear.

A strange feeling swept over her. Something was very wrong. She had flown more times than she could count, and this was more than turbulence. Maybe something was wrong with the engines. Now she could feel the plane losing altitude. It seemed to drop faster by the second, and all at once Lauren became acutely aware that it was thrashing about in the black sky, out of control. Terror gripped her, a terror so paralyzing that she couldn't think. Pitiful questions came from every direction: "What's wrong?" "Are we going to crash?" "Why don't they do something?" The same questions bombarded Lauren's thoughts. And where was Diane? She must have been caught at the rear of the plane and told to sit down, strap herself in.

Bedlam reigned as the aisle came alive with a flurry of activity. Tight-lipped stewardesses rushed about, pulling out pillows, quickly issuing them row by row, desperately trying to comfort and keep hysterical passengers in their seats. Small pieces of luggage and personal belongings dropped like flying debris from the overhead compartments to the floor below. And all the while, the plane continued its wild descent.

The captain's voice suddenly blared on the loudspeaker, but Lauren couldn't seem to comprehend his words: *Stay calm . . . seatbelts . . . lost power . . . altitude . . . forced landing . . .*

Panicky thoughts sped in and out of Lauren's mind. The plane was out of control, and there was nothing anyone could do about it. Maybe it was all a bad dream and she would wake up soon. If only that could be true. But this was real, and it was happening to her. Agonizing seconds went by, and her breaths came in gasps; her heart beat in her ears. She thought of her desperate attempts to get away from Alex and his man at the back of the plane. It all seemed so insignificant now. If she hadn't tried to run away none of this would be happening. And now she was going to die. The screams were deafening, but Lauren felt too frightened to utter a sound.

She was barely aware of taking the pillow from the stewardess's hand. And then a feeling of utter numbness swept over her as she placed her head on the pillow, reached for her purse, and waited.

Chapter Three

Fear crept into Lauren's consciousness as she lay unmoving on a small, narrow bed. Her ribs throbbed with pain, her head ached, her mouth felt parched, and her limbs felt like lead. Her eyes seemed all she was able to move. They turned to take in the blurry details of the stark-white room: a small chest of drawers, a vinyl-covered chair, and a bedside table. Alex had found her. He had done her bodily harm and now she was his prisoner. Her eyes filled with terror as she stared at his dark form looming over her.

"Don't be frightened, Miss Roberts." The words were uttered by a strange male voice.

"Who—?" Momentary relief flooded her body. She forced her gaze away from the concern in the man's eyes and realized there was someone else in the room. A woman in a white uniform. A nurse. She became vaguely aware of a medicinal smell. This must be a hospital. "Where—?" She felt so stupid. She couldn't seem to put a whole sentence together.

"Start I.V. fluids with 1,000 c.c.'s of five percent glucose with ringers—lactate, so we'll have a line open until we see what else we may need. And give her 75 mgs of Demerol for the pain," the man said. "Keep a close check on her vital signs, and I'll be back later."

The nurse moved closer to the bed, and Lauren noticed the syringe poised in her hand. "Oh please, no!" She couldn't allow herself to be knocked out. She was trying so hard to be alert and now they were putting her to sleep. She had to keep her wits. Alex could be here any minute, and God only knew what he would do if he found her unconscious. "Please, no shot. Please . . ."

"Now, now Miss Roberts. You're suffering from shock and pain, and we're trying to help you."

"But you don't understand. I'm not . . . There's been a mistake . . . Please wait until . . ." The needle entered her arm.

"Now let's not try to talk. Rest is what we need right now after that terrible ordeal. Let's be a good girl and close our eyes." The nurse's voice was sugary sweet, as though talking to an imbecile.

Lauren felt helpless, defeated. She fought to stay awake as long as she could, but minutes later, she drifted into unconsciousness.

Alex Compton felt uneasy as he stared at the mangled corpse in the temporary morgue set up in a school gymnasium in Evanston, Illinois. It wasn't just the gruesome ordeal that made him feel unsettled. From the minute he set eyes on it, he knew that this was not his wife's body. The face was so badly crushed and burned that the features were not discernible, but what was left of the hair was not the same. Lauren's was much darker. "What about identification?" he asked the official. "Did you find her purse?"

"It was almost destroyed in the fire, and the contents were scattered and burned in the debris, but we found enough of her driver's license to make the identification."

"May I have her luggage?"

The official shook his head. "The baggage area was hit the hardest, and I doubt that anything can be salvaged."

"Have all the dead been identified?"

"Not yet, but we're working on it."

It was possible that Lauren was dead, but this was not her body. "What about survivors? Were there any?"

"Fortunately, yes. I don't have the official count, but there were close to thirty."

"Maybe my wife was one of them."

"I know it's hard to accept, but we have the documentation to identify her. Besides the driver's license, she was in her assigned seat. I'm very sorry, Mr. Compton. You have my deepest sympathy."

Alex ran his fingers through his silver hair. Even though this was not Lauren's body, the odds were against her survival. He forced himself to look at the poor dead woman again. He had to be sure. Even though the body was in bad shape, he could tell at a glance that it was not as slender as Lauren's. He stepped a little closer and examined the hands, surprised that they were in better condition then her face. The fingernails were very short, almost as if they had been bitten to the quick. Lauren always took such good care of her nails and kept them long and perfectly manicured. And there was still the matter of the hair color. No, this was not Lauren. He was sure of it.

"If you can identify the body, we'll need your signature before releasing it," the official said.

Alex hesitated a long time before answering. If he went along with this, the Senate committee would not seek testimony from a dead woman. And, too, if she had the tape with her, it had probably been destroyed, and that would get the pressure from his associates off his neck. If Lauren *had* survived, she would naturally grab the chance to run again, but he would deal with that later. On the other hand, if she had been killed in the crash, no harm would be done by going along with it now. All things considered, the announcement of Lauren's death would help matters considerably.

"It—it's my wife," he said, his voice breaking. "Give me the paper to sign and I'll make arrangements to take her home." He was glad that he had had the presence of mind to put Jason Lawrence, one of his best men, on the scene. Lawrence had a knack of knowing precisely how to get to the heart of a matter. If anyone could find out if Lauren were alive, he would be the one. As soon as Alexander could find a phone, he'd get in touch with Lawrence and instruct him to move with full speed on an investigation.

"Well, how are you feeling today? Time to wake up."

Lauren opened her eyes and focused them on a man with a shock of white hair and a kind, cherubic face. Her head hurt, and she was barely awake. She felt as though she were in a fog.

"You're a very lucky young lady." He gave her a broad smile. "I'm Dr. Jeremy Arnold. You look a lot better this morning after that nasty bump on your head." He was studying her chart, nodding his head as he spoke. "Good, I see your vital signs are normal." He smiled at her. "No broken bones or internal injuries. We'll keep you a few more days for observation, and if all goes well, we'll release you on Monday."

Lucky? While the doctor was talking, she discovered bandages on her right hand and around her rib cage. *The flight to Chicago! I was on a plane!* Memories came rushing back too fast—vivid memories of pitiful screams and an airplane out of control.

She could almost hear the pilot's voice and his words that had made her numb with fright. And then she had had the presence of mind to hold her purse so there could be no question about identifying her body. She could hear the doctor speaking again, yet it was so hard to force her mind back to the present. But she had to know more of what happened.

"I feel so dull and uncoordinated. Would you mind telling me what happened when—?"

"Just the effects of shock and the strong sedative, nothing to worry about. Don't try to think about anything right now, Diane, except getting back to normal. There'll be plenty of time for details later . . . Need anything?" His voice sounded kind.

Why did he call her Diane? Lauren was furious at her sluggish thinking. Never had she felt so out of touch, so bewildered in her life. Maybe if she had some food, she could sort things out. "I feel a little hungry," she said.

"That's good news. Your breakfast should be here any minute." Dr. Arnold went to the door and asked a nurse to hurry with the tray.

"May I have a newspaper, too? It's strange, but I don't even know where I am." She thought of the plane again and the terror of those last few minutes. Everything seemed so unreal. She felt disoriented and haunted by memories of panic.

"You're in Evanston, Illinois," he said, smiling. "I think you'd like it here, but I understand Mr. Saunders is anxious to take you to Chicago." He glanced toward the door as it opened and nodded to a nurse who was bringing in the breakfast tray. The beeper in his pocket sounded just then, and he gave her a wave and headed for the door. "Get a good rest. I'll look in on you later."

"Wait, Dr. Arnold. How long have I been here?"

"Two days," he said.

Two days. She had vague pictures of people coming

37

in and out of the room, but everything had been a blur. She felt she had lost two whole days of her life.

By now the nurse had deposited the tray and was in the process of raising the head of the hospital bed. "Just ring when you're finished," she said, and left Lauren alone in the room.

Bits and pieces of conversation crept into her thoughts. Who was Mr. Saunders and what did he have to do with her? And why did the doctor call her Diane? Maybe *he* was the one who was confused. She did feel muddled, but at least she knew her own name. It was possible the plane hadn't crashed—just a bad forced landing. She had likely been dazed, bruised a little. That was probably it. Maybe after a cup of coffee she could sort everything out. She took a sip from the steaming cup and tried to put the trauma of those last moments on the plane out of her thoughts. She didn't know if the food was actually as good as it tasted, but she savored every bite.

Just as she finished eating, a volunteer appeared, offering her the local newspaper and any books or magazines that might interest her. The middle-aged woman lingered after Lauren chose only the newspaper. "I just have to tell you that the whole hospital staff can't wait to see you. We're all so glad to have the survivors here in our hospital—especially you, since you were hardly hurt at all. I heard that one man actually walked away from the wreckage. Isn't that amazing? But those poor people, especially those at the back of the plane—just awful! Some crushed and burned so badly they couldn't even be identified."

Lauren felt the color drain from her face. The plane had crashed. Oh, why didn't this woman leave! She suddenly felt panicky.

"Oh, I hope I didn't upset you." Noticeably startled by the change in the patient's appearance, the volunteer, still uttering apologies and rolling the cart before her, hurried out of the room.

Lauren stared at the newspaper, almost unwilling to unfold it. But it was something she had to do. Her fingers trembled as she took it in her hands. And then black headlines screamed out at her: DEATH COUNT MOUNTS IN AIRPLANE CRASH and underneath, 220 PEOPLE DEAD—28 SURVIVORS. A cold sweat broke out all over her body as she kept reading, words blurring one into the other. She was barely able to comprehend the catastrophe so objectively related in print . . . *list of those who died taken from the manifest . . . some unidentifiable . . . plane broken in half on impact . . . cause of crash under investigation . . . survivors taken to area hospital.* Tears filled her eyes, and she dreaded reading any more gruesome details. Fortunately, the pilot, co-pilot, and one stewardess, along with many of the people who had been sitting near the front of the plane, had survived. The rear half of the plane had been destroyed. Oh, my God! Her hands grew cold. She remembered she had moved from the back about an hour before the crash. She lay back on the pillow, stunned, barely able to comprehend the reality of her good fortune.

Finally she picked up the paper again. She had to know more. On the next page she noticed a smaller article, listing the names of the survivors. Lauren Compton was not among them. She scanned the list again, more carefully this time, just to make sure, but her name was not there. Surely there was a logical explanation. In all the confusion, her name had obviously been left out.

She read on, trying to glean more information, especially concerning the women who had survived. One name in particular caught her eye—Diane Roberts, the name everyone had been calling her. It was a case of mistaken identity, pure and simple, and she had to straighten it out right now.

Her thoughts tumbled over each other. Where was her purse? She leaned over, acutely aware of the pain in her ribs, and reached inside the drawer of the night table. It was there. She breathed a sigh of relief. Drawing it out and onto the bed, she gasped in disbelief. This was not her purse. She dumped the contents on the bed, reached for the wallet with shaking hands, and pulled out the driver's license, then studied the information it held: *Diane Roberts, Los Angeles, California, color of hair: brown, color of eyes: blue, sex: F, height: 5'6"*. And printed on the side was a picture of the young woman. How on earth did she happen to have Diane Roberts' purse?

Lauren stared at the face, and recognition stirred her senses. Of course! Though it was not a good likeness of her, this was the young woman on the plane who had been so kind to her and offered her a seat near the front. She felt a stab of guilt. She remembered that she had been so absorbed in her own problems that she hadn't thanked her enough for her kindness. Diane had been at the back of the plane at the time of the crash. Diane Roberts was probably dead and their identities had been mixed up!

She looked at the picture again and tried to relive those last few minutes on the plane before pandemonium broke loose. Diane had asked for her purse. That was it. When she handed it to Diane, she had obviously given her the wrong purse. The bags looked so much alike, and she had been so preoccupied at the time, she hadn't paid close attention. No wonder everyone assumed she was Diane Roberts. She must tell someone about the awful mistake! And then another thought hit her. If this were another woman's handbag, then her own purse was lost to her forever. It wasn't the money inside she mourned; it was the tape she had so cleverly hidden. That tape had been her only hold over Alex.

A thought crossed Lauren's mind. Could she get away with it? Did she dare try to lose her identity and live the life of Diane Roberts? Where was a mirror? She riffled through the contents of the purse spread on the bed, found a compact mirror, and looked at her reflection for the first time since the accident. What she saw was a pale, bewildered face, blotched with light purple and green bruises on the forehead, one cheek, and one side of the chin. No wonder no one questioned the mistake.

Lauren looked again, more objectively this time. She could pass for Diane Roberts if this were the only photograph of her available to the officials. It hardly looked like the woman she remembered. It would mean the end of running, no more threats from Alex. She'd be free to breathe, to live. Destiny had handed her a way out of this nightmare she had been living since she became his wife. But could she live a lie?

She looked at the contents of the purse again, trying to find out more about Diane. On the bed lay a small plastic folder containing Diane's passport. This picture of Diane looked even less like the woman she remembered. There was also a fat brown envelope. Lauren unsealed it and gasped. It was stuffed with money, most of it large bills, maybe as much as twenty-five thousand dollars. Incredible! Why on earth would anyone carry around such a large sum? She realized that her own purse contained a lot of money, too, but *this* was a small fortune. She suddenly felt like an intruder and quickly put the envelope back in the bag, along with all the other items on the bed, closed the purse, and put it back into the drawer just as a nurse poked her head inside the door. She was a heavyset

41

woman who appeared to be in her late fifties.

"I think it's about time to get you cleaned up if you're up to it. Oh, I see you found your handbag." The nurse walked in and proceeded to fill a plastic washbowl with warm water. "My, you look a whole lot better today." Taking Lauren's silence as assent, she began to give Lauren a sponge bath. "Gee, we need to do something about your hair, too. It's all matted."

Finally, after about an hour, she had Lauren clean and comfortably settled against fresh linens. "Why, you're really beautiful, you know?" She gave Lauren a broad smile as she rolled the tray-table in front of her and flipped up the top, uncovering a large, attached mirror. Surveying her patient with obvious pride, she went on. "Gosh, it's a shame your cosmetic case was lost because you sure could cover a lot of that discoloration with a little makeup. Do you have a lipstick or anything in your purse, Miss Roberts?"

Lauren stared at her image, barely noting her face. She was confounded by the fact that everyone accepted her without reservation as Diane Roberts. "Yes, I think so." She had shoved everything back so quickly that she hadn't paid much attention to all the items. "Would you look for it, please?" She felt a shiver run up her spine as she continued to study her image in the mirror. How could she be two people? She must tell everyone who she really was or she would truly lose her identity.

"Here it is, and a powder compact, too," said the nurse. "Now you'll really look great when the television crew gets here."

"Television crew! Oh, my God, what are you talking about?" Lauren quickly closed the top of the tray-table and stared at the nurse.

"Why, the whole lobby's been filled with newsmen and photographers since the crash. You're one of the survivors who's well enough to be interviewed, and

42

they've been waiting all this time to talk to you, so just as soon as . . ."

"Oh, no! There's no way I'll see anyone from the press!" Alex and his men would be upon her immediately if her picture appeared on the television news. Calming somewhat as her mind raced ahead, she changed her tone. "Won't you help me—What's your name?"

"Isabel Scott. Just call me Isabel. Everyone else does."

"Please forgive me, Isabel. I'm not quite myself." How true, not exactly herself, because she was seriously considering becoming someone else. Lauren flashed her most winning smile. "You're so efficient, I know you could handle this whole thing, if you don't mind. I'm just not up to talking to reporters or having my picture taken. Would you see if you can get someone in charge to ask them to leave? I can't remember much about the crash, and what I can remember, I don't want to talk about." She gave Isabel a pleading look, frantically hoping that she would agree.

"You poor dear." Isabel was obviously flattered by Lauren's confidence in her. "You just lie there and rest. I'll see that those newmen don't bother you." She marched out of the room with determination.

Lauren sank against the pillow and closed her eyes in relief. Imagine what could have happened if all those media people had access to her! It was too frightening to think about. Yet if she were to go on with this deception, things like this might crop up over and over again. She wondered if she were strong enough and clever enough to pull it off. It wouldn't be easy. She'd have to be on her guard constantly. But the alternative was to be under Alex's thumb.

The morning newspaper still lay on the night table.

Lauren picked it up and scanned the names of the survivors again. They were right here in this hospital. She studied the names of the men. Could *he* have lived through the crash? He was sitting near the back, where the damage had been the worst. The swarthy man who had followed her might have perished along with all those innocent people. It was a ghastly thought, but she couldn't help but feel relieved that he probably hadn't lived.

As her eyes traveled down the page, she was suddenly arrested by her own obituary. Oh, my God! she thought in horror, her eyes riveted to the words. *"Alexander Compton, international financier, mourns the death of his wife, Lauren Townsend Compton, who was killed Wednesday in the crash of Flight 333 en route to Chicago."* The article went on and on and Lauren's vision blurred with rage. Alex mourn her? Right now, he was probably congratulating himself on his good fortune, knowing she would never testify against him. At last he could call off his dogs. Why shouldn't the news of her own death be her good fortune, too?

The news of her death also confirmed the fate of Diane Roberts, who was carrying Lauren's purse, along with her identification. Diane, the woman who inadvertently might provide her with her freedom, was obviously dead. Lauren felt the heavy hand of guilt on her head. What was she to do? Would anyone be hurt if she assumed Diane's identity? Diane had told her about her father's death, which had left her alone in the world. That was why she was so happy about starting her job with the artist Lucrezia. So no one, absolutely no one, would be hurt or the wiser if she went through with it. Poor Diane. It didn't seem fair. And it was so gruesome. It would almost be like dancing on her grave. But she had to decide one way or the other and

44

soon. It had to be done before Mr. Saunders arrived on Monday, expecting to take her to Chicago.

Determined to go over every detail, Lauren studied the driver's license. Diane's hair had been brown; her own was very dark, but the difference was not noticeable in the photo. As far as eyes were concerned, the license stated that Diane's were blue, and hers were green—not the same color at all, but at least Diane's weren't dark. Everything else seemed to fall into place as though for a purpose. Diane was five feet six inches tall; Lauren was five feet seven and a half, so that would be no big problem.

Diane was about to take a position with one of the most famous women in the world. For the life of her, she couldn't remember what Diane had said about her job and what she would be doing. She had been so preoccupied with her own problems that she hadn't paid much attention to what Diane was saying; but she did remember hearing her mention that Lucrezia had some kind of health problem. Nephritis, or something like that. She couldn't be sure. She hoped that Diane wasn't a nurse. If that were the case, she would blow the whole thing and make an utter fool of herself since she didn't know the first thing about nursing.

Just then, Nurse Scott appeared with Lauren's luncheon tray. "Well, I did it," she said as she set the tray on the table. "I had a little trouble at first, but I finally convinced Mr. Abernathy to shoo all those newsmen out the door. I don't think you'll be bothered."

"Thank you, you're a real jewel," Lauren said. "Tell me, have I had any visitors since I've been here?"

"Just that one man."

Lauren froze. Oh, God, here she was thinking she might get away with this deception, and Alex had it figured out all along. He was probably lurking somewhere in the hospital right this minute. She felt panicky, urgently needing to get out of there. "What did he look like?" She could barely get the words out.

"Tall, blond, rather young, and oh, gee, so good-looking."

Lauren felt a little relieved. That description certainly didn't match Alex's, but it could have been one of his men. "Did he tell you his name?"

"Sure, it was Mr. Saunders. He came the first night you were here, not long after they brought you in. Said he'd be back to pick you up. Is there anything else? I have all these other trays to deliver, and patients are waiting."

"No thanks, you've been a big help."

Lauren breathed a grateful sigh, but her hand was still shaking as she picked up her fork. The time had come to make a decision. She could go through with this identity switch or call the authorities and straighten the whole thing out right now. But she really had no choice. The fright only moments before had made the decision for her.

Chapter Four

On Monday afternoon, Lauren was sitting up in bed when a young blond man walked into the room. He was handsome with a loose, casual manner and a commanding masculine presence—broad-shouldered, and well over six feet tall. She could sense an aura of wealth and power about him.

"If my guess is right, you're Mr. Saunders," she said. "Dr. Arnold said you'd be here today. I—I'm sorry I was so out of it the last time you were here." She extended her left hand awkwardly in greeting and held up her other hand to show that it was still bandaged.

"Well, you guessed right." Cole gave her a grin and held her hand in his. "I'm Cole Saunders—just call me Cole. I was here the first night, but you were asleep. When Lucrezia heard of the crash, she sent me right down here. Anyway, we're both relieved that you're not only alive, but well enough to leave this place." His voice had unusual resonance, along with a definite British accent. Lauren felt immediately comfortable with this man, as though she had known him for a long time.

She smiled. "I'm just glad you're here now so I can finally leave." She pushed the sheet away and started

47

to get up.

"Hold it a minute," Cole said, laughing. "I think you'll be interested in what I have in this box—that is, unless you plan to walk out the front door in that skimpy hospital gown."

"What on earth?" She had been so mesmerized by Cole's voice and manner, she hadn't even noticed the box in his hands. She loved the sound of his laughter.

"Just a gift from Lucrezia, something I think you need right now."

"I haven't given much thought to my clothes, but I suppose they were ruined when—" She remembered she didn't even have any luggage.

"Try not to think about the accident. It will probably bother you for a long time, but right now, why don't you just try to forget it. So—why not have a look at what's inside?" He opened the large dress box and pulled out a sea-green silk dress with a matching cardigan-style jacket of a woven fabric. "Lucrezia said to tell you there are hose and underthings in here, too. She put everything together herself."

"How thoughtful! This dress is lovely," Lauren said, running her fingers over the soft material. "But how did she know my size?"

He grinned. "Well, that's where I came in. Did a little detective work the other night. A nurse let me see the clothes you had on when they brought you in. I just wrote down the sizes, and Lucrezia took it from there." He suddenly looked somber. "God, that must have been some impact! Did anyone tell you your dress was split straight down the back? No . . . don't answer that. Here I go, talking about the crash when the last thing you need is to be thinking about it. Ready to get dressed?"

"You bet I am, Mr. Saunders."

"Cole, remember?"

"Okay, Cole, if you'll ask a nurse to help me, I'll be ready to go in no time. You can get a cup of coffee or something, and we'll call you when I'm ready."

When Cole left, Lauren fingered the beautiful dress and slip. She remembered so many such garments, clothes and furs, she had bought without a thought to the cost when she was living with Alex as his wife. Idly she wondered if the bulk of her wardrobe was still hanging in those huge closets in their home on Long Island. She hadn't wanted anything from him, so she had taken just the necessities when she left. She had wanted only her freedom. The summer things she had thrown into the bag when leaving Los Angeles were a few of the better dresses she had left over from her days with Alex. She realized it was good that she had been wearing the inexpensive beige dress and shoes when she arrived at the hospital. Diane Roberts probably would not have had an expensive wardrobe. Things were working out well so far, but she couldn't let down her guard for a moment.

There were cosmetics in the box, too. Lauren was delighted. Cole must have described her battered face to Lucrezia, because she had included a jar of cover-up, which would probably do wonders to camouflage her bruises.

She was standing before the mirror in the bathroom, almost finished making up her face, when Isabel Scott came in.

"I told you makeup would help," Isabel cried in amazement, "but I had no idea it would cover so well. Why, you look like you're ready to go dancing! And I love what you've done to your eyes."

"Dancing in this charming thing?" Lauren laughed, pirouetting in her white hospital gown and exposing her bare backside. "I think I'd better get into some clothes."

49

"You're really something special, Miss Roberts." Isabel was still giggling when she handed Lauren a bra, panties, slip, and a pair of panty hose. "No wonder your boyfriend looks so happy."

Lauren's hand was arrested in midair. "Boyfriend?" She hadn't heard that term used in years. It suddenly made her feel very young again. She was only twenty-eight, but the years as Alex's wife had made her feel old beyond her years.

"I'm sorry, I just took for granted that . . ."

Lauren laughed. "Actually, I've just met him. He's my new employer's attorney."

"Oh, you're starting a new job?"

"As a matter of fact, I am. I'll be working for Lucrezia Saunders, the artist."

"My, that sounds interesting. You'll be living in Chicago?"

"Yes, but Lucrezia has galleries all over the world, so I suppose I'll go where she goes."

"What an exciting way to make a living. Sure she couldn't use a nurse or a companion? I wouldn't mind that kind of work at all."

"You'll be the first to know if she does. You've been so good to me, and I'll miss you."

"And I'll miss *you*. It isn't often we have anyone as pretty as you in this hospital. My, you look just like a fashion model." By now Isabel had finished helping Lauren slip into her dress. "I'm sure glad Dr. Arnold let me remove that tape and bandage from around your ribs this morning, but just because the X ray didn't show any broken ribs, don't think you won't hurt for a while, so you be careful, you hear?"

"I promise. Now will you find Mr. Saunders and tell him I'm ready to go?"

As Isabel was leaving, Lauren reached for Diane Roberts' handbag and winced. The physical pain was

50

almost a welcome distraction from the mental anguish she had endured the past two days. *I can't do this. It's all wrong. When Cole Saunders comes back, I'll tell him the truth and figure out some other way to get out of this mess.* She walked into the bathroom to make sure she had everything, and glanced up at the mirror. When she looked at her reflection, an eerie feeling swept over her. It was as if Diane were on the other side of the mirror smiling and giving her permission to go through with the deception. She felt better somehow, and braced herself, knowing that once her "boyfriend" came to call, she was committed to the lie.

When Cole walked in, his eyes lit up at the sight of her. "I'd say you made a remarkable recovery, Miss Roberts."

"Please call me Laur—Diane." She felt color rise in her cheeks.

"It's a deal."

Lauren caught his gaze, and their eyes met and held for a moment of mutual discovery. She stopped in her tracks, mesmerized by the intensity of his blue eyes. Neither seemed able to move. Finally forcing herself to break the spell, she fumbled in Diane's purse, searching for the wallet. "I'd like to leave something for the nurses." Her voice was soft and whispery.

"That's already been taken care of." Cole forced his gaze away from her. "I came loaded with perfume and candy for the whole staff." He grinned. "Don't thank me. Lucrezia is the thoughtful one. Say, that dress looks great on you—a perfect fit.".

"Thanks. I love it."

Lauren smiled her good-byes as they walked down the corridor and into a waiting elevator. Neither spoke a word as they descended, tension continuing to build as they avoided looking at each other.

Once in the lobby, Lauren froze when they ap-

51

proached the door. Groups of reporters, armed with their cameras, were camped on the front steps. "I don't think I feel up to answering questions out there—a little unsteady on my feet, I guess. Is there another way out of this place?" She looked around frantically.

"Oh, sure, there's a side door. I wasn't even thinking." He took her arm and guided her down a side corridor until they came to an exit sign. "Wait here a minute, and I'll be back with the car in no time. Sure you're all right?"

Lauren could only nod. She watched Cole disappear through the door. Almost wishing she could vanish inside it, she leaned against the wall. Here she was, not even out of the building, having to hide her true identity. Maybe it would be better to find another exit, slip outside, and start over some other way. Her life was such a mess. She thought of Diane Roberts. In an act of sheer kindness, she had forfeited her own life, and now her name was being stolen from her. It was all so frightening. She couldn't possibly go through with this. She wouldn't.

But Cole walked in the door just then, abruptly cutting off her urge to flee. He steered her toward the rented Mercedes waiting for them in the driveway.

Once Cole had her seated beside him, he started the motor and maneuvered the car away from the building. Lauren looked back one last time and saw the newsmen and camera crews still milling about the front lawn of the hospital. The car sped on, turning onto the highway that led to Chicago. Lauren leaned back against the leather upholstery, resigned and ready to begin her strange new life with no idea of what would be expected of her as Diane Roberts.

Chapter Five

Gia was gentle as she pulled the brush through Lucrezia's thinning black hair, trying to work it into a chignon with the pile of hairpins on the dressing table. The roots were beginning to show their true color, she noticed.

"Don't be afraid of pulling too hard. I'm not going to break. That last birthday has everyone acting like I've got one foot in the grave." Lucrezia's voice was filled with annoyance. She was impatient to finish dressing, eager to be alone with her thoughts. That phone call from London a few moments ago with news of still another art forgery had sent her into a tailspin. It was hard to concentrate on Diane Roberts' impending arrival with so many worries nagging at her. Her illness was always on her mind, but she tried to force herself not to dwell on that now. If these dialysis treatments didn't help for any length of time, she would deal with the inevitable later.

Death is the word, you old fool, she thought with a wry smile on her face, a face that belied her seventy-odd years. But now was not the time to die. She had to finish doing the important things that needed doing. There were too many loose ends. For instance, who the hell was copying her paintings? Who dared to duplicate and sell her life's blood? It was an unthinkable situation. How to best handle it was something that must be decided tonight.

"Ouch, you're hurting me!"

"I'm just trying to cover all these white roots." Gia had been with Lucrezia most of her life and had always felt free to say exactly what was on her mind. The two women had long ago established a comfortable relationship, and they never minced words with each other.

Over fifty years ago, Gia had stumbled, half starved, into Lucrezia's tiny apartment in Rome. The struggling young artist barely had room for herself, let alone a decent place to paint, but that hadn't stopped Lucrezia from filling canvas after canvas with magnificent works of art. She had taken Gia in, fed her with whatever the two of them could scrape up between them, and had let her stay on as a part-time model, full-time housekeeper, and trusted friend. Years later, after Gia's husband died, Lucrezia took Gia and her young daughter with her when she moved to Paris. Now, even though Gia was heavy and had trouble getting around, Lucrezia still let her pose occasionally, which pleased the old woman no end. No matter how many servants were on hand, Gia was the only one who personally took care of Lucrezia.

"White roots!" Lucrezia was furious. "I was born with coal-black hair, and I'll die with the same color, no matter what abomination time has wrought on my poor, dead roots. Make an appointment, Gia."

"Don't worry. I've already made a note of it in my head. I just don't want that new young lady who's coming to think of you as an old woman."

"If I hear the word old one more time today, I'll

scream." Lucrezia automatically sat up straighter. She was a tall woman with a straight back and a long, slender neck that supported a proud Italian head. The skin on her face was pale and surprisingly free of wrinkles. Even at her age, she was still referred to as one of the great beauties of the century. "I'll have you know I can still hold my own with the best of them, even when it comes to sex. Ha, I shocked you that time, didn't I?"

Gia placed the last hairpin in Lucrezia's chignon and stood back to admire her work. "You talk like that in front of the American lady, and she'll turn around and leave faster than Mussolini left Rome." Nothing Lucrezia said ever seemed to shock or surprise Gia. She was the only one who knew how ill her benefactress was—that is, besides Dr. Mario Rossi, Lucrezia's dearest friend, as well as her nephrologist.

As if Gia had mentioned Dr. Mario Rossi's name, Lucrezia asked, "Did the good doctor happen to call while I was in the shower? He should have phoned by now." She glanced at the gold-embossed clock on her dressing table. "Mario promised to be here when Cole arrives with Miss . . . What's her name again, Gia?"

Lucrezia rarely waited for answers to her questions these days. She knew she was forgetting more and more and resented the frustration of searching her memory for something she felt should be on the tip of her tongue. "My God, according to Cole's description of her, I can't imagine why they would release her from the hospital so soon. He described the blood and bruises as though he'd been on that jet with the poor girl. Why can't I think of that damned name?"

Gia held up a flame-red hostess gown and helped Lucrezia slip into it. "No, Dr. Mario didn't call. Maybe he'll come directly from work." She zipped the gown up

55

the back and grinned. "I gotta admit, you look plenty gorgeous in this dress. Your figure is still as good as the day I wandered into your studio." Lucrezia could see Gia's eyes become misty with the memory. "You've been so good to me all these years and to my grandson, too. It's a shame he didn't go to college after you offered to pay his way."

"But Angelo's doing what he loves. Where else could I find a chef and chauffeur with all his talents?" Lucrezia didn't object to Angelo's decision. He had chosen to study under one of the best chefs in Paris, and she felt very lucky when he came to work for her. He had traveled all over the world with her and was as devoted to her as he was to his grandmother.

Lucrezia viewed herself in the full-length mirror, noting that the triple strand of pearls was trying valiantly to hide the wrinkles on her neck. "Oh, hell, I look at least two years older than God." She tried in vain to find the young beauty she had been when Brewster Saunders first fell in love with her. Fortunately, the doorbell rang before she had a chance to become maudlin. She hurried out of her bedroom, confident that the caller was Mario.

The tall, portly doctor with a shock of thick white hair was handing Angelo his umbrella when Lucrezia reached the landing at the top of the stairs overlooking the floor below. "Lucky for me I remembered this," Mario said. "It started raining about an hour ago." He brushed some extra water from a well-tailored, Italian-cut silk suit.

Lucrezia realized how distinguished her friend looked. He had never married, and had reached the age and financial position when he felt he could do whatever he wished with the rest of his life. She knew that medicine would always be his first love, but his

56

friendship with her ran a close second. She was glad that he was invited to work this summer in the new kidney dialysis clinic in Chicago. It would be an interesting change of pace from his life in Rome. Because he was treating her nephritis, she doubted that he would have accepted if she had not come with him. He had made the trip very enticing for her, landing her the assignment to paint a mural for the new clinic, owned by a close friend and colleague. As soon as she was contacted, she began making sketches, hired a crew of established artists to work with her, and was now comfortably ensconced in the State Suite of Chicago's Ritz-Carlton Hotel.

"Mario, I'm so glad you got here before Cole arrives with Miss . . . Roberts." Lucrezia was elated that she had remembered the young woman's name at last. She floated down the spiral stairway into the living room, a cloud of red chiffon billowing around her slender body, her voice an octave below that of the average woman, her flamboyant manner that of the undisputed female lead in one of life's continuing performances.

"Aren't you overdoing the grande dame bit?" the doctor asked with a touch of amusement in his voice.

"Not at all." Lucrezia was indignant. "Diane Roberts is expecting to meet the famous Lucrezia. How sad it would be for her to be greeted by some old biddy in a bathrobe and curlers. She'd be miserably disappointed. Really, Mario, you've still so much to learn about women. You should have married, you know. Men learn all kinds of essential trivia from the fairer sex." She turned to Angelo. "Don't just stand there grinning. Bring in the tea before we die of thirst."

Lucrezia sank onto one end of the large sectional sofa that seemed dwarfed in the spacious living room. She sighed with satisfaction as she noted that the maids

57

had been in to clean this downstairs area as well as the two bedrooms upstairs. She had ordered fresh gladioli for the tall vase on the grand piano. The violet-colored flowers blended beautifully with the brown and mauve shades of the fabrics and wallpapers decorating these rooms. She patted the cushion next to her. "Come join me over here, Mario, there's so much to discuss before they arrive. I thought I'd explode before you got here . . . Oh, yes, Phoebe called," she added.

Mario looked worried. "Phoebe from the London gallery? What is it? Oh, damn, not another fake painting?"

"Exactly. She called about an hour ago. Lucrezia's International just bought another 'Interlude.' Remember when I told you a while back that the Mag Mile Gallery here in Chicago had bought the original canvas? Well, Phoebe checked with them thinking maybe they had sold it. But no, it's still hanging on their wall. Poor Phoebe was terribly upset."

"Didn't she have it authenticated before the seller got away? That would have been the perfect time to nail the bastard!"

"Unfortunately she didn't have anything to do with the transaction. A young man was right there waiting for his money. When they discovered that it was a fake, he was quietly arrested, but, according to Phoebe, the police soon became more interested in the case because the man swore that the copy of my painting was given to him by a junkie to pay for a large amount of drugs. Of course they completely forgot about the piece of art when they heard of that and are hot on the trail of cocaine . . . or whatever. Phoebe has the forged canvas tucked away so no one else will ever see it." She sighed, feeling even more distressed. "By the way, she said it's an excellent reproduction. How do you like that? Oh,

58

Jesus, this has really gotten out of hand. Maybe I should have gone to the police instead of hiring such a novice. This forging of my artwork has been going on far too long."

Angelo returned, placing a silver tray containing tea and finger sandwiches on a huge cocktail table in front of Lucrezia and proceeded to fill the china cups.

"As long as she's on her way, I can't see that it will hurt to give her a go at it. You know how we've always felt about calling in the police. Yes, I firmly believe you should give Miss Roberts a chance." His voice was calm, but the look in his eyes told Lucrezia that he was more concerned than he was willing to let on.

"Georges Carnot tells me that she's really quite plain," Lucrezia said as she handed Mario a steaming cup. "He says that she's honest and capable, but rather nondescript. The poor doctor has called at least twenty times to make sure she really survived the crash. He feels so guilty that he sent her to us on that particular flight."

"You assured him that we were expecting her today?"

"Of course." Lucrezia tossed her head in annoyance, then looked thoughtful. "Yes, I suppose we might as well try her out, but who the hell is doing this to me . . . and why?"

"You can't keep asking yourself that same question. Right now you really need to be thinking of Miss Roberts. She must have suffered an awful experience, and she could very well be traumatized." He shook his head. "You'd better prepare yourself. I wouldn't blame her if she were sorry Georges Carnot ever mentioned her name to you. She could very well be ready to back out of the whole thing."

"Yes, that's possible. Anything seems possible to me

59

right now. First, my female detective is in a strange plane crash, and second, another painting has been copied. God knows how many more are out there somewhere—anywhere—in the world. It's damned frightening." Lucrezia could not sit still. She stood and began pacing the large living area, stopping to straighten a flower in the vase on the grand piano, and running a finger over keys to check for dust.

"I hope Miss Roberts can tell us more about the accident," Mario said. "They've given out so little about the cause that I wonder if they're not trying to hide something." Dr. Rossi was obviously trying to shift the conversation to spare Lucrezia's nerves. The fact that someone out there was copying her paintings and selling them for originals was not only criminal but extremely harmful to Lucrezia's reputation.

"She'll probably tell it over and over again until we're all ready to die of ennui. They've repeated so many ghastly details on television that I'm bloody tired of the whole story."

"Bloody? You're sounding more like Cole every day."

"Association begets assimilation," Lucrezia said, pouting.

"Now you're being childish. That's not like you, Lu." Dr. Rossi was the only person alive who could get by with calling her 'Lu.'

"I know, I know. I'm just undone today . . . sorry. I really do feel lucky that Georges Carnot found this girl for me and recommended her so highly. I just hope she'll be able to do the job. Her résumé looks impressive, but what if Georges' judgment isn't what it used to be?" Lucrezia was still walking the floor.

"When he came to see you so soon after we arrived, had you been in touch all along?"

60

"No, I hadn't seen him since he took the post in California nine years ago. Poor thing, I know he still misses Paris and all his old friends. We had such a short visit that he promised we'd get together again at some point this summer." Lucrezia stopped pacing the floor and returned to her seat next to Mario. "Do you realize I've known him since he was ten years old? I gave him lessons at my studio in Paris for years. But going into medicine was perfect for him." She shook her head. "Poor dear just never had quite what it took to be a professional artist, but he came damned close."

"Is that why you confided in him about the bogus paintings?"

"Probably. We've been friends all these years. It was so fortunate that Diane Roberts' name came up. Georges went on and on about how she cleared up a case at the hospital where he practices. Did I tell you about that?"

"Yes, dear, several times."

"You know, I'll have to tell Diane everything about my illness and trust her not to tell Cole." At the mention of Cole's name, Lucrezia's face lit up. Just the thought of her newphew, Cole Saunders, gave new meaning to her day. He was her only living relative, an in-law at that, and she openly adored him.

Just then she heard a key in the lock. Cole had keys to all her doors, including this hotel suite. "Just in case of an emergency," he always said. Both she and Mario stood in anticipation and watched as Cole held the door open for a young woman who was dressed in the green silk outfit that his aunt had chosen for Miss Roberts. Lucrezia never dreamed that it would suit her so perfectly.

"Come in, my dear," she said with a generous wave of her arms. She turned her cheek for Cole's greeting.

Her keen, artistic eye automatically assessed Miss Roberts. She was surprised at the quiet beauty of the young woman. In spite of the bruises on her face, she could see immediately that this was no ordinary woman. Diane Roberts had a definite presence. She was tall and slender, yet quietly curvaceous. Her dark hair fell to her shoulders, framing a heart-shaped face that was dominated by large, clear green eyes. She wore the expensive dress with ease and did not seem in awe of the luxury of the surroundings. She was used to quality, that Lucrezia could tell immediately. This was the plain young lady that Georges Carnot had described?

Chapter Six

Lauren entered the Ritz-Carlton's State Suite, hurting and sore all over. She was breathless in anticipation of meeting the famous Lucrezia, for more reasons than anyone in the room knew. It was an honor to meet a living artist of her stature, a woman whose painting hung in her home—in Alex's home—in Oyster Bay, and whose name was often mentioned in the same breath with the great masters. This was the woman whom she intended to lie to and deceive. Lauren already felt like a criminal, and now finding herself face-to-face with Lucrezia, she wondered if she could actually go through with this fraud. But it was literally a case of life and death.

She straightened up in spite of her aching ribs and managed a smile as she was welcomed into the room. She heard the name of the large, well-dressed man, but it didn't register. She tried to concentrate, knowing how important it was to her future, but her head was heavy. Lucrezia was everything she expected and more. She had black hair and eyes and the whitest skin Lauren had ever seen. She resembled one of her own portraits. In fact, Lauren felt that she had seen that portrait in one of the many galleries she and Alex

63

had visited while abroad.

"We're all so happy to have you safely with us at last." Lucrezia motioned for everyone to be seated. "But we want to give you time to get your strength back and be perfectly well before putting you to work." She looked at Cole and Mario as though seeking help with the conversation, but when neither spoke, she went on. "Would you like to tell us what happened on that plane, my dear—as best you can, that is."

"It was an awful experience, but if you don't mind, I'd rather not think about it. I feel very well, but it's painful to talk about the details right now." As long as Lauren was given a choice, she had no desire to relive those terrible moments. She had to put all of that behind her and have the strength to carry on with this charade, this character exchange with a poor, dead woman who really should be enjoying herself at this very moment in the company of these elegant people. Cole had been the epitome of kindness and consideration during the ride to Chicago. And here was Lucrezia, world-famous artist, so concerned with her well-being. Lauren felt weighted down with guilt. Wouldn't Diane Roberts have cherished this moment! She probably had never in her life been in such an expensive and luxurious suite.

Lauren glanced around to get the feel of observing with Diane Roberts' eyes. The room was two stories high, with a spiral staircase that rose up to a spacious landing which probably led to the bedrooms. As she took a few more steps into the living area, she could see a large dining room on her left, and to her right, a stunning, oversized circular sofa, several occasional chairs, a large cocktail table, and a baby grand piano. Beyond that she could see what was probably a small library or study. She assumed that the suite also contained a fully equipped kitchen. There were few people who could afford to stay in this suite for even one night, much less an extended length of time. It reminded her of Alex's personal suite at the Saint-Saëns, the hotel he owned in Nice, though Lauren thought this one might be even more luxurious.

"I'm sure you must be feeling a little shaky right now, so I'll have Gia show you to your room a few floors down and you can freshen up. Then we'll talk." Lucrezia called to Gia, introduced her to Miss Roberts, and asked her to take the young woman to the room she had reserved for her new employee.

"You're very considerate." Lauren smiled for the first time, touched at Lucrezia's thoughtfulness. "I'll be back shortly. Unfortunately, I don't have anything to unpack."

Lauren left with Gia, wondering for the thousandth time if she could pull this off. She had never felt quite so uncertain and lost in her life. She had no idea why Diane was coming to these people and what would be expected of her. She would wind up being found out before this first day ended. Now was the time to leave before it was too late. But this was her chance. She was safe with these people, and Alex thought she was dead. She could start all over with an entirely new identity and he would never know. Maybe she should give it a little time. But, God, she felt unsure of herself walking in another woman's shoes.

As soon as Lauren was out of earshot, Lucrezia told Cole about her phone call from London and the appearance of another Lucrezia painting that turned out to be a fraud, a deliberate copy.

"Are you still so sure that you don't want the police involved?" Cole asked. "Scotland Yard probably has some kind of information on art frauds, some connections with people who know how to deal with crooked galleries, that kind of thing."

"No, not yet." Lucrezia was adamant. "We'll handle it as planned. As Mario suggested, we'll give Diane Roberts a chance, as long as she's already here."

"I'd sure like to get my hands on the thief who's running this show!" Cole was furious at this latest development. He realized that they couldn't even guess at how many forgeries might be floating around the world. Lucrezia was only thinking in terms of three or four, but there might be ten, twenty, or more. It was frightening to think of what could happen to the impeccable reputation Lucrezia had built up over these years. In his own investigating, he had managed to locate three copies of her work, but had not come close to discovering the forger.

"Well then, let's discuss Diane Roberts, shall we? I'm anxious to know how she impressed both of you. I, for one, was surprised by her appearance."

"Quite a beauty, I'd say." Mario was the first to respond. "She's being very brave. I think I'll follow after her and make sure she's all right."

"Oh, would you? She looked rather dazed." As Mario left the room, she turned to Cole. "Also, most attractive, wouldn't you say?" Lucrezia poured tea and handed him a cup.

"God, yes. I was shocked when I picked her up this morning. Almost thought I was in the wrong room. You know, you told me she was sort of plain. She's not my idea of plain at all. Georges Carnot must need new glasses."

"Well, Georges is in his sixties. Maybe he stopped looking at women that way."

"Oh, come on, Frenchmen never stop looking until they die, and even then, they're probably wondering who they're going to meet in heaven that they already haven't bedded down in this life." Cole smiled at his aunt as he sipped his tea and stuffed a small sandwich in his mouth.

"Bedded down? Really, darling, you don't have to use archaic expressions with me just because I'm centuries older than you. What's come over everyone today? I'm constantly being reminded of my age, and I don't like it."

"You'll never be old, and you know it." Cole reached for another sandwich.

"Four-letter words happen to play a vital part in my vocabulary. I've just not had the occasion to use them with you." Lucrezia gave her nephew a knowing look. "But tell me," she asked with concern in her voice, "how is she, really? What an awful experience for a young woman to have gone through. Can't you imagine how she must feel, wondering why she lived when so many died?"

"We spoke about it on the way here from the hospital. Diane—that's what she wants to be called, by the way—is trying to be philosophical about the accident. There just aren't any answers. She did say she was glad she didn't know any of the other passengers personally. That would have been even worse. Frankly, I don't think the full impact has hit her yet. I'm not even sure she realizes she's a survivor."

"Oh, my, we'll have to be very patient with her. The pictures on TV are horrible . . . everything scattered for miles. That poor child. I even heard there might have been some kind of sabotage." Lucrezia paused as Dr. Rossi walked into the living room and sat down.

"Pour me a fresh cup, will you, dear? I did a cursory examination of our patient. She'll be all right, I think, but we all need to help her with her mental turmoil. People always think survivors should thank God and go on their way. It's just not so. There's a tendency to

67

feel terrible guilt."

"She seems to be a strong, sensible young woman, though, don't you think?" Cole realized none of them knew Diane well enough to answer his question. Mario just shrugged his shoulders and Lucrezia shook her head.

Lucrezia took her friend's hand. "I'm glad we had a doctor here when she arrived. Thank you for coming."

Mario smiled and stood, circling Lucrezia's waist when she rose to follow him to the foyer. "I've a good deal of paperwork to finish before tomorrow. Think anyone will be up to going out for dinner tonight?"

"Oh, let's not ask Diane to go out," Lucrezia said. "Angelo can fix us something here. He's been dying to try a new angel hair pasta recipe. He can surprise us tonight. Eight o'clock?"

"That sounds wonderful." He kissed her on the cheek and waved good-bye to Cole.

"Wait a minute, I need to leave, too, and check with the office, that sort of thing." Cole kissed the top of his aunt's head. She was a tall woman, but he towered over her. "Take good care of Diane."

A surprised smile played around the corners of Lucrezia's mouth. "Smitten already?"

"Oh, for God's sake, can't I show some compassion without your rushing out to have her fitted for a trousseau?"

"Well, I hadn't thought that far ahead yet, but . . ."

"You're impossible." Cole was used to his aunt's constant attempts to marry him off since his divorce. "See you later." He hurriedly left to catch up with Mario, shaking his head in amusement.

When Lauren returned to the suite, she found Lucrezia alone in the living room. "Oh, did the men

68

leave, Mrs. Saunders?"

"'Lucrezia,' please. No one has ever called me Mrs. Saunders, not that I haven't loved the name all these years and the man who gave it to me. Yes, they left, work to do, you know. They'll both be back for dinner."

"I'm glad. I never had a chance to thank Mr. Saunders."

"We're not at all formal around here. It's 'Cole.' I'm sure that's the way he wants it. Look, my dear, your work will be personal, more like a member of the family, understand? We'll just be an informal little group."

Lauren smiled, hoping she could cover her confusion. She supposed they had explained everything to Diane Roberts in detail. "I never dreamed I'd meet the famous Lucrezia, and now I'm practically a relative. It might take some getting used to, but I'm game. Just give me orders and I'll try to follow them."

"I hope you mean that, since I may be asking more of you than you bargained for. Well, first things first." Lucrezia rose and looked Lauren over from every angle. "You're going to need some clothes. Even if they recover your luggage, I'm sure everything will be ruined or scattered. I'm sorry, my dear. How stupid of me to remind you of the crash."

"You don't have to walk on eggs with me. The accident will be on my mind for a long time, I'm sure, so you're not bringing up something I've managed to block out." Lauren was far more concerned at the turn the conversation was taking in regard to her clothes. Soon the money would be discussed, too, no doubt. What explanation could she give for not putting the twenty-five thousand dollars belonging to Diane in a bank? Even if Diane intended on doing just that, Lauren couldn't open an account in either Diane's name or in her own. She couldn't bring herself to use Diane's identification for that purpose.

There were too many questions and she had no answers. Diane Roberts should have transferred her account to a Chicago bank, as any normal person would have done. She should have already opened a checking account. But on the other hand, maybe the money in the brown envelope belonged to someone else or, worse, maybe she had obtained the money illegally. Poor Diane, dead because of her and being blamed for twenty-five thousand dollars in an envelope.

"Come, let's sit down," Lucrezia said, and Lauren followed her to the sofa. "It's good that you have your purse. Cole mentioned that you were still clutching it when they . . . well, anyway." Lucrezia looked embarrassed by her constant reference to the tragedy. "I mean, it's such a nuisance to have to report missing credit cards. You're lucky you don't have to do that."

Credit cards? Lauren hadn't used a credit card in over a month because of her constant fear of being traced by Alex. But what American didn't have a billfold full of them these days? Only fugitives, she thought, feeling more and more guilty with each passing moment. There were credit cards in Diane's purse, but she had better destroy them as soon as possible.

"I did have credit cards, and I've already reported them. I called from the hospital," she lied. "I had put them all in my cosmetic case. Now it seems ridiculous, but I carried the case along with me on the plane, and I thought if anyone were to steal my purse, they wouldn't get my credit cards." Lauren was speaking more quickly, thinking if she got it out faster it would have a truer ring. "Luckily I closed out my account at home and thought I'd wait to open one when I got here. Every cent I have in the world is still in my purse. It must have

70

been some kind of instinct . . . in case I survived, I mean. It's funny how you think of such unimportant things in the face of death."

"That's not at all unusual. I've heard of people doing all kinds of strange things in emergencies. I'm just glad you came through this with relatively minor injuries. But believe me, I can understand that they don't seem minor to you right now." Lucrezia's black eyes were misty as she spoke of Lauren's miraculous escape.

Lauren couldn't remember when anyone had cared enough for her to lift a finger, let alone shed a tear, since her dad died. Lucrezia was becoming a symbol to her, an embodiment of everything a woman should be in life. And here she was lying to her. *Oh Lord,* she prayed, *don't ever let me betray her!*

"You know," Lucrezia said, obviously trying to get the conversation back to normal, "I can't imagine why you closed your bank account. We both agreed that you would be here only on a trial basis at first. Don't you remember?"

Lauren wished she had paid more attention to what Diane Roberts had said on the plane. She didn't remember her saying anything about only being in Chicago temporarily. What else had she missed? Damn that miserable man in the brown turtleneck and those wire-rimmed eyes that hadn't left her for a second! She'd been so preoccupied with how to escape him that she had only half listened to Diane. Everything was even more difficult than she'd imagined. This change of identity was bound to cause more and more problems. And this was only the beginning.

"Yes, of course I remember, but after my father died, there was so little money left that I just sold everything, knowing I'd have to make a fresh start somewhere, even if it didn't turn out to be here." Lauren had lowered her head while she spoke, but now she raised

71

what she hoped were innocent green eyes and thankfully saw only sympathy on Lucrezia's face.

"Let's not worry about anything I said regarding a trial basis. With your credentials and what you've been through, I wouldn't dream of allowing you out on your own. You're here to stay. If you have enough money for clothes, fine. If not, well, just look what a good job I did without even seeing you first." They both looked at the green silk dress that Lauren was still wearing. It was a remarkable fit.

"Thanks, you did a terrific job, but I do have money . . . Do you like to shop?"

"Doesn't every woman?"

"Well, then when you have time, will you go with me to buy my things? I'm not familiar with the stores in Chicago."

"Will I! My dear, we have a date. We'll have a . . . how do you say it in English? Yes, yes, we'll have a ball."

Lauren was enjoying herself, and she began to relax.

Lucrezia was apparently trying hard to make her feel comfortable by drawing her out. "Were you able to spend a lot of time in San Francisco with your father?"

San Francisco? Lauren was dumbfounded. What had San Francisco to do with Diane Roberts' father? "Yes, as much time as I could manage." Once more she felt on guard, hoping for some clue as to what she was getting herself into.

"I understand the facilities at the American Hospital are some of the finest in your country. Were you satisfied that they did everything possible? Being an investigative reporter, you probably were very critical, right?" Lucrezia was probably asking questions for her own purposes. No doubt she was curious to know how caring and sharp a person she was.

So Diane Roberts' father must have had cancer,

Lauren thought, putting that little piece of the puzzle in place. The mention of the American Hospital cleared up her confusion about San Francisco and why they had been there. That hospital was known all over the world for its outstanding work in cancer research. And Diane was an investigative reporter. She remembered now hearing Diane mention her work.

"They're amazingly efficient." Lauren was improvising. She had never seen the hospital, but she had certainly heard of the wonderful work being done there. In fact, she had been to San Francisco several times with Alex, but she had mainly gone shopping while he carried on his business. "I was very impressed with how much personal attention is given to each patient. That's important when people are so ill. Yes, in my father's case, I felt that nothing was overlooked." The palms of her hands were wet. Lauren felt as though all that was missing from this questioning was a naked light bulb shining into her eyes.

"Did you have any family with you for moral support?"

"No, I have no family anywhere . . ." This was becoming unbearable. Lauren was afraid she might panic. She wanted to cry out the truth to this beautiful woman who was being so kind to her.

"I shouldn't have brought up such a sad subject, my dear. It was in terrible taste, and I'm afraid I made you nervous." She handed Lauren a steaming cup of tea. "I can't understand how Dr. Carnot could have thought you plain," she said, apparently attempting to change the subject.

Lauren almost blurted out, "Who?" but caught herself in time. Instead, she cast her eyes down modestly while helping herself to a tea sandwich. *I'm learning,* she thought with a rueful smile. *Living with Alex has certainly taught me to be devious.* The thought of Alex made her hands tremble. She put the cup down carefully, hoping she could keep it from rattling. "I'm ready to begin working when you are. What exactly is it that I'm supposed to do?" She uttered a silent prayer that what she was about to hear would have nothing to do with nursing, something she couldn't possibly fake.

"All right, if you feel up to it. First of all, let me explain my illness to you again. I know we spoke of it on the phone, and I mentioned having nephritis, but I didn't want to say too much before you arrived. Dr. Rossi thinks I'm mad to carry on in secrecy, but I'm determined to go through with my plans. I think I have most of the details worked out in my mind." She took a deep breath and swallowed hard. "Nephritis is a disease of the kidneys. I won't go into all the details right now, only that my kidneys can't function without artificial help. Dr. Rossi wants me to begin a dialysis program with the possibility of a kidney transplant in the future."

Lauren was aghast at the thought of an organ transplant. She had no idea that Lucrezia's illness was so serious. "Can't some other surgery be done?" Diane Roberts had mentioned Lucrezia's nephritis, but she had been so preoccupied with that miserable man to pay much attention. and now he was probably dead, too.

"No, surgical treatment won't correct this disease, and medication doesn't help much. This is the way we're prepared to go for the time being. As it happens," she went on, "Mario doesn't want me to wait any longer before beginning the dialysis. He's gone to great lengths to make the arrangements for me right at the Hudson Clinic where my artists and I are painting a most unusual mural. We start treatment tomorrow morning." Lucrezia leaned against the back of the sofa,

74

her brave facade crumbling for a moment as she closed her eyes.

Dark shadows became visible to Lauren, even through the layers of carefully applied makeup. *This dear, talented woman is actually facing death, and I'm worried about troubles that are nothing in comparison,* Lauren thought. *I swear I'm going to do everything I can for her. Maybe I can eventually make it up to her for all these lies.* "Just tell me what to do."

"I know you told Dr. Carnot that you know nothing about nursing, but I explained my medical condition to you because I need someone to field any questions about my whereabouts while I'm getting these treatments. While I'm away, it will be up to you as my, let's say, *companion* to find excuses for my absences and carry on with my friends and associates as though I were delayed by shopping, water skiing, playing polo—anything you can think of to avert suspicion. You see, it's Cole I'm trying to protect."

"Forgive me for interfering, but Cole seems like a big boy, levelheaded and all. Wouldn't it save you both a lot of pain if you were to confide in him now?" Lauren was involving herself in someone else's life for the first time in years. She thought of Cole, his strength, his clear blue eyes, so filled with understanding when he had rescued her from the mob of reporters and cameramen at the hospital. But even more important, he had taken charge with authority and complete control.

"Cole is strong, of course, and could stand to hear that I'm probably not going to live much longer, but his reaction would kill me. He'd drop everything to give all his time to me. Oh, he'd think he was being clever and subtle, but I'd feel guilty, he'd feel guilty. No, my way is best. And there's a definite reason why I wanted someone outside our circle of friends, someone no one in my organization would know. I don't want any whispering about 'poor old Lucrezia.'"

"Oh, I'm sure your friends would never let you know—"

"That's just it. They'd be so careful, I'd die of boredom." She laughed, a deep, throaty sound. Lucrezia became serious again, and her eyes grew distant. "They would no longer allow me to paint since it's such exhausting work for me. You see, my dear, every waking moment, my mind is actively creating images. I see things differently from most people. When I look at anything of beauty or form, a scene automatically comes to my mind, often already in a mental frame, and I must go to work on that picture as soon as I can get my hands on my brushes. And when I don't have a brush in my hand, I'm frantic because I must capture that mental picture on canvas. I'm compelled to make it live. Sometimes I feel as though my brain is putting pressure on my hand, urging me to paint, paint, paint until I drop. I'm afraid not many people can understand." Lucrezia was in a world of her own.

Lauren felt a shiver up and down her spine. She knew that for the first time in her life she was in the presence of greatness. "I wish there was some way to express my admiration for you and your work." She wanted so much to help this dear woman that she forgot for a moment that she intended to deceive her and ultimately break any trust they might build between them. "I promise to honor your confidences in every way." And after a moment, she added, "I'm really very good at secrets."

Lucrezia laughed. "I really like you, my dear. We're going to get along famously. "That will come in handy when we discuss the real reason you're here. I know Dr. Carnot has faith in your abilities along those lines.

Let's drop the problem with the paintings until after dinner. and we're dining in tonight, by the way. Angelo will fix us a light supper. We all thought it best that you take it easy for a while. The men will be back around eight."

Problem with the paintings? The real reason she was hired? If this Dr. Carnot had been Diane's father's doctor, Lauren had to assume that he was an oncologist. But how had Diane and the doctor become so chummy? And why would he recommend Diane for a job that had anything to do with artwork? Oh, God, he could very well call her to ask how she was getting along. He would surely recognize that her voice was not Diane's. *There's no way I can carry out this identity switch. I was a fool to think I could.*

In as normal a voice as she could muster, Lauren said, "I wish you hadn't changed your dinner plans for me. I'm here to help you."

"Yes, yes, I know, but it will be easier for me to get to know you if we spend time together here."

"In that case, do you usually dress for dinner?"

"You look lovely in the dress you're wearing, and there's no need to change for the men. They're family, and we're only having an informal meal. Tomorrow, if you're up to it, we'll pick out a few new things . . . essentials. You will let me buy you a thing or two? . . . I want to."

"Absolutely not. You've already given me all I'm wearing now, and I want to pay you for it."

"Please, it always embarrasses me to discuss money. Besides, it was all a gift."

"You're being so wonderful and kind to me."

"Not at all."

Lauren felt embarrassed to discuss money, too, and longed to change the subject. "I understand your husband was English. How did you meet?" She was falling under Lucrezia's spell and wanted to know all about her.

"Oh, my, way back. When Brewster Saunders wandered into my little Venice studio with some British friends, it was Gia who saw the light in his eyes and told me he would return, but not just to buy paintings. Sure enough, he was back, and a love blossomed between us and lasted over twenty-five years—until he died. It was really Brewster's money and social position that launched me so successfully at such a young age. I became the toast of Europe because of him. Those were days, years, when every breath was a joy, and every day a new wonder. We began opening our own galleries— Lucrezia's International Galleries. My reputation was established, and I was painting so fast that Brew said it was the only proper way to market my works. From then on, everything sold for higher and higher prices." She looked Lauren in the eye. "Sure you want to hear this?"

"Oh, yes, I do. Please go on." She was flattered that the artist was taking the time to tell her about her life. Listening to her was like watching an actress on stage. She spoke in a low, vibrant voice that had just enough of an Italian accent to make it melodious.

"Brewster Saunders was the youngest son of a wealthy English family. They frowned on any activity that faintly resembled labor. And here was dear Brew, throwing away his life on an artist! To them, that was a few steps below an actress. Well, my Brew was a maverick. He all but abandoned his holdings in Devonshire and devoted himself to managing my affairs. A job Cole has recently taken over, by the way."

"Cole said he spent a lot of time following you around the world. Now I understand why."

Lucrezia sighed, and a wistfulness crept into her voice. "Those were the good days all right. Our fortune expanded along with my reputation. Then suddenly my whole world fell apart. Brewster died of a heart attack. The pain of his not being with me was unbearable. I couldn't eat or sleep or paint. All the beauty was gone from the world. If it hadn't been for Gia, I doubt that I would have survived."

"I don't mean to interrupt," Lauren said, sniffing, "but I need a tissue. I don't want to drip on my only dress."

They began to laugh. "If there's a stain, I'll pay for the cleaning! But, young lady, you've heard enough for one day. To be continued." Lucrezia was still smiling. "I'm going to rest before dinner, and I suggest you do the same."

Both women walked down the hall together. At the foot of the stairs, Lucrezia called, "Gia, come help a poor old lady get comfortable for her nap."

Lauren stood in the living room for a long time after Lucrezia disappeared up the staircase. She had learned very little about her new job and what was expected of Diane Roberts. It had something to do with artwork, and Lucrezia had mentioned that Diane was an investigative reporter. She hoped to God that it had nothing to do with an investigation. She wouldn't know where to start. She left the suite and took the elevator to her own floor. At least she'd know after dinner if she would be able to stay here with Lucrezia.

Chapter Seven

"Shall we have dessert in the living room?" Lucrezia was obviously pleased that the little pasta supper Angelo prepared had turned out so well.

"Nothing but coffee for me." Dr. Rossi patted his stomach in satisfaction. "I don't think I could eat another bite."

"Angelo tells me he's made his special chocolate mousse," Lucrezia said, "and he who can pass it up is stronger than I. Cole won't refuse a helping or two, will you?" Lucrezia turned to her nephew, smiling as she rose from her chair, her red chiffon gown floating about her as she moved.

"I've never refused a dessert in my life." Cole turned to help Lauren.

Lauren folded the black-and-silver napkin before rising. The simple little supper had not only been delicious but had been elegantly served at a dining table that could easily have served twelve. Lauren was impressed with the wonderful food as well as the lavish appointments—the black lacquer-and-silver service plates and glass candlesticks in varying heights, for example, that held lighted black tapers and circled a centerpiece of fresh pink peonies. She had hoped that she might glean some information about her job during dinner, but the conversation had been light, and not a word was mentioned about what was expected of her. She had felt too tense to enter into the chatter and had eaten very little.

As they moved into the living room, she noticed again the richness of her surroundings. She had been so dazed when she arrived this afternoon that she hadn't taken it all in. This suite was as elegant as any fine home she had ever seen. The windows reached the full height of the two-story room, enclosing the outside wall with glass. She looked out the window, fascinated by the tiny, moving ribbons of lights, twinkling as they curved around a continuous expanse of black water twenty-odd floors below. "This is a fabulous view," Lauren said as Cole joined her at the window.

"You're looking at Chicago's pride and joy, its famous Outer Drive. See how it meanders around the shores of Lake Michigan? Spectacular, isn't it?" Cole moved closer to Lauren, looking down at the stream of cars, their headlights shining a brilliant white as they came forward and a glowing red as they headed north.

"No description can really do it justice." Lauren continued to stare in awe. "I've seen pictures of the Outer Drive at night, but only seeing is believing." She looked at Cole and laughed at her trite remark. "Wow, when I want to be profound, pearls come out of my mouth."

Cole grinned. "And I think I might apply for a job at the Chamber of Commerce. Let's go have some dessert." They both took a seat facing the circular sofa.

"Just in time," Lucrezia said as she handed each of them a cup of steaming coffee while Angelo served the chocolate mousse. It was obvious that she was waiting for Angelo to leave the room, but when he had gone, it was Cole who started the conversation. "Isn't it about

82

time we told Diane about the bogus paintings?" he asked Lucrezia.

Startled, Lauren looked at Cole, hoping he couldn't see how unnerved she felt. At the mention of the bogus paintings, she knew she would be expected to do some sort of detective work, and having to leave Lucrezia's home seemed more likely than ever. She braced herself for what was coming next.

Mario turned to Lauren. "Dr. Carnot has already filled you in on all that, hasn't he?"

Lauren had no idea how to answer, but she tried to look innocent and composed. "I never did understand all that was involved. Dr. Carnot didn't make himself very clear. Will you start from the beginning and tell me everything?"

Lucrezia needed no further urging. "I've wanted to get to this all evening, but Mario thought we should wait. Where do I begin? Two years ago—?"

"It may have even started before that," Cole interrupted. "Remember, we've never been able to find out which one was copied first."

"That's true," Lucrezia said. "All right, we think it all began about two years ago. It's so damned frustrating that I can't think coherently. Cole, tell Diane what has been happening, what may well ruin me."

"Okay," he said, "but feel free to jump in if you think I'm leaving out something."

"Believe me, I will." Lucrezia sat up very straight, her black eyes glittering.

Get on with it! Lauren wanted to scream, but she kept her composure and waited, hoping she could understand what they were trying to tell her.

"As you know," Cole went on, "Lucrezia has always been a very prolific artist. Her early works were sold so fast that some of them weren't even titled and are in public and private collections all over the world. But

83

fortunately she's always left her personal mark on each canvas."

"It wasn't that I was so clever," Lucrezia added, "but when I first started out, a local artist told me to put my thumbprint on every single painting because one day I would be famous and some of my work might need identification."

"How right he was," Cole said. "About two years ago, an auction house in New York contacted Lucrezia after they received an untitled painting that had been sold about two months beforehand by a gallery on Fifth Avenue. It was so unusual to see the same painting up for auction so soon after it was sold that they contacted the gallery, who in turn called the buyer to see if she had been unhappy with the painting and had sold it to someone else. Of course, they were discreet with the buyer, but the outcome was that she loved her Lucrezia and it was hanging on her library wall that very minute."

"Hold it a second, you're losing me." Lauren felt desperate. She hadn't the least idea what he was talking about. "What are you trying to say?"

"I'm saying that someone was copying Lucrezia's work. Sorry if I'm confusing you, but the problem of forgery is getting bigger every day . . . monstrous. Copies of Joan Miró, Marc Chagall, to say nothing of Pablo Picasso, are showing up all over the world so fast that no one can keep up with them. But our forger works in a different way, and so far, we haven't found any connection to similar cases. We drew a blank two years ago. The woman still had her painting, but there was an identical Lucrezia for sale on the open market. So the question was: would the real Lucrezia please stand up?"

"Oh, be serious, please!" Lucrezia said, obviously annoyed.

"Sorry, old girl. Guess I've been working on this so long without any luck that I'm trying not to bore the audience." Cole looked so sheepish that everyone smiled, including a reluctant Lucrezia. "At any rate, after months of investigation, we resolved the situation, dropped the matter, and hoped that was the end of it."

"Wait a minute, you've lost me again," Lauren said as she took a chair closer to Cole. "Which painting was the real one? I don't understand."

Mario jumped in, apparently ready to have his say. "Oh, for God's sake, I've already had two desserts and you still haven't come to the important part."

"Don't rush me." Cole looked at Lauren as though enjoying her wide-eyed attention. "The painting that surfaced at the auction turned out to be the original. In other words, the woman who bought the Lucrezia from the gallery had a fake painting in her home, and there didn't seem to be much we could do about it."

"Until you got the bright idea that saved my reputation," Lucrezia said, and held up her hand to stop Cole from continuing. "His plan was so simple we wondered why we hadn't thought of it sooner. Cole bought the original at the auction and had the gallery call the woman to ask if they could pick up her painting for reframing. They made up a story that the frame was defective. Then the exchange was made, the woman had an original, and the fake was destroyed. But that wasn't the end of it. One year later, the same thing happened again, this time at our Paris gallery. It was a different painting, and luckily we were able to learn that the buyer had the original."

"How awful!" Lauren was nonplussed. "Who would do such a thing? Did the police ever catch the guilty person?"

Lucrezia shook her head. "Police? No, no. We couldn't let the police in on it. A juicy story like that would be all over the news in no time at all. From that moment on, everyone owning my paintings would worry about the possibility of having a fake in their homes. Oh, no, we couldn't tell anyone. We had to solve each case ourselves—and take hundreds of thousands of dollars in losses, I might add, but that was the least of it. Whoever is copying my work, brush stroke for brush stroke, is doing it for the huge sum of money a Lucrezia brings on the open market. The copies are so damned good that the forger has to have the original for the whole time it takes to copy it, but that's not possible. The first case proves that theory wrong. So how and where is the thief doing it?"

"Since then, there have been two more forgeries that we've been able to handle in the same way—until now." Cole was completely serious now. "This time, we don't have the slightest hint where to start looking. We found two copies of 'Interlude' in a New York auction, which we've been able to buy, and have authenticated the original. Fortunately now it's here at the Mag Mile Gallery on Michigan Avenue, not far from this hotel."

"Of course they haven't been told that we have any problems," Dr. Rossi said. "The gallery has no idea that there are forgeries around, but somehow we have to get to their records and find the name of the original owner, then try to trace subsequent owners from there. And then, confound it, Lucrezia got a call from London today. Another 'Interlude' has just surfaced!"

Lauren hated to have to ask, but she had no idea of why Diane Roberts came into the picture with this little group of amateur sleuths. "Excuse me, but are you suggesting that I was hired as a detective?"

"Of course! Why else would we have needed you?" Lucrezia looked astonished. "Oh, damn, I had a feeling Georges didn't make himself clear enough to you. He's French, you know, and sometimes he gets so carried away he just rambles." Lucrezia rose and began pacing the room. "Shortly after we arrived in Chicago, Georges called me here at the hotel. He was in town for a medical meeting and read that I was here to do a mural at the Hudson Clinic. He brought his wife with him. I had never met her. They married about eight years ago. She's stunning and very young, considering Georges's age, and from one of the most prominent families in France, I've been told. Anyway, her clothes were magnificent. We lunched at the Pump Room, and over a drink or two, I wound up telling him my problem about the forgeries. He was as mystified as the rest of us, but came up with a great idea. He suggested that I hire you to be my secret private detective."

"Me? But why?"

"Because of the case you solved in San Francisco, when you were researching a story about the hospital. Georges recommended you highly, and told me all about how you solved the case of some missing drugs while your father was his patient there." Lucrezia shook her head. "Didn't Georges even tell you that much? He went on and on about how good you were at your job. I understand your story even made the wire services." Lucrezia sat down beside her and patted her hand. "You're much too modest, my dear."

Diane Roberts was involved with exposing drug dealers! Lauren couldn't believe what she was hearing. Her insides were shaking so hard that she could barely speak. *Good Lord, what have I gotten myself into?* These people were expecting her to be an expert at uncovering crimes, and the only criminal she knew was her own husband. The thought made her shudder. "Well, yes, I guess he tried, but what I did at the hospital was so insignificant that I didn't think of it as detective work." *What am I doing to these people who trust me and believe in me? Damn you, Alex!* she silently screamed. *Look what you've caused! One day I'll see you behind bars if I have to die trying.*

"You're a celebrity, young lady," Dr. Rossi said. "I was impressed at how you single-handedly broke up a ring of thieving hospital aids. That was a damn good piece of detective work. Tell us how you did it so we'll know where to start in this case."

"Well, I . . ." Lauren could go no further. She had no idea how that damned case had been solved. What in God's name was Diane planning to do? Where did she get the nerve to pretend to be a detective? Diane Roberts had been a reporter, and not a very professional one at that. She never should have told a complete stranger on a plane about Lucrezia's illness when the artist was going to such great lengths to keep her nephritis a secret. "It just took a lot of legwork, and luck, too, I guess." She had to take a stab at some kind of answer, as feeble as it was.

"Legwork! That's it!" Cole's eyes left Lauren's legs long enough to come up with an idea. "Suppose Diane and I do just that . . . a lot of legwork. We'll start right here on Michigan Avenue. Once we find the original owner of 'Interlude,' we'll be closer to the person who had it long enough to make these copies. Then we can stop at all the galleries in this area. If one of the major museums in the world had added the painting to their collection, you'd have been notified, wouldn't you, Lucrezia?"

"Of course I would, but what has that to do with—"

"It means that a copy of the painting isn't likely to be found in a museum. First off, that eliminates the Art Institute and the Field Museum. The chances of finding it here are pretty slim, though. So all Diane has to do is visit every other gallery and look for 'Interlude.' That shouldn't take but about ten years. There are more than a few galleries in this world."

88

"Well, it's a place to start." Lucrezia didn't look too optimistic.

Lauren was quick to grab at a straw. "It's worth a try." Her heart was pounding, wondering what she would do if Georges Carnot decided to pay them a visit. "I'll be glad to go, first thing tomorrow, only I don't know Chicago very well." She looked at Cole, who seemed deep in thought. "Did you mean that about going with me?"

"Sure I did. I've been here so often, visiting these galleries, that I can get you started and make a list of the most likely ones for you to carry on with." Cole rose and stretched his long, lean body, yawning audibly.

"Nothing like a subtle hint." Lucrezia smiled, getting to her feet, too. "Then it's settled? You both know how important this is to me. You won't give up?"

"Of course not." Cole gave her a big hug. "I'll never let you down." He kissed his aunt's manicured hand. "We're here only to serve you."

"Oh, go on with you. I can see that we can't do more tonight. Sleep well, Cole." Lucrezia's black eyes sparkled.

Lauren could see the love between Lucrezia and her nephew. It was something she hadn't known since she was fourteen years old, not from her own aunt, and certainly not from her husband. She ached to be a real part of this circle. She knew that she would be fumbling in the dark, but she decided right then and there to give it a try. Tracing owners through records shouldn't be all that hard to do. At least Cole had given her some idea of where to start. She would try for a decent length of time, and if things didn't work out, she would explain everything to them and go on from there. She owed these wonderful people that much.

*   *   *

Jason Lawrence sat alone in a booth near the back of Swenson's Bar, an out-of-the-way joint located on the outskirts of Evanston, Illinois. He was a rail-thin man, well over six feet tall, with thinning black hair. Anyone in the bar who happened to notice him would probably take him for a mild-mannered bookkeeper, but the brown eyes behind his dark-rimmed glasses were as cold and calculating as a cobra's.

He glanced at his watch: 11:25. The old dame was late. Her shift ended at eleven, and she should have shown up by now. He felt slow anger rise. He had given the woman a picture of Lauren Compton and slipped her a hundred-dollar bill with the promise of a full grand if she came up with something. Hell, she probably stuffed that bill between those fat breasts and considered this her lucky day, had no intention of sniffing around. It was worth a try, though. So far he had come up with nothing to back Compton's theory that his wife was alive. Chances were damned good that there was one less rich bitch in this world. He downed the last of his whiskey and water and held up his hand to signal the waitress for another. He'd wait fifteen minutes more, then give Compton a call. This case was going nowhere.

The waitress brought the fresh drink, and as Jason took the first swallow, he spotted Isabel Scott, still wearing her nurse's uniform, standing in the doorway, scanning the dimly lighted room. He sat motionless, but stared at her until he caught her eye.

"Oh, there you are," Isabel sang out. She hurried to Jason's booth and slipped into the opposite side. "I guess you'd about given up on me. Sorry I'm late, but I had a hard time getting away. Why, you wouldn't believe—"

"Keep your voice down," Jason said in a terse voice. "I don't have time to waste. Got anything?"

90

"Sure do."

"Well?"

"You have to understand I'm not used to this sort of thing. But if I can help that poor man find his wife, I'm glad to do it."

"Cut the crap."

"Well, to begin with, there were only four women survivors in that particular age group. I eliminated three right away—two were with their husbands on the plane and the other's folks showed up the next morning. Still, there was one I noticed from the beginning, but her face was so bruised up, I couldn't be sure at first if she matched the picture. Say, how about a drink? It's been a long day."

Jason leaned forward, his dark eyes glittering. "Just get on with it. There's time for that later. What about the picture?"

"It wasn't until today right before she left that I felt sure about her. A man named Saunders came to get her and brought her some clothes. She's the right one, all right, and oh, my, how beautiful! No wonder your friend wants to find her."

"Then she matched the picture?"

"Oh, sure, and then I thought back to how she was scared to death of the television crew and realized why. She was hiding from something . . . or someone."

"Who's this Saunders guy?"

Isabel shook her head. "Seems like she said he was the lawyer of a woman she was going to work for—new job, she told me. The woman's an artist, I think she said, but I can't remember her name. It was foreign-sounding, kind of Italian, I know that much."

"Think hard, it's very important."

"Oh believe me, I've tried to remember, but I can tell you this much, she's probably famous." She laughed. "I'm just not into this art stuff, and the name didn't register. But I'll still get my money, won't I? I found the right one, you know."

"It all depends. Go on."

"She said something about traveling all over the world with this artist, so I figured she wouldn't be in Chicago long."

"Chicago?"

"Sure, that's where he was taking her."

Jason stroked his chin. This could mean their living arrangements were temporary, likely a hotel. "Can you think of anything else?"

"Just give me a minute to think."

Jason's mind churned. It looked like Alex Compton had it figured right after all, and his wife had almost pulled it off. Too bad this old bag couldn't remember the artist's name, but what the hell, he had found people for Compton with less to go on than this. "What name is she using?"

"Diane Roberts—that's how she was registered. Had identification and everything. I had a chance to check her purse while she was asleep, and she sure didn't match the picture on her driver's license. And there's something else. There was an envelope full of money in the purse . . . lots of it, maybe thousands. It's a good thing I'm honest, 'cause I sure could use it." She held out her hand. "That reminds me, where's *my* money? I did what you asked. I found her, and that's what I agreed to do."

"Sure that's all?"

"There's one more thing. I just thought of something. The artist's last name was the same as the lawyer's—Saunders, I'm sure of it. I remember wondering at the time if they were related."

Jason smiled and pulled out a thick envelope filled with small bills, then signaled the waitress. "How about a drink?"

92

"Now you're talking."

Isabel ordered a Tom Collins, and Jason tuned out her idiotic chatter. His mind was on his job and how in hell he'd go about finding Lauren Compton in a place like Chicago with so little to go on. It wasn't the first time Compton had given him such an assignment, and he sure as hell hoped it wouldn't be the last. He'd keep the rental car and drive to Chicago. Tomorrow would be soon enough. He had a matter to clean up here before he left. He waited impatiently for Isabel Scott to drain the last drop of her drink.

"Finished?" he asked.

"Sure could use another one." Isabel was about to signal the waitress.

"Sorry," Jason said. "One's enough. I've got work to do." He stood and waited for the old broad to slide across the seat on the opposite side of the booth.

"I can't thank you enough for all this money," she said, beaming. "Believe me, I needed it. Why, you wouldn't believe how hard nurses work for such low pay. Did you know that—"

"It's been a pleasure doing business with you. Good night."

He walked with her to the door and watched her get into her car and drive away. Then he ran to his own car and pulled out to follow her.

The next morning, Jason sat in his car across the street from Isabel's small frame house in a quiet suburban neighborhood. Her compact car was still parked outside in the driveway. He looked at his watch. Shit! It was nine forty-five, and he'd been waiting since seven. Almost half a day had gone by, and he needed to get on the road to Chicago. If Isabel Scott's shift started at three, the whole damned day would be wasted.

But then, as though on cue, a side door opened, and Isabel Scott, dressed for work in a white uniform, bustled out the door and hurried to her car. Jason felt his adrenaline start to flow as he gave her time to fasten her seat belt and locate her keys.

He heard the sound of the ignition, then saw a flash, just for an instant, before the whole neighborhood rocked with a deafening explosion. The car burst into a ball of orange-and-yellow flames, with pieces of metal and glass flying like missiles in every direction.

Jason's dark eyes gleamed. He never left a trail behind, and he never did a job halfway. But he had to admit, this one ranked damned close to the top. It was spectacular.

Chapter Eight

Lauren and Cole were silent as they rode the elevator down to the lower lobby. It was a hot summer day in Chicago. Lauren still wore the green silk dress that Cole had brought with him to the hospital but had left the matching jacket in her room. Her body ached in more places than she could count, but she didn't want to complain.

Once in the lobby, the doorman pushed the revolving door for them and they stepped outside. Cole took her arm and led Lauren across the covered passageway that carried cars to and from the hotel garage. Before she knew it, Lauren was going through yet another revolving door that opened into a large, air-conditioned department store.

"Marshall Field's," Cole said as he guided her past fresh plants and flowers, past various counters and aisles, skillfully skirting avid shoppers. They finally pushed through double doors that put them onto Michigan Avenue.

"That wasn't fair," Lauren said, out of breath. "Here I am in my only dress and you have the nerve to rush me through Marshall Field's."

Cole laughed. "Just be grateful I didn't go the other

way and pull you through a different maze of aisles, doors, and a huge atrium. We'd have wound up in Lord and Taylor."

"And I'm supposed to thank you for that, when I don't have a stitch to my name?" There was humor in Lauren's voice, but she would have loved to stop just long enough to buy a pair of walking shoes. She was still wearing the heels she bought at Henri's in Los Angeles, and they were far from comfortable. They were already heading south on Michigan Avenue on foot. "What exactly was that place anyway?"

"Water Tower Place—quite a unique complex. The atrium I mentioned is the entry to seven floors of shops and restaurants." He smiled. "Don't worry, I promise to show you all of it. The building goes up and up from there. On the twelfth floor is the lobby of our hotel. And then above the hotel are the Water Tower Apartments—rather nice, I've heard. Condominiums, they're called."

Lauren smiled at the idea of an Englishman explaining a condo to an American. But she didn't want to embarrass him by calling attention to it. "How many floors altogether?"

"Now you've got me. Seventy-two, I think."

"And you'll show me all of it?"

"Glass elevators, McDonald's and all." He laughed. "That look on your face is making me feel guilty. We can postpone the visit to the gallery if you like."

"Lord, no. We set out for a purpose, and I can go shopping any time. Right now we're going to find the original owner of Lucrezia's 'Interlude,' no matter what it takes. The thing is, I'd like to know how many miles we're planning to walk, since I'm not in the most comfortable shoes."

"Oh, I'm really sorry." Cole looked down at Lauren's feet as though he expected to see blood gushing forth.

"We could have taken the car or hailed a cab, but I like walking on Michigan Avenue and assumed you would, too, without a thought to your comfort. Well, it's too late now. The gallery is directly across the street. I guess you think I'm a clod."

"Don't be silly. I wanted to walk, too." Lauren couldn't mention that she wasn't used to wearing such inexpensive shoes. Instead, she concentrated on the gallery Cole had pointed out. It was large, with an imposing facade—black granite extended upward three stories, and the display windows were equally high, exposing an elegant staircase on the inside. "Come on," she called when the light turned green and she hurried to cross Michigan Avenue. "I have a feeling this traffic doesn't wait."

And she was right. Horns blared, crowds scurried, people jostled one another. Those slower souls who stopped on the middle island to wait for another signal watched carefully for any sign of a careless driver, ever ready to retreat a few feet one way or another.

Cole caught up with her in front of the carved black double doors whose heavy brass pulls dominated the entrance to the Mag Mile Gallery. She took a deep breath, mustering her courage, ready to see if she was any good at all at this investigating thing. "Okay," she said, "I'll do the talking since you're my client. Let's go inside."

"Sorry, but I'm afraid I'll have to do the introductions. They know me."

"Oh, sure, I forgot. All right, you start the chatter while I case the joint." Lauren looked up at Cole with an impish grin. All that was missing was a rumpled trench coat to complete her character. Cole squeezed her arm in appreciation. They entered the gallery with Lauren feeling more than a little foolish and having no idea where to begin.

"Cole Saunders, how nice!" A sleek blonde greeted Cole with extended arms and planted a kiss on his cheek. "We all know that Lucrezia is in Chicago doing a mural, and I've spoken to her several times about our recent acquisition of 'Interlude,' but I didn't realize you were here, too. Had I known . . . well, there was a formal exhibit last night . . ." Lauren decided she was the epitome of the intimidating salesperson, the kind who makes the customer feel she couldn't possibly afford anything in that department and makes her want to slink away in shame for daring to invade her sanctuary.

Cole smiled and put his arm around the woman's narrow waist. "Lydia, I'd like you to meet Diane Roberts. She needs to check through your files for the names of some of Lucrezia's original purchasers, to trace present owners, that kind of thing." He was deliberately vague, his face all innocent smiles.

Lydia barely glanced at Lauren. Her eyes were busy devouring Cole. "Darling, of course, anything you want, but you must know our files are very private. I would have loved taking you to the exhibit last night at the Four Seasons. Everyone who is anyone in Chicago was there."

"Sorry I missed it. That would have been fun, but at the moment, Lucrezia is very anxious to have your cooperation in letting Miss Roberts search certain files, very discreetly, of course, just for certain buyers."

"Right now? Sorry, darling, but I don't have the keys to the vault where we keep records, and even if I wanted to . . ."

"And you don't want to?" Cole's blue eyes were cold steel.

"Now don't give me that look." Lydia obviously preferred to disregard Cole's insinuation, not willing to play anymore. "No one, and that means no one, can search our books, period. End of conversation. It was so nice to meet you, Miss Robbins."

Bitch, Lauren thought, barely able to control herself, but in a calm voice, she said, "Roberts. Diane Roberts. It would be a shame if we had to get a court order to examine all your books. The IRS might be interested in doing a little checking, too. I understand they're pretty good at finding discrepancies that take months and sometimes years to clear up. Besides . . ."

Lydia glared at Cole. "Who is she? Did you bring someone from the IRS here?"

"Not yet, but that's a thought. We're only interested in Lucrezia's clients for the time being." His voice was pure ice, and Lauren didn't dare look at him for fear she would burst out laughing. "We're not interested in financial records, just names of purchasers."

Lydia seemed relieved. "Why didn't you say so? You just want to check on Lucrezia's painting sales? How far back? We're always anxious to cooperate with anyone working for Lucrezia."

Lydia must have had her hand in the till for some time to have capitulated so easily, Lauren thought. She was proud of herself for putting a scare in the bitch. She suppressed her emotions and tried to look as professional as possible. "If you'll show me the records as far back as the very first sale, Miss . . . ?"

"Just call me Lydia, dear. Everyone does." Her voice and attitude toward Lauren had changed considerably in the last few minutes.

"That's kind of you, but for the record, I'd like to know your last name, too. Funny, but I feel better when I know the full name of my friends . . . and enemies." Lauren could hardly believe the words had come out of her mouth. When had she become so hard? She had heard these very words somewhere before. Of course! When she'd listened to the tape she made of conversations in Alex's study, someone had said something very similar, only in a much more ominous voice. And now that tape was lost forever in the fire and rubble of a shattered airplane.

"Lydia Patterson. My grandfather, Sylvester Patterson, opened this gallery in 1926." Lydia's head rose a little bit higher, and her shoulders squared proudly.

"May I see the books now, Miss Patterson?" Lauren wasn't anxious to be on a first-name basis with this barracuda. She had to admit, though, as she looked around the gallery, that she was very impressed with the quality and quantity of the paintings for sale.

Cole was doing the same thing, walking from wall to wall, examining the artwork on display. "I see you have two Lucrezia prints on hand, along with this wonderful 'Interlude.'" He motioned for Lauren to join him in front of an oversized canvas that was almost all white. A second look revealed shadings ranging from pale violet to soft pink, then to a pink beige and off-white, and back again to pure white, all done in graceful swirls and curves. It was the most restful painting Lauren had ever seen. Cole seemed pleased that Lauren seemed to truly appreciate the quality of Lucrezia's work. He turned back to Lydia, who had a puzzled look on her face. "How much do you think the prints will bring?"

"Oh, they'll sell quickly, 'Lucrezias' always do. They're priced rather low since more prints were made from the cuttings than usual. About two thousand dollars each." She looked at Lauren. "I hope you can come back this afternoon. I really don't have the key right now." Her voice sounded about as sincere as a packet of artificial sweetener.

"Diane will be back at two-thirty, Lydia. Think you can find some desk space for a few days, with a phone, of course?" Cole was all business.

"Anything you say." Miss Patterson was obviously

trying to recapture the easy, flirtatious note that had begun this conversation.

She watched Cole Saunders and this stranger walk out the door. She had lost ground, and she knew it. Being haughty didn't pay off with everyone, she realized too late. What in hell was Cole up to? He was looking for something, and until she found out exactly what it was, she would play along for her own protection.

"Well, now you know what the 'Interlude' looks like." Back on Michigan Avenue, Cole was holding Lauren's arm. A cool wind suddenly swept over them as it drifted in from Lake Michigan, a few blocks away.

"Oh, that feels good." Lauren closed her eyes for a moment and relished the sudden relief from the heat of the city. "It reminds me of what the 'Interlude' is saying to anyone fortunate enough to see it: 'Relax, rest, and let me wash over you like a cool breeze.'"

"You're going to relax all right," Cole said as he quickly hailed a passing cab and they both got in. "You look so great I keep forgetting that you need pampering for a few days. After that clever little maneuver you pulled on our Miss Patterson, I think you're entitled to lunch on me. Do you realize I don't know what kind of food you like?"

Lauren was grateful for the cab ride since her feet had begun to swell in her new shoes. She had bought them in such a hurry that they probably weren't even her size. "How could you be expected to know anything about me? We only met yesterday." She felt her eyes crinkle in pain, but hoped Cole took it for amusement.

Cole smiled. "Just yesterday? I feel like I've known you forever. Sure we didn't meet in a past life?"

"Well, even if that's the case, I think I'd have liked a

hamburger for lunch then, too."

"And I was about to suggest ambrosia."

"You caught me. I'm just plain Jane after all." By now they had reached Pearson Street. Lauren was anxious to check on Lucrezia to see how her first dialysis treatment had gone. She didn't think she'd be back from the clinic yet but wanted to call the suite just in case. "I see we're right back where we started. Is there a coffee shop or something in the hotel?"

"As a matter of fact, there's a great cafe where they serve a mean hamburger. How about it?"

"Sure, if you have the time to waste on me. You've been more than kind, and really, if you have something else to do, please do it. Don't worry about me."

"Enough of that." He ushered her into the elevator that would take them to the lobby floor of the Ritz-Carlton.

The cafe was located on the left side of the lobby, concealed only by low plantings so one could watch all the activity at the bar and the main lobby. Even though it was early for lunch, the cafe was already crowded. Most people had made reservations, but fortunately Lauren and Cole were able to be seated.

Lauren excused herself for a moment and rang Lucrezia's suite on the house phone. Gia told her that Lucrezia had not returned but had said that her treatment would last for at least three hours and that she planned to do some work on the mural afterward. She returned to the table, her mind on Lucrezia, wondering how this elderly woman could be so ill and still drive herself so. She felt guilty that Lucrezia was going through her first treatment alone.

"What a wonderful life you must have led, being so close to your aunt and living around such talent. When you were young, did she let you watch while she worked?"

102

"Oh, yes. Lucrezia can be caustic when something interferes with her work, but she's the kindest, dearest . . . well, don't get me started on the wonders of Lucrezia as a woman. I was six when my mother died. Aunt Lucrezia and Uncle Brewster had been married for twenty years and weren't able to have children. Father was always traveling on legal business, so it seemed to work out better for me to spend my holidays from school in Italy with them. I cared about them very much, and I'm afraid they spoiled me beyond repair."

"I'll pass on that one until I know you better."

He laughed. "To answer your question, yes, I watched and I watched, not quite believing how any one person could create such beauty. By the time I appreciated her magic, Lucrezia was well established but still covering canvas after canvas as fast as she could. Right before my eyes, an empty canvas became a living, almost breathing symbol of pure beauty under her flying brushes. And the colors! She used combinations of the most blazing tones anyone ever dreamed of." Cole looked sheepishly at Lauren. "It's your fault, you know—you got me started on my famous aunt."

"But I love hearing about her. I've always loved her work. And now, to be actually working for her. We had a Lucrezia in our . . ." Lauren stopped abruptly, startled at her near blunder.

"Anything wrong?"

"Wrong? Why no. I—I was just thinking about someone I know who owns one of her paintings. He was so proud of it and would be so jealous if he knew where I was right now. Please go on."

"Well, okay. It was her flower period that I was describing," Cole said, "yet nothing was ever painted in the shape of flowers. She just borrowed color from them. Lucrezia said that no one could improve on the original. Ever since she could afford it, great bouquets

103

of fresh flowers have always been a part of her life, no matter which of her homes she's in. Before she married, they tell me, when she was poor and lived in Rome and Paris, there were flowers in wicker baskets when she could afford them. Now the Oriental porcelain vases they're in are almost as costly as one of her paintings."

Cole looked at his watch. "I have a lot of business to take care of before this day ends. Look," he said as he signed the check, "why don't I call Lydia and tell her you'll be in tomorrow instead of this afternoon? Lucrezia will probably appreciate having some time alone with you before you're all involved in your heavy investigating."

"That's a good idea. Say, are you making fun of me?" Lauren's green eyes searched Cole's face with peculiar intensity. She was more curious than hurt, wondering if Cole thought there wasn't a chance in hell of her finding the forger. After all, he'd been trying to track him down for two years or more. And she couldn't blame him. She certainly had no confidence in herself as a bogus, novice investigator.

Cole's businesslike look brushed aside any answer or any more questions. Lauren could tell that his thoughts were already far away from her, probably on some legal work that he'd neglected while helping her. They parted at the elevators.

Lauren was grateful to be alone in the elevator. Her pulse was still banging like a kettle drum at her close call with Cole when she'd almost given herself away by mentioning that she had lived with a Lucrezia in her home. Alex had acquired "Beginnings" shortly after they married, and it was one of his most prized possessions. He had found it at Sotheby's in New York, and was fond of bragging about the fortune he'd spent on it.

If only this elevator ride could go on and on and take

104

her away from Chicago and this whole mess of a new identity. If only she could wake up, miraculously free, unmarried, unscarred, unafraid. But she was afraid. She didn't feel competent enough to pull off this ruse. She took deep breaths, trying to regain her self-control. Damn Alex! He left her no choice.

Chapter Nine

When Angelo opened the door to the State Suite, he informed Lauren that Madame had returned and was waiting for her in the library. Lauren hurried to join her.

Lucrezia looked surprisingly well. Lauren hadn't known her long enough to make positive comparisons, but she did seem to have more color, even through the layers of makeup. Once more she marveled at how handsome a woman Lucrezia was.

"Well, tell me!" Lucrezia rose, pulling Lauren over to the sofa. "I want to know what you found out at the gallery." She looked at Lauren in amazement. "Good God, you're still in that same dress? We've got to get you some clothes before everyone thinks you're in uniform. We can talk while we shop. Come on, come on. What in hell are you waiting for?" Lucrezia was halfway to the door.

"I don't believe this! How can you even think of clothes? *My* clothes, I mean, when you've just returned from such a traumatic experience. Why, I've been on pins worrying about you. And I don't even know you."

Lucrezia stopped in her tracks, then walked slowly back to the study where Lauren was standing. "You were really worried about me?" She seemed amazed.

"Of course I was. Is something wrong with that?" Lauren felt embarrassed. Lucrezia looked so confident. Her white silk suit was immaculate and complemented her sleek black hair to perfection. She looked like a woman in full charge of her emotions.

"No, I guess I've kept this damned nephritis a secret for so long that I'm grateful for anyone's concern. Right now I want to throw my arms around you and maybe cry."

Lauren melted. She knew only too well what it was like to keep a secret walled up inside. If only she could tell Lucrezia about Alex and his threats, about the tape and all that had happened as a result, and about stealing a dead woman's identity. The temptation was overwhelming, but she didn't dare. Instead, she put a comforting arm around Lucrezia. "How long did the treatment take?" They sat down again.

"Too long. I thought it would never end. But," and her face was again animated, "it wasn't too bad, and I do feel much better for the moment. So maybe . . . maybe." Lucrezia crossed her fingers, holding them for Lauren to see. "There's really nothing more to tell, not yet. Mario says it will take a while to know how much help dialysis will be and how long it will last. I have to get these damned treatments three times a week. But thank you, my dear, thank you." Lucrezia pulled out a lace-trimmed handkerchief and blew her nose with vigor. "Now, shall we go shopping?"

There was no stopping her this time. Lauren and Lucrezia spent the rest of the afternoon buying an entire wardrobe for Lauren. It was the first time either of them had a reason to purchase every item of clothing possible, from nightgowns to evening gowns. Lauren filled Lucrezia in on the visit to the Mag Mile Gallery while they had the time of their lives, as only women who enjoy fashion can. They returned to the suite, exhausted but triumphant.

Two days later, Lauren waited for Lucrezia as she was leaving for the Hudson Dialysis Clinic.

"Just where do you think you're going?" Lucrezia asked.

"With you, so don't fuss." Lauren stopped Lucrezia as she started to protest. "You told me I could see your mural, and I was hired as more than an investigator. You wanted me to be a companion and a trouble-shooter. So, I'm going with you." Lauren faced Lucrezia, putting her hands on her shoulders, looking her right in the eye. "And I'd like to see what a dialysis treatment is like. May I?"

"Well, I guess so." Lucrezia's voice was gruff, but Lauren could tell that she was secretly pleased.

They found Angelo waiting in the limousine at the front entrance to the hotel. He jumped out to assist the women, his greeting as cheery as always. He was one young man who seemed to love his job.

"Did you learn anything at the gallery?" There was always anxiousness in Lucrezia's voice when she spoke of the forgeries.

"I've found the name of the original buyer, but not much else so far. I hope you don't mind my taking the afternoon off to be with you."

"My dear child, I'm flattered."

After a twenty-minute drive, they pulled up in front of a contemporary stone-and-glass, two-story building that appeared to be void of windows. A large brass and stainless-steel sign designated its purpose: LINCOLN J. HUDSON DIALYSIS CLINIC. Once inside, they walked into a wide, glass-enclosed atrium where people, ladders, pulleys, and paint covered one entire wall. The artists greeted Lucrezia excitedly, everyone talking at once, all wanting advice on various aspects of the unfinished mural.

Lauren took a few steps back for a better view. Lucrezia's concept had the effect of a stained-glass window, each odd-sized panel depicting several people —men, women, and children, in various stages of growth and development, glorious colors surrounding them. The mural was magnificent, overwhelming in size and scope.

"So what do you think?" Lucrezia seemed pleased by the look of awe on Lauren's face.

"It's . . . it's . . ." Lauren was speechless. There were no words to describe her enchantment.

"It's not finished. Is that what you're trying to say?" Lucrezia obviously couldn't hide her pride as she let her artists know what a great job they were doing in following her carefully conceived blueprints and diagrams.

"When it's finished, could I take a photograph of it?" Lauren asked. "Nothing like this has ever been done that I know of, and it's perfect . . . beautiful."

"Of course. In fact, we'll have some professional prints made and you can have all you want." Lucrezia looked at her watch, then gave a great sigh. "Now it's time to launder my blood. Shall we enter Dracula's lair?"

Dr. Rossi was waiting just inside the door and introduced Lauren to his friend, Dr. Richard Hudson, and explained that he was a distinguished nephrologist, as was his deceased father, for whom he had named the new clinic. Dr. Hudson was duly modest when answering that he hoped to earn the reputation that his father had enjoyed.

Lucrezia was shown into a large room and seated in a leatherlike chair that resembled a recliner surrounded by equipment. The room contained about thirty such chairs, all of them occupied by patients in some stage of dialysis treatment.

"Does the sight of blood bother you?" a nurse asked Lauren.

"I don't think so."

"My name is Betsy. Be sure to let me know if it bothers you." Betsy pulled a stool over to Lucrezia's chair, and Lauren sat down to observe the procedure. Next to the chair was a huge machine with all kinds of colored dials, buttons, and tubes.

"We call this the kidney," Betsy said, "because it actually takes over the work of the kidneys while the patient's here."

"Just watch the size of the tool they have the gall to call a needle," Lucrezia said. "They're going to stick two of them in my vein—fistula, really, the one that was made surgically. Look, there's one coming and one going. Just watch those tubes and you'll see my dirty blood getting cleaned of nasty toxic waste, then returned to the other tube. Fresh and clean for another two days, I hope."

"Isn't she something else?" a male technician said. "She kidded with us the whole time we were getting her fixed up the first day she was here. At her age, you'd think she'd be scared, but . . ."

"If you mention my age one more time, sir, you'll know what it is to be scared!" Lucrezia scowled at the young man.

Lauren grimaced as Betsy slid a long needle attached to a tube into a veinlike area of Lucrezia's arm, then inserted another a few inches lower in the same arm. "Doesn't that hurt?" she asked when Lucrezia didn't flinch. "Are you being brave just because I'm here?"

"Believe me, I'd be screaming so loudly they'd hear me in Rome if this really hurt. I keep quiet for no man!

111

There's Mario—ask him if you don't believe me."

Dr. Rossi smiled. "She's very special, but this part of the procedure usually isn't painful. I think Dr. Hudson could make you understand better than I can, though."

Lauren turned to the other doctor. "Oh, please, I don't want to take you away from your patients."

"That's all right, Miss Roberts. Everyone is in good hands." Dr. Hudson looked around the room with pride. It wasn't that the patients necessarily looked happy, but they seemed resigned to undergoing this procedure to keep on living. "Ordinarily, unless the patient has unusually large veins, we perform a Gortex graft, but since Lucrezia's veins are very small, we did a Bovine graft by inserting extra materials obtained from a cow to strengthen the area of the fistula."

Lucrezia laughed. "If I start mooing and walking on all fours, you'll understand why."

"See what I mean?" the technician said. "This old lady's a real card."

"Young man, I may have to kill you!" Lucrezia said. "There's been enough talk. My favorite soap opera is on, and I want Angelo to take Diane back to the gallery so she can get some work done. This will go on for an eternity." Lucrezia placed earphones on and manipulated the miniature TV set that was attached to the right arm of her chair. They were all dismissed so far as she was concerned.

Dr. Rossi shook his head and smiled as he led Lauren out of the room.

"Just a minute, you two!" Lucrezia called. "There will be about thirty people in for cocktails tonight, so don't be late." Her earphones were on again, not giving either of them a chance to reply.

*　　*　　*

Checking the books at the Mag Mile Gallery turned out to be a tedious job for Lauren. She had never had a job before and didn't know anything about organizing her work. Before she left for the gallery on the days that Lucrezia was having dialysis, she spent a couple of hours answering the phone, accepting or declining various invitations. Since Lucrezia was a celebrity in town, Chicago's society and art circles fought to entertain her.

By the end of the second week, she felt discouraged trying to trace people, only to find that they were no longer living and no one knew what had become of the family. But she did find the name of the original owner of "Interlude" and learned that it had been bought from Lydia's grandfather. But other than that, she had come to a dead end.

One evening after dinner, Cole observed that Diane seemed more discouraged than usual. He never dreamed she would be so diligent in so fruitless a search. He knew only too well how she must feel. He'd been there several times himself. It was a hell of a job to try to track down a painting if it had changed hands several times over a period of years. It was even worse to try to search for an elusive art forger.

He was disappointed that he had seen very little of Diane these past two weeks. They had had dinner together almost every evening, along with Lucrezia and Mario, but she seemed to go out of her way not to be alone with him. Usually they had cocktails before Lucrezia left for some dinner or affair that she felt obligated to attend. Often his aunt invited some of her Chicago friends in for drinks and hors d'oeuvres and it seemed that there were always people around.

Diane Roberts was a beautiful, vibrant young woman, yet she hadn't tried to make any friends of her own and seemed content to go to her suite and spend

113

each night alone. Pleasing Lucrezia seemed to be her main objective in life. He had never met a woman quite like her—so honest, so honorable, so guileless, and so unpretentious. Everything she did or said solidified his first impression of this lovely young woman.

Enough of this polite chatter, Cole thought as the group sat having coffee in the living room. He had to get Diane alone. The more he saw her, the more he wanted her. There it was, plain and simple. He wanted her so much that he could think of nothing else, day or night. He could almost taste her. It just wasn't right for both of them to be alone in separate beds night after night. He looked over at Diane, who was talking to Mario Rossi, so composed, so unaware of him. He scowled and ran his fingers through his blond hair. He'd had his share of affairs, had been married and divorced, but had never felt quite like this. And he'd never even touched her. Jesus! What it would be like to make love to her!

Just then, he noticed her looking at him, motioning for him to join her. He felt as if she had been reading his mind as he excused himself and followed Diane to the study.

"Oh, I'm really at a dead end here in Chicago," she said. "What I need to do is go to London to check out the forgery, maybe find out more about who brought it in, who the check was made out to, that sort of thing."

She had never looked more lovely to Cole. The bruises on her face had completely disappeared, leaving a flawless complexion. Her green eyes, though troubled, were the exact color of an emerald necklace his mother had owned, the one piece of jewelry he had managed to salvage after his divorce from Iris. The clothes Diane had selected were tailored and understated, just right for her willowy figure, and in impeccable taste.

114

"That's not a bad idea. What's your problem?"

"Everything is taking so long, and I know Lucrezia must be annoyed with me. I hate to mention London."

"So you want me to do it." Cole gave her a crooked smile and looked at her with interest.

"Would you? It's asking a lot, I know."

"What's in it for me?" He kept his tone casual, but his heart was doing crazy things.

"What do you mean?"

"Exactly that. If I suggest this jaunt to Lucrezia, I think I ought to go along to watch the expense account."

"You're joking! I wouldn't dream of taking you away from your work."

"But how would you find your way around in a completely foreign city?" He had made up his mind. He would introduce London to Diane. She would love his hometown, his favorite city in the world, and how it would love her!

"Foreign? London isn't foreign to me. Why, I've been . . . I mean, that is, people do speak English there."

Cole didn't notice her slip. He was already anxious to pack. "Sure they do, but the money is different, and it's so big. There's no way you could get along without me. I'll go with you, and that's the end of it."

"Well, Lucrezia might have other ideas. When will you ask her?"

Cole winked at Diane. "Right now. In fact, I'll make our reservations and we'll try to leave tomorrow. Where's your passport?"

"Passport. Sure, I need a passport." She looked crestfallen. "How long does it take to get a new . . . I mean, a passport?"

"You don't have one? I remember telling you on the phone before you left for Chicago how Lucrezia can

115

make up her mind in a flash to be off for any part of the world, and to be sure to—"

Lauren interrupted, her face brightening. "Wow, you must think I'm ready for the funny farm. I just remembered, I do have a passport. It's in my purse." She ran into the foyer to get it, rummaging through it on the way back. "I don't know why, but I carry it around with me all the time. I'd just never had a chance to use it and forgot I had it." She finally dumped everything into her lap until she came up with a passport and handed it to him. He noticed that her hands were shaking.

He smiled indulgently at her and shook his head. Women carried so damn much junk around in those bags, it was no wonder they couldn't remember what they had in them.

"Oh, one more thing, before I forget that, too . . ." Lauren said. "Since there's no need for me to go back other than to pick up my notes, can we save me a trip and stop by the Mag Mile Gallery on the way to the airport?"

"No problem." Cole couldn't wait to make all the arrangements. He hoped to God they could leave tomorrow. He would finally have Diane all to himself and intended to make the most of this unexpected windfall.

Jason Lawrence propped the yellow pages against the wall of the phone booth to skim the listings of galleries one more time. Only three were left. For days he had pounded the sidewalks of Chicago, checking out all the hotels, art galleries, museums, and auction houses. At least he had come up with something. He finally found someone who would tell him that the Saunders woman was known professionally as Lucrezia. If she happened to be registered at one of the hotels, the people running the desks had obviously been told to keep her registration confidential. That was the trouble with these damned celebrities. They were far too grand to let their public in on their whereabouts. On the other hand, Lucrezia might just as well be living in a private residence. He shuddered at the thought. Finding Compton's wife through that route could take as long as a month, if it were possible at all.

His eyes fell on the address of the Mag Mile Gallery located on Michigan Avenue. That was only a few blocks away from here. Maybe he'd have time to check this one out before closing time. It was worth a try. Shit, Alex Compton would be ready to have his head if he didn't come up with something soon.

He headed down the sidewalk, walked two blocks, and turned the corner, checking the street numbers every now and then. The Mag Mile Gallery finally turned up in the middle of the next block. He opened the door and stepped inside, walked past the reception desk, and entered the first room on the right. The walls were filled with paintings, ornately framed, and small benches were spaced strategically for viewing. Jason pretended to study the paintings, one by one, and now and then he ran across Lucrezia's signature. He didn't know the first thing about art and didn't care to, but damn, the dame was pretty frigging good if he said so himself. He had been in the room a few minutes when a well-dressed, rather snooty-looking woman approached him.

"May I help you?"

Jason was about to launch into his usual story about needing to get in touch with Lucrezia Saunders and could she please help him when he caught sight of a young couple standing in the doorway.

"We're leaving now, Lydia," the man said. "See you in a week or so."

"Have a good trip," the woman said, and turned her attention back to her unlikely-looking customer. "As I was saying, may I help you?"

"I think I've found what I'm looking for," Jason said, and ran out the door behind the couple. Damn, if that wasn't Lauren Compton, he'd screw his own mother. It had to be. Compton had furnished him with several clear eight-by-tens of his wife, and this woman was the living image of the pictures. He reached the sidewalk, just as the pair climbed into a white limousine. The chauffeur trotted around to the driver's side and quickly sped away.

"Damn! Shit!" Jason growled. Furious, he raced up the street, waving his arms to attract the attention of an approaching cab. It stopped. He jumped into the backseat and yelled at the driver. "Follow that white limo!"

The driver turned around to look at him. "You're kidding, aren't you, not another car chase?"

"I'm not kidding, dammit. Catch up with that limo and I'll give you fifty over the meter."

"Hell, man, you're on!"

Jason's luck ran out at the second red light. The limo had stayed well in sight for two blocks, but the cab was caught at the light behind two other cars. By the time the light changed, the limo had turned the corner and was nowhere to be found. Finally, after searching every side street, Jason gave up and decided to try the next best thing. "Take me back to where you picked me up."

He returned to the Mag Mile Gallery again just as the woman called Lydia was about to lock the door.

"I'm sorry, but we're closed. You'll have to come back tomorrow. We open at ten."

Jason pulled a switchblade knife from his inside

118

jacket pocket. "I think I'd rather come back now."
Lydia took a few steps backward as Jason pushed the
door open and entered. The gallery had the quiet sound
of an empty building. "All alone?"

"Yes . . . uh . . . no," Lydia stammered.

"What is it, yes or no?"

"I don't know . . . I think . . ."

"You're alone, right? You were locking up, weren't
you?"

Lydia nodded, her eyes wide with fright. "Please
don't hurt me. We don't keep much money in the safe,
but if that's what you want, you can have what's there."

"I'm not after money, and I'm not going to hurt you.
I just need a little information. If you cooperate, I'll be
out of here in no time."

"Just tell me what you want to know." Lydia's voice
was shaking, and so low that he could barely hear her.

"That's better, but you need to speak up." He kept
the knife pointed at her throat. "First of all, who was
that couple who just left here?"

"C—Cole Saunders and his assistant. Diane Rogers
or something like that."

"Roberts?"

"That's it. I'm sure of it."

"You mentioned something about a trip. Where are
they headed?"

"The airport."

"And?"

Lydia hesitated for a moment, and Jason stepped
closer, touching the point of the knife into the hollow
of her throat.

"And?" he said again.

"They're going to London on the seven-thirty flight.
I think they mentioned the Concorde."

Jason glanced at his watch. Six thirty-four. He had
time to make the flight if he hurried and could get a

119

seat. "Just one more thing and I'll be gone. Where are they staying in Chicago?"

"The Ritz-Carlton." Lydia looked relieved to be almost rid of him.

"Good girl," he said. He turned and headed for the door, pausing just as he reached the exit. "You've been a big help, and I want to leave you with something." He pulled out a revolver with a silencer from his pocket, aimed at her heart, and fired.

She dropped to the floor, facedown. Jason walked to her side and rolled her over. Blood oozed from the wound, painting her well-tailored jacket with a red stain. Her eyes were wide open, staring a dead stare, but Jason fired another shot into her body for good measure. One could never be too careful, and he liked to wrap things up nice and neat.

Turning off the lights, he left the gallery, walked casually down the sidewalk about a block, and crossed the street to the opposite side. He hailed another cab, this time promising the driver a hundred dollars above the meter if he could get him to O'Hare in half an hour.

The cabbie earned his extra fare, pulling to a stop at the terminal at 7:05. Jason dropped the money on the front seat, jumped out of the cab, and made a dash to the first pay phone in sight, then quickly dialed Alex Compton's private number in New York.

"I found your wife."

"It's about time. Where?"

"In Chicago, but she's leaving for London in a few minutes. I'm calling from the airport."

"Do you have a ticket?"

"Not yet."

"Hell, man, have you lost your mind? Move!"

"Right. But do I grab her in London or put a bullet in her?"

"Just keep up with her. She can't hurt me as long as

120

the world thinks she's dead, but I need to know what she's up to. Understand?"

"Right, Mr. Compton. I'll get back to you."

Jason hung up the phone and hurried to the British Airways ticket counter. "I need a coach ticket on the Concorde on the seven-thirty flight to London."

"I'm sorry, sir," the ticket agent said, "but there's no coach seating on the Concorde." She punched a few keys on the computer. "I do have an available seat, though, if you're interested."

Jason grinned. "That's wonderful." He opened his wallet and paid for the ticket in cash. Hell, planes like the Concorde were the only way to travel. Now he could sit his ass in a comfortable seat, sip champagne from a crystal glass, and have Lauren Compton in plain sight all the way to London. Damned good deal if he said so himself.

Chapter Ten

It was raining lightly and the air was chilly when they landed in London. As Cole checked Diane into the Dorchester Hotel, he felt a sense of déjà vu. He should have chosen a different hotel. It was good that he was staying around the corner in his own condominium. Iris was everywhere he looked. They had spent many afternoons here in the months before their wedding— the wedding that should never have taken place. It all came back to him as he watched Diane sign her name on the register.

"Darling, you simply cannot keep me bare-assed and cooped up in this room forever. It's time you made an honest woman of me. I haven't seen the light of day in ages." Iris Wickersham was the only daughter of Valerie and Archibald Wickersham, first cousins to an aunt of the Queen of England. She was a tall, graceful girl, with flaming red hair and alabaster skin.

"Clothes are for gilding a lily, and you, my pet, are definitely not a lily." Cole laughed as he poured more champagne in Iris's empty glass.

"But we're so perfect together, and, besides, everyone expects us to marry. We shouldn't disappoint them." Iris wrapped a satin sheet around her body, carelessly dragging it off the bed as she moved toward Cole. "We are in love, aren't we, darling?"

"If you say so."

"I don't say so! That's why I'm asking you, silly. We've been friends for years and years, so we know we'll be good together and probably live happily after ever."

"Ever after."

"I like after ever better."

Cole took Iris into his arms, allowing the sheet to slip to the floor. "In that case, will you marry me so we can live happily after ever?"

Iris tossed her glass into the fireplace and threw her arms around Cole's neck. "Damn, I thought you'd never ask. Now let's go practice being married some more."

And so the wedding had taken place. But ever after or after ever turned out to be neither nor. Not that they hadn't both tried to make a go of it. They were two very decent people. The problem was that they had separate careers that meant a great deal to each of them. Cole, who was becoming a distinguished barrister, had a growing interest in criminal law. And Iris was an editor for one of the top fashion magazines. And, too, they were both brought up in households where they usually got their way in all matters.

The beginning of the end of their marriage came on a cold, windy day in February after six years of marriage.

"Darling, I've been trying to have a serious conversation with you for several weeks," Iris said as she pulled on her driving gloves. She was dressed for work in boots, a suede skirt, and a matching jacket, and looked as chic as any one of her fashion models.

"I knew something was brewing in that red head of

124

yours. If you'd wanted to talk, I was here to listen."

"Oh, rot. You're never home."

"I'm only gone at dinner . . . don't relish eating alone, my pet."

"You know very well that this is our busy season, and Harrington is an excellent cook. You hired him yourself, remember?"

"You're right," he said, "but you had something to discuss?"

Iris took a deep breath. "They've offered me the New York office, and I can't turn it down." She looked up at the expression on Cole's face. "Well, I must say, you don't seem overjoyed for me. I'd be managing editor there—my own boss at last, and I've worked hard for that job."

"Well, I can testify to that all right, by the evenings you've been gone."

"Come on, you're gone as often as I am."

"Just when it concerns an important case."

"Every case is important to you, but you can't see the importance of anything I do."

"There's a difference, don't you think, since I'm the breadwinner?"

"Breadwinner? That's a laugh. You could eat cake the rest of your life and never make a dent in your inheritance from your father, so don't tell me you're working to feed me. You're only feeding your own ego, sweetie."

"In that case, there's nothing more to be said. When will you leave?" Cole didn't care anymore. Iris's blows were getting pretty low.

"The first of the month. I've already rented a lovely place near the park. Please come with me, Cole. You could open a New York branch of your law firm. Hell, you'd probably even make another fortune. You and that aunt of yours have a knack for coining money."

"It's not a knack," he said in a cold voice. "It's called talent. No, I don't think I'd like your place near the park. I'd be reminded too often of the children you don't care to have."

"Oh, for God's sake, let's not get on that subject again!" Iris looked at the clock. "It's getting late. I'd better go." She closed the door with more of a bang than she had ever done before, Cole thought. She wasn't brought up to slam doors.

But that hadn't been the end. After weeks of transatlantic calls with much pleading on her part, Cole decided that he was being much too chauvinistic. Iris had as much right to a career as he did. She loved her work. It gave her a sense of being, accomplishment. It was the wee hours of the morning in New York right then, but he'd call her anyway and tell her he'd changed his mind. By damn, he'd open an office there after all.

Iris's phone rang several times. He was about to hang up when a sleepy male voice mumbled, "Hello." At first it didn't register. He must have gotten a wrong connection. But then, he heard Iris's unmistakable voice in the background. "Who is it, sweetie? Who's calling at this hour?" Cole quietly replaced the receiver. A speedy divorce was all he wanted right now. He would find it hard to trust a woman ever again.

Lauren felt some jet lag but wouldn't admit it to Cole. He seemed so excited about showing her his town. She had almost given herself away again the other night. That was turning out to be the most difficult part of trying to be Diane Roberts, having to pretend that she'd never had anything material in her life, never worn fine clothes, never been to Europe. And now she had to act as though she didn't know London at all, when it was one of her favorite cities.

She would have to go sightseeing with Cole and pretend it was a whole new adventure. Everything was becoming more and more difficult.

But she had come to love Lucrezia, and working for her was an experience she would treasure the rest of her life. That is, if she could count on any kind of life that didn't include Alex or the threat of him. Alex. Lauren shuddered, and a cold chill ran down her spine. Her obituary had been formally published. Legally, she no longer existed. Were Alex to find her this time, he could kill her without fear of punishment since officially she was already dead.

And if he killed her, who would mourn her? Who was there to care if Lauren Compton lived or died? What had she ever done to make anyone think twice about her? The friends she made in college were no more. Alex had seen to that by making them feel uncomfortable and scaring them off. She had lost touch with them years ago. For a short time, she had thought Trudy might become a friend. What a fool she had been, so trusting, so naive. She was now convinced that Trudy worked for Alex. There was no other way that anyone following her could have gotten enough information about where she was going and what flight she would take. There simply hadn't been enough time to check all that out and then appear like an evil phantom to haunt her on the flight. That is, until the crash. Hopefully, that was the end of one of Alex's hired killers.

At least, Lauren thought, maybe she was becoming more sophisticated, less gullible, more realistic when it came to judging people. And yet, it was all a complete fraud at the expense of the real Diane Roberts. But, she had to admit, it was more desirable to be a live fraud than a dead wimp. Disgusted with herself, Lauren picked up the phone and called Cole's condo. She had better let him show her London and be thankful she was alive to see it again.

As Lauren sat down at the restaurant for dinner, she felt sure she wouldn't be able to eat a thing. She was bone-tired after sightseeing for hours, especially after that long plane ride. She could tell Cole had enjoyed taking her to the places that visitors to London always haunted, like Westminster Abbey and Buckingham Palace, where they saw the changing of the guards. At her request, because she thought the average tourist would be interested, they visited the crown jewels and the famous Tower of London, where Henry VIII imprisoned his wives before having them beheaded. She was glad that Cole felt they should postpone their work at Lucrezia's International and the Tate Gallery until tomorrow. She had to get some rest and clear her head.

As it turned out, the food was delicious, and she felt rejuvenated. Cole was excellent company. They hadn't been alone much in Chicago. Lucrezia adored people, and there were always plenty of them around. Lauren thought that Lucrezia was frantically trying to cram as much living as she could into each day, knowing that her time was running out. Dr. Rossi had confided to her that he didn't hold out much hope for the dialysis treatments to work for Lucrezia much longer. Lucrezia was no fool. She, too, was aware of Mario's opinions but never discussed it, was always cheerful and as active as ever, working on the mural at a frenzied pace.

"Well, tell me, how do you like London so far?" Cole asked.

He was wearing a navy silk-linen blazer with a white turtleneck shirt, and looked positively dashing. Lauren had noticed heads turn as they were ushered to their

128

table. She had been concentrating so on being Diane Roberts, trying so hard to get some concrete information on the forger, worrying so about Lucrezia's reaction to her dialysis treatments, and keeping Cole from finding out about his aunt's true state of health that she hadn't really looked at him since that first warm meeting in the hospital. Besides, no matter what she thought of Alex, she was still married to him and had never once looked at another man. Wouldn't the women's libbers make mincemeat out of those archaic thoughts!

"I love it," Lauren said.

She smiled at Cole across the narrow table and lifted her wineglass, intending to take a sip. He did the same, and their hands accidentally brushed against each other. For a split second, delicious currents of forgotten passion surged straight to her very soul. Now his hand rested on the table and was so close to hers that she could easily touch it. She ached to touch it again. What was he saying? She couldn't concentrate. She wanted desperately to allow her fingers to move toward his in such a way that her hand would be protected. The urge was almost uncontrollable. Lauren was frightened by this sudden, all-consuming desire, powerful enough to carry her emotions into a state of utter chaos.

Cole seemed to be studying her with a new intensity. "I know so little about you. Tell me about yourself. For instance, what were you like as a little girl?"

"Strictly a tomboy. I was always pretty good in sports, especially baseball, but the boys in our neighborhood didn't let me play with them very much. But when they needed a few r.b.i.'s, they always knocked on our door and asked my dad if I could come help them finish the game." At least she could finally answer a question with honesty. "My life is so uninteresting and ordinary; why don't you tell me more about yours. Didn't you say that you'd been married?" Suddenly she wanted to know all there was to know about Cole Langston Saunders.

And Cole evidently wanted Diane Roberts to know all about him. "There's not too much to tell. I guess this scenario has been played out time and time again. It's just that I recognized all the flaws too late, after a good deal of soul searching, I mean." Cole casually picked up Lauren's hand and absently touched his lips to her fingertips as he spoke. She could scarcely breathe. "I was young. Iris was even younger. We both came from fairly prominent families and had partied together as children, gone horseback riding when we were both at our families' country estates. You know, the old story of children growing up together and parents expecting them to marry eventually. Well, we went right along with tradition, all that sort of thing. A large wedding followed, with all the right people invited. The gifts were duly catalogued and acknowledged."

"You sound bitter," Lauren said. "What happened to your storybook marriage?" Lauren silently prayed that Cole was not still carrying a torch for Iris, then wondered why in the world she suddenly cared what he thought about his former wife, or anyone else, for that matter. He had let go of her hand, but her fingertips were still sending strange messages to her brain.

"Bitter?" Cole appeared to be examining the word, turning it over and over as though looking at a flawed jewel. "Yes, that's as good a word as any. I didn't know it showed."

"Oh, not much, just when you mention her name. If it's too painful, please, don't go on."

"The pain is long gone, but so is a lot of my trust. I'd like you to know that you're completely different."

"I hope that's a compliment." Lauren was sorry she

130

had asked about his marriage. She was afraid to hear more about Iris.

"Getting married spoiled everything, for Iris anyway. You see, I'm sort of old-fashioned. Marriage to me meant commitment, giving, sharing, even having children. Iris had a career of her own and was completely devoted to it. Still is, I suppose. When she was given the chance to move to New York as the editor of a posh magazine, there was never a thought of turning it down. She did the right thing, because divorce for us was inevitable."

"But she was at fault. I don't blame you for not forgiving her."

Cole laughed. "It was as much my fault as hers." He stretched back in his chair. "At any rate, it all worked out for the best, as the old saying goes, and we're friends again. You know, thinking back, there was never a time when we actually thought we were in love." He reached for Lauren's hand again. "Let's call it a night."

The ride to the Dorchester in Cole's rented car ended all too soon for Lauren. She could have stayed at the restaurant and listened to him talk for hours, but in no time they were standing outside her room.

"I guess it's good night," Cole said at the door. "We have a busy day ahead of us tomorrow."

"Yes, and we need an early start." She couldn't keep from looking into those sky-blue eyes. He was so handsome. She felt a sudden lump in her throat as she stared at him.

"Very early," he repeated. Before she realized what was happening, she was in his arms, her eyes still on his, her face tipped up. "Oh, Diane," he said as he brought his mouth down upon hers.

His lips were soft and warm and her own trembled slightly at first, but within seconds they became

131

urgently responsive. Something close to paradise soared through her as he gently kissed her, searching with his lips. The spicy scent of his aftershave enveloped her as he tightened his grip around her body. This was so wrong. Wrong for every conceivable reason, but somehow it felt so right.

He lifted his head and tilted her chin with the tip of his finger. He looked at her, searching her eyes. "Diane . . . Diane." He repeated her name as if for the utter pleasure of saying it.

"Good night, Cole." She couldn't keep the huskiness from her voice.

"I want to go inside with you."

"No, not now. We have to get up very early . . . so much to do tomorrow."

"The investigation can wait. I want you and you want me. There's no way we can get around it." He bent to kiss her again.

She turned away slightly and his lips found the side of her face. "I can't. This isn't right."

"But it is right . . . so right." He pulled her closer. "Can't you see what's happening between us?"

She gave him a nervous little smile. "As far as I can tell, what's happened is that I've just been kissed by a very handsome man."

"That's not it at all, and you know it."

"You hardly know me. There's so much you don't know, and we simply can't do this." Her voice was bright and social, the expression on her face tightening. Her body, so yielding just seconds before, became stiff and quivering with the urge to be free. She felt self-conscious, aware of the lighted hallway, the people coming and going to and from their rooms. "I'll see you in the morning. Good night."

Lauren's hands shook as she closed the door behind her and leaned against it. This couldn't be happening.

132

Every ounce of her longed for Cole, but she simply couldn't allow herself to fall in love with him. Cole had made it plain that he had a hard time putting his trust in women, and everything about her was a lie. She couldn't let anything happen between them. But deep down she knew that she would not be able to resist him.

Chapter Eleven

Lauren stood over the bathroom sink staring at the puffs and circles under her eyes. *It serves you right,* she thought, furious with herself. *You didn't deserve a good night's sleep after the way you acted last night.* Cole had expected her to jump into bed wiht him. And why not? She had let her feelings spill across the dinner table as carelessly as the tipped milk glass of a small child. How close she had come to telling him everything—that she was married, whom she was married to, and why she was pretending to be Diane Roberts.

Oh, there was just too much for anyone to understand, let alone forgive. But what a relief it would have been to unburden herself and let Cole take over completely. And he would have. That was one of the wonderful things about him. When would she ever learn that she had to stand on her own two feet before she could respect herself as a human being? It just wasn't easy to juggle all these new pieces, along with the realization that, yes, she was in love with Cole Saunders.

No teeth had ever been so vigorously flossed and brushed as Lauren's were that morning after she had admitted her feelings for Cole. She had to wash him out of her system. There wasn't room in her dangerous, involved, mixed-up life for this kind of complication.

She picked up the phone and dialed Cole's condo. It was only six A.M., she realized too late.

His voice was slightly slurred but brisk when he answered the phone.

"Did I wake you?" Lauren could scarcely believe it. She was feeling so guilty about everything, even the time.

"Why no. I always sit around at the crack of dawn hoping maybe the phone will ring. Of course you woke me. What is it, you're sorry about last night and want me to dash over to your room right now?"

He was laughing at her, but Lauren didn't care. At least he wasn't angry. His deliberate, husky tone did all kinds of strange things to her. "Yes, I'm sorry in a way, and no, I definitely don't want you to rush over here. As a matter of fact, I'm calling to tell you that I'd rather work on my own today. And I know you probably have a lot of work to catch up on here in your London office."

"So you were scared, hmm?" She could still hear amusement in his voice.

"As a matter of fact, yes. Now will you let me go my own way today? I have a job to do and can't concentrate with you laughing at me all the time."

"If I let you out of my clutches today, will you wear something green and filmy tonight? I want to show you off at Simpson's on the Strand."

"I have something chiffon, but not green."

"Go shopping, my love, go shopping. Charge anything to me. London has never seen the likes of you. I'll call for you at nine."

He was off the line before Lauren had a chance to argue. She'd *never* charge a gown to him. Impossible.

136

Maybe she could spend some more of Diane's twenty-five thousand dollars. She'd think about it when she took a break for lunch.

It might have been better to have Cole with her after all, Lauren thought as the cab dropped her at Lucrezia's International. But she knew Lucrezia had told Phoebe to expect her, so there shouldn't be a problem getting any information she needed.

Phoebe was in her midforties, a small blond woman who certainly seemed to know all about the artwork she was selling. She immediately showed Lauren the "Interlude" forgery. She took Lauren into her office, locked the door, and asked not to be disturbed over the intercom, before uncovering the fake painting. Lauren was shocked. To her eye, it looked identical to the original that she had seen hanging on the wall of the Mag Mile Gallery.

"Why, it's beautiful! I had no idea a copy could be this good," Lauren said.

"Yes, it's good. That's why it's so hard to catch art forgers. These copies sometimes hang in someone's home for years." Phoebe sat at her desk, angrily tapping her pencil.

"But how in the world can you tell one from the other without an expert on the scene all the time?"

"By instant identification," Phoebe said. "That is, if the forger hasn't been too careful—and you'd be surprised how sloppy some of them are and still get away with it—there is usually some small identifying mark that each artist will hide somewhere on his canvas. Of course, we know Lucrezia's mark. Then, too, most galleries number their paintings on the back of the canvas to identify the origin of the purchase."

"But how did you know this was a fake and the one in

137

Chicago was the original?" Lauren was becoming fascinated by the work she was doing as Diane Roberts.

"I can tell you that it was not my decision," Phoebe said. "Mr. Merriweather has been with this gallery since it opened over thirty years ago and has an eye for fakes. However, this one was so unusually good that he did a bit of scraping on the edge of the canvas that covers the frame. He wouldn't have touched the actual painting—that's left to an art expert. At any rate, he found wet paint! Can you imagine the nerve of someone in such a hurry for money that he or she couldn't even wait for the canvas to dry?"

"Then why did you buy it if Mr. Merriweather knew it was a fake?"

"Because Lucrezia wants to take any and all forgeries off the market, no matter what it costs her."

Of course. Lucrezia had explained that when she first told her about the forgeries, Lauren thought.

"Actually, we're lucky in this case, since at least we know that this painting hasn't had time to have another owner," Phoebe said.

"But when could the forger have gotten the original to have it long enough to copy it? It must have been recent, since the Mag Mile Gallery hasn't had it too long."

"Did you ever find out whom they bought it from?"

"Oh, yes. I worked that one out in Chicago." Lauren smiled apologetically. "However, I don't feel at liberty to discuss any of that. I hope you understand."

"Certainly." Phoebe covered the painting and propped it against the wall. "How about some coffee?"

"That sounds great."

Phoebe pushed a button and a small wall of the bookshelf slid back to reveal a bar area and an electric plug where a glass container rested with fresh, hot coffee. She poured two cups and handed one to Lauren. "It never fails to amaze me, the way these forgers operate, I mean. I don't know if you realize it, but the modern forgers didn't really take hold until the early 1980's. Dali prints were copied by the hundreds of thousands at that time. And, like I said before, some were unbelievably sloppy, but they still sold for two and three hundred thousand dollars each."

When Lauren first began her job, she had started to carry a small notebook and pen, just to make herself look more professional, but now she actually found it quite useful. She rapidly took notes on what Phoebe was telling her.

"There was so much competition among forgers that they had to smarten up," Phoebe went on. "Now they go to the trouble of duplicating the water marks on the papers used to forge their prints so it will resemble the paper used in the original more closely. Now, if they're copying a living artist, they have the gall to buy the paper from the very same source as the artist." Phoebe glanced at Lauren, who was still furiously taking notes. "Stop me if I'm boring you."

"Are you kidding?" Lauren felt that she was finally learning something about what she was being paid to do. "I never dreamed anything like this could go on without the law being able to put its hands on the forgers."

"Well, after a six-year hiatus, Scotland Yard has reinstituted its art and antiques crime squad. In your country, the Federal Trade Commission and the Department of Justice are conducting sweeping art fraud investigations. These scandals are coming to light and even written up in papers like *The Wall Street Journal*. It's high-tech crime, and believe me, these criminals are hard to catch. I know Mr. Cole has come close several times in the past, but so far, he's come up empty-handed."

"Have there been any arrests that you know of?" Lauren was curious to know how Lucrezia's forger would be treated if ever caught.

"So far they've been very discreet, but I happen to know that one of the largest art gallery chains in the country has been indicted."

Lauren stood. "You've been very helpful. I can't thank you enough, Phoebe. I'm sure Lucrezia warned you how confidential my investigation is. She doesn't want any publicity."

"Oh, yes, I know. As I said, I worked with Mr. Cole in the past. You can trust me."

"I was sure I could." Lauren smiled as she shook Phoebe's hand. "Before I leave, I'd like to wander through the gallery if you don't mind. Lucrezia's work is so outstanding, I get goose bumps just looking at it."

"Be my guest. If there's anything I can help you with, please don't hesitate to ask."

Lauren couldn't help but wonder if Phoebe was a little too anxious to help. She certainly had access to a major part of the collection. Did she dare ask if she ever tried to paint herself? No, she decided, she was probably loyal and innocent and would be so hurt that Lucrezia would lose one of her most prized managers.

Instead, Lauren walked from painting to painting, studying the different periods of Lucrezia's work. Her personal life must have had a great influence on her paintings. She felt so privileged to know and work for such a famous woman.

She stood in the middle of one of the gallery rooms, letting the wonder of Lucrezia's art surround and envelop her. She turned her body slowly, absorbing the emotional impact of each lovely canvas. Suddenly she stopped, her eyes wide with terror. Cautiously, she turned her head, fully expecting to see Alex's silver head and powerful body behind her, hear his voice taunting her, or feel yet another blow, one that might kill her this time.

There was no one. She was alone in the room. But his painting was hanging on the wall. "Beginnings," the Lucrezia painting that Alex had bought for them shortly after their honeymoon, the piece of art that he had gone to such trouble to have authenticated, then had hung with such pride in their library, was here, right on the wall in front of her.

Lauren reached a nearby cushioned bench and eased herself down, her pulse racing. She had to think. She took a deep breath and wondered if Alex could have sold his treasured Lucrezia. Never. She knew him well and he never gave up any possession. How difficult it had been trying to escape from him after his brutal nature became a reality to her! She had pleaded so for a divorce before resorting to hiring a professional to tape his library, to plant bugs in the room and his phones. No, this had to be a forgery.

She rushed toward Phoebe's office, trying to decide if she should call Cole first or make an overseas call to Lucrezia. She stopped. What would she tell them? That her husband had "Beginnings" in his library on Long Island? That she was terribly sorry and she thanked them very much, but she was not Diane Roberts after all, but really the resurrected dead wife of an infamous racketeer? Oh, no, she wasn't ready to give up yet. Not when she was beginning to function as Diane Roberts, not when Cole was trusting her and maybe, maybe falling in love with her. And most important of all, not when she was almost relaxing in her new role without the terror of Alex hanging over her head. Her fear of Alex would linger until he and all his associates were either dead or in jail, stripped of all their worldwide political power. She wondered if she would ever live to see that day. She doubted it. Alex seemed more powerful than the government that sought to investigate him.

No. She couldn't tell anyone about her discovery of still another forged painting. Lauren knew she was doing Lucrezia a terrible disservice, but her own life hung in the balance, and telling them would probably bring them no closer to the solution than they were now.

Lauren couldn't wait to leave the gallery, but first she had to have a place to work for a few days. Finding the identity of the forger could possibly involve Alex. She shook her head. She was becoming hysterical. It was too preposterous to think that Alex could be masterminding a gang of nefarious artists. No, she didn't believe it would be lucrative enough for him. Alex was inclined to go for much bigger bucks and the sweet smell of world power. He would never wait for his money until the paint on a canvas became dry enough to pass as an original. Besides, even though he had little respect for human life, he did revere the arts. Still, she had better make sure by checking every possibility.

She poked her head into the manager's office. "Phoebe, do you have a desk with a phone I could use for a few days? It can be in any corner. There are some things I want to check out while I'm here."

"Certainly. Lucrezia made it clear that you were to have anything you needed."

"Good, I'll be back after lunch." Lauren hurriedly thanked Phoebe again, then almost ran down the lengthy aisle to the outer door. She hailed the first cab she saw, grateful for a chance to relax.

"Where to, mum?"

Where indeed? Lauren hadn't thought that far ahead. If she were to go shopping as Lauren Compton, her first inclination would be to phone Jean Muir or

Sonia Rykiel to see if either designer had any clothes on hand that might interest her. They would both recognize her in a moment. As Diane Roberts, she'd better pick a department store. "Harrods," she told the driver. She could lunch there or somewhere nearby, if nothing else.

After wandering through Harrods, looking at bags and sweaters, shoes and hose, but not seeing anything but Alex's face, Lauren left the exotic fresh flowers and wonderful take-out foods behind and settled for a cozy restaurant right down the street. It was small, picturesque, and intimate, and not too crowded. She ordered a sandwich and tea and tried her best to gather her wits.

It was no use even trying to swallow lunch. All thoughts of shopping for a dress to wear this evening had long since left her head. In spite of having been frightened half to death by the appearance of "Beginnings," Lauren couldn't wait to get back to the gallery. She hailed another cab and soon settled herself in the tiny office Phoebe had arranged for her.

From the start, while working in the Mag Mile Gallery, she had found that the "Interlude" painting had been bought by a Mrs. Rita Gardner Rhodes in 1950. The Rhodes family had been prominent in Chicago for generations. In checking, Lauren had determined that Luther Rhodes had made a good deal of his money from the sale of illegal alcohol back during the twenties. It seemed that the painting remained in their home on South Shore Drive until Mrs. Rhodes's death. At that time, since the painting had increased in value, it was left to a daughter, Martha. Martha married . . . who? Lauren rummaged through Diane's ersatz Louis Vuitton bag until she found the notebook.

It was almost funny. When she had begun her investigating in Chicago, Lauren felt like a bumbling fool. She had no idea what she was doing, but decided to keep notes on every little detail so anyone checking on her in the future would think of her as a true investigative reporter She had no idea that any of the information would ever amount to anything. After all, Cole was an attorney with all kinds of people on his staff, and none of them had discovered the identity of the forger. Not that she was even close, but somehow, seeing "Beginnings" and knowing that she could check on everyone who had been in her home on Long Island—until she ran away, that is—gave her some kind of edge and a certain feeling, a feeling that maybe she was on the right track. She felt excited. Now wouldn't it be something if she could catch the thief!

Ah, there it was. Martha's last name was Clover. Her death preceded her husband's, so "Interlude" had been in his possession for some time. When John Clover remarried, he gave the painting to his son, Edgar, who sold it for a nominal amount of money. So far, end of trail.

But now, even though the trail seemed lost for "Interlude," Lauren could start checking out "Beginnings." She couldn't tell anyone that the painting hanging on the wall of Lucrezia's International was probably not an original at all. But if someone wanted to buy it, she'd have to tell Lucrezia. She shrugged. She'd worry about that if and when it happened. Right now, she had a lot of work to do.

She heard a soft knock on the door and Phoebe's voice. "Miss Roberts . . . ah, Diane."

"Yes, come in." Lauren leaned back in her chair and rubbed the back of her neck as she turned to Phoebe.

"I hated to disturb you, but you've been working so hard, and I have an idea that might help you."

"Anything will be appreciated, believe me."

"Well, if I were looking for an art forger, I'd put an

144

ad in the newspaper."

"What kind of ad?" Lauren knew Phoebe meant well, but she was wasting her time.

"Well, if the ad said something about doing a retrospective on all Lucrezia's works from such and such a date to whatever date, and that top prices were being offered for any originals, I think the forgers would fly out like termites, anxious to sell their copies as originals."

Lauren rose and threw her arms around Phoebe. "Then all we'd have to do is have Mr. Merriweather decide which of the fakes were done in the style of our forger and we'd have him! Phoebe, you're a genius!"

"And," Phoebe continued, obviously touched by Lauren's typically American display of warmth, "if authentic originals do show up for one reason or another, we'll gladly buy them. We always have plenty of customers for them."

"This is the best advice I've had since I started this job. I can't wait to get the ad in. Will you help me word it and tell me the names of the papers to call?"

"How's this for a starter? 'Lucrezia's International is having a retrospective of all Lucrezia paintings from . . .'"

The two women put their heads together until they felt the ad was exactly right. After they had finished and called the newspapers, they were ready to call it a day:

"Good Lord, what time is it?" Lauren looked at her watch in disbelief. "Eight o'clock? Why didn't you throw me out sooner? I lost all sense of time."

"I didn't mind staying late. I'm as anxious as you are to catch the forger."

Lauren began gathering her notes. "I'm sorry I kept you, but you've really been a big help. And now I have to hurry to keep an appointment." Cole was calling for her at nine. She'd have to call him and tell him she wasn't going to be on time.

"I have my car," Phoebe said. "Can I drop you?"

"I'm at the Dorchester, if you're sure it's not out of your way."

"Not at all. I go right past it."

"Would you wait a second? I need to make a fast phone call." Lauren used the directory to look up Cole's number. There it was with all the other Saunderses, but it looked so special. Cole Langston Saunders. What a nice, strong name! She shook her head, hoping to clear it of this schoolgirl crush or whatever else it was that caused her heart to beat faster every time she so much as thought of him.

A manservant answered the phone. Mr. Saunders was not in at the moment. Lauren was disappointed, but left her message and hurried out to join Phoebe.

A rented blue Cadillac pulled away from the curb in front of the gallery right behind the two women. Damn, Jason thought, he'd been out there all day and here it was eight o'clock already. What was the pretty bitch doing all this time? He hadn't figured out what she was up to. He didn't even know why they were in London. He liked his room at the Dorchester, hobnobbing with all those rich bastards, but hell, he hadn't had much of a chance to spend any time in it, having to follow Lauren Compton around. But last night it was kinda fun watching the broad give that Saunders guy a hard time at the door. He smiled, wondering which one of them would win tonight. His money was on Saunders.

Chapter Twelve

"Oh, Miss Roberts . . . Miss Roberts . . . Miss Roberts!" The third time the concierge called, Lauren realized he was speaking to her. She turned to the desk acting as though she had been preoccupied. "Yes?"

"There's a message for you. I thought as long as you were passing . . ." The concierge handed her an envelope. It was sealed, but not stamped.

"Thanks." Lauren turned the envelope over in her hand. No return address She didn't recognize the handwriting. Who in London but Cole knew she was there? She walked toward the elevators, still mystified. It wasn't Alex's handwriting, but it could be that of someone he hired to follow her. *Oh, God, has he found out I'm alive?*

Once in her suite, her hands shook as she opened the envelope, careful not to tear any part other than the flap. Her eyes widened as she read the brief contents.

Ms. Roberts,
   You don't know me, but I know of your work through our friend in California. Right now, in addition to what you are doing for him, I have need of your services. Meet me tomorrow at 6 P.M.

147

in the bar of your hotel. Will explain then.

A Friend

Lauren was frozen with fear. Who was this friend? What friend? She had no friends. That was the trouble. She had no one in the world to go to with her problems . . . with this problem.

Once she stopped shaking, Lauren reread the note. She sat on the edge of her bed, going over each word. The writer obviously didn't know she was really Lauren Compton. That was a good sign. Why, she didn't know, but somehow it made her feel safer. Okay, how did he know Diane Roberts was in London, even know the name of her hotel? There could have been many ways for someone checking on her to find out. Cole had her passport; he'd bought the airline ticket in her name. He also must have alerted his branch offices of his flight to London with Miss Roberts. Lucrezia knew, and so did Dr. Rossi. Angelo and Gia knew, too. And there were probably several others.

Lauren decided a bath would be more relaxing than a shower. She ran water into the tub, liberally sprinkling it with bubble bath. She would soak some of the fear out of her system. It had been a long, exhausting day. She didn't want to think about the world of art or forgers and how they managed to get their hands on fine paintings long enough to copy them in every detail.

But most of all, she didn't want to think about whether or not she would meet the stranger who wrote the note demanding an appointment as though she were an employee of someone he knew. She couldn't figure out what he meant by "in addition to what you are doing." Doing for whom?

It felt good to slide down among the bubbles and let her mind become a complete blank. She wished she

148

could stay right here, feeling warm and comfortable, relaxed, even a bit sensual. She still hadn't heard from Cole. Maybe he was going to be on time after all. She'd better move her bloomin' arse!

Once out of the tub, she liberally slathered lotion over every part of her dripping body, then reached for one towel to wrap her wet hair and another to pat herself dry.

"Can I help?"

Lauren almost jumped out of her skin. There stood Cole, dressed for dinner, smiling broadly and calmly holding two stemmed glasses along with a bottle of wine.

"What are you doing here? How did you get in? And how long have you been standing there?"

"I came to take you to dinner, your door was unlocked, you evidently didn't hear my knock, and I've been here long enough to know that you have the most beautiful body I've ever seen." The smile left his lips. "Oh, God, I've scared you." He swept her into his arms, murmuring apologies. Their lips came together, stilling words that both had begun to utter. Everything was forgotten in the kisses that followed. Lauren was lost, her senses swimming.

"Your clothes are getting all wet," she finally said.

"So they are. Help me get out of them. I can't take my hands off you." There was laughter in Cole's voice, sexy, tremulous laughter.

Shuddering with desire, Lauren began unbuttoning pieces of clothing that she'd never touched before, all the while being kissed, stroked, and caressed by Cole until she was one quivering mass of human arousal.

At last he, too, was as naked as she. He pulled her down beside him. "Diane . . . I need you so."

Her moisture lotion anointed him with every movement of their bodies. Lauren felt her very soul had been forever crying out for just this kind of affection. She couldn't believe her hunger for him, his hands, his lips, his tongue. For the very first time, she was experiencing the true, joyous excitement of what it was to be a woman—a woman in love. It was wrong, but she couldn't feel guilt, not now, not yet. Her desire for him stilled all thought. She wouldn't let herself think. All she wanted was to give in completely to these persistent sensations. "Oh, Cole, please!" she begged, desperate for blessed release. His hand came under her, and soon he was deep inside her. And then she cried out in sweet agony.

"One day," Cole said, "when we're old and gray, we can tell our grandchildren that the first time we made love, we were on the floor of the Dorchester Hotel in London." He picked Lauren up and deposited her on the bed.

"If that was a proposal, I'm not only speechless, I'm freezing." Lauren tried to pull the sheets that had been so tightly tucked in but they wouldn't budge.

"Here, I'll help." Cole climbed on top of Lauren as if that were the only way to release the sheets and blankets.

"You're no help," Lauren said, laughing at his pretended attempts.

"But you'll have to admit, I'm warming you up!" Cole was kissing her again and stroking her to the point that she would have kicked off any blankets. This time they were unhurried—exploring, discovering, building, until the tension between them was so compelling that they both rose to emotional heights they never before dreamed of.

Cole smiled as he held her in his arms. "This would be a perfect time for me to light two cigarettes and hand one to you so we could both take deep drags, blow out the smoke, and contemplate our future."

Lauren laughed. "There's just one problem. Neither one of us smokes."

"Neither did a lot of the stars in those great old movies, but the cigarettes made good props. And here we are with our naked emotions showing, and we don't know what the next move should be."

Lauren sat up in bed. "I've got it— Cut! Now we can both come down to earth, get dressed, and go out to dinner, like we should have done in the first place."

"Are you suggesting that the last hour had no meaning at all?" Cole studied Lauren's face as he waited for an answer.

"Pleasure, yes. Meaning? I just can't answer that right now."

"You didn't believe my proposal, Diane?"

Lauren came back to reality with a thud. She was not Diane. That was the whole trouble. She not only couldn't marry Cole, he wouldn't even want her if he knew the truth about her. The sweet, wonderful girl Cole thought himself in love with had died in an airplane crash, and the one who took her place was a lying, deceitful, selfish bitch who was married to a notorious gangster. But instead of pulling away, Lauren clung to Cole, showering him with kisses. It was her way of showing her love without giving him a verbal reply. There were no words. He would never understand. His response was immediate and demanding.

"What does a lady have to do to get some food around here?" Lauren asked sleepily after they woke.

"That's the nice thing about hotels, love, they wash and iron, make beds, and cook." Cole hopped out of bed and searched until he found a hotel menu and climbed back into bed. "Now then," he said, careful to touch Lauren with every move, "what do you feel like eating?"

151

"Since this was to be our night at Simpson's on the Strand, I'll have to have some time to think. Any suggestions?"

"Anything's okay as long as it's not alive."

Lauren looked thoughtful. "What about champagne and caviar for starters and for an entree, a big, juicy hamburger with fries and lots of catsup and, let me see . . . I know . . . cherries jubilee for dessert. How's that?"

"Ye gods, girl, I'll never be able to take you anywhere. A hamburger at the Dorchester? And catsup? They'll probably throw us out! But you know, it sounds good, and I'll have the same. If we hear any complaints, we'll buy the damn place."

"My, how you brag! Are you sure you don't already own this fine establishment?"

"Wait until I make the call. If they don't hop to it, I'll make them an offer." His eyes devoured her. "Wait—don't pull the sheets up. I want to feast my eyes on you while my stomach growls in anticipation."

Some time later, after they had eaten to their hearts' content, Cole grew serious and held Lauren close. "I have something to tell you, but I didn't want to spoil your evening."

"Nothing could have spoiled our night on the town."

"Remember Lydia Patterson from the Mag Mile Gallery?"

"Do I? You'd better believe it. There's one nasty gal."

"You have to admit she was very attractive."

"Well, if you say so, but she has fat fingernails."

"You're impossible!" Cole said, hugging her even closer.

"I spoke with Lucrezia this afternoon. That's when she told me, and I didn't want to frighten you."

152

"What?" Lauren was losing patience with Cole's British calm.

"There's just no way to tell it but to tell it. Lydia was found dead in the gallery."

"Oh, dear God!" Lauren sat bolt upright. "How? A heart attack? She was so young." She couldn't imagine anything like this happening to someone she knew.

"According to Lucrezia, she was shot. Murdered. It didn't seem like a robbery, and the weird thing is that the police estimated the time of death at just about the time we were at the gallery. So the murderer might have even been there when we left. Do you remember seeing anyone still there when we said good-bye?"

"Oh, Lord, let me think." Lauren stared at the empty wall as if it could mirror the happenings of the last evening. "I know Lydia was getting ready to lock up, but I just can't remember seeing anyone else."

"Are you all right? You're shaking." He pulled her to him and held her close. "We're so lucky we left when we did. If it had been a few minutes later, I shudder to think . . ."

Chapter Thirteen

The day could not go fast enough for Lauren once she decided to meet the stranger. Six o'clock seemed an eternity away. There wasn't much to do at the gallery since the ad wouldn't appear until the evening papers. They had called it in too late to make the early editions.

So she would just have to wait and wait, think and think about Lydia Patterson's death when she would much rather go over every moment spent with Cole last evening. She wondered why life couldn't be simple so their love could grow and thrive without the disaster that was bound to manifest itself when she was confronted with her lies.

Oh, it was so painful to think about Lydia no longer being alive. She felt so ashamed. She had joked about her and said nasty things to Cole when he was trying to tell her of Lydia's murder. She felt sick. She couldn't imagine who could have done it and what possible reason the killer could have had if it weren't to steal something. The gallery was filled with millions of dollars worth of artwork. But according to Cole, nothing was touched.

She had called Chicago to speak to Lucrezia about the murder and to ask about her health. Lucrezia was shocked, of course, and said the police had absolutely no leads so far. She planned to check with Lucrezia every day.

Lauren's head was already going around and around from too many whys. Thank goodness for Phoebe. The two of them had lunch together and spent the day wondering who would answer their ad.

Finally it was five o'clock. Lauren had kidded with Phoebe, telling her she'd be in early tomorrow to help with the crowd of artists waiting at the door with their trusty fakes, eager to sell them for the exorbitant prices authentic Lucrezias would bring. They both laughed then Lauren hailed a cab, ready to do battle in the bar of the Dorchester Hotel with the anonymous note-writer.

She had time to go up to her room to freshen up. Though the weather was exceptionally cool for July, she felt hot and sticky. Running cold water on her wrists and splashing her face gave her new confidence.

Dressed in a white linen skirt and a navy jacket with brass buttons, Lauren sailed into the bar at six o'clock looking smart and efficient. Cole's love gave her new courage and self-confidence. Also, she was learning from Lucrezia. How would she know him? He would have to approach her. And he did. Unless he had begun his drinking elsewhere the man must have been waiting for some time. His breath was so strong, she had to avert her head as he introduced himself.

"Miss Roberts? I'm Felix Barrendo. You're a hell of a lot better-looking than our friend led me to believe. Why don't we sit down?" She followed him to a table that he had evidently been occupying. "What will you have?"

"Nothing, thank you." Lauren studied Felix Barrendo. He was a small, heavyset man with a bald head that seemed too large for his body. His eyes were black

156

and hard and looked as though they were ready to pop out of his head. She hated the way those eyes roamed over her body.

"Are you a teetotaler?" Felix hailed a passing waiter and ordered a double whiskey, all the while looking at Lauren from every angle.

Lauren didn't dignify his question with an answer. *Get on with it,* she thought, anxious to get away from this character. "Who are you and why did you contact me?"

"Our mutual friend in California said he hadn't had time to give you instructions before you came over here. He didn't think it was very smart to call you in Chicago. He wants you to do some extra work for him. Said to tell you your cut would be the same as usual."

"I hope you realize that I don't know what or whom you're talking about." Lauren had no intention of being friendly or making anything easier for this man. He was pure sleaze. That was apparent the moment she set eyes on him. She felt embarrassed just being seen with him in this bar, and she didn't even know anyone here.

Felix went on as though Lauren hadn't said a word. "Our friend wants you to photograph as many Lucrezias as you can while you've got the chance, and you'll get the same deal as always—twenty-five grand. I'm sure he means while you're spending so much time at the gallery. You're a crafty one to have gotten yourself planted right here, I'll say that for you."

Lauren had no idea what he was talking about, but she was becoming more unsettled by the minute. She would have thought the whole thing a big mistake if this Felix's note hadn't been addressed to Diane Roberts. She had to find out what he wanted of her and why he thought she was a photographer. "Why are you playing these games with me? Who is this friend you keep mentioning? And how does anyone know I spend so much time at Lucrezia's gallery? And one more thing, tell me why in the world someone would want pictures of paintings— Oh, my God! The man. The man in California. Our friend . . . is the forger?"

"Such innocence isn't especially becoming, considering your take in this little caper. Forget the act, Miss Roberts. I know who you are." Felix breathed enough alcohol in Lauren's direction to make her feel lightheaded. "If you weren't so good with a camera, Carnot wouldn't be nearly so rich. Now, I've got some plans of my own, and I pay, not only better than Georges, but in cash just like he does."

Felix's bug eyes were fixed on Lauren's to the point that it was difficult for her to think or breathe. He seemed to be watching every expression, yet she couldn't help but react in disbelief. "Wait a minute! Are you talking about Georges Carnot, the famous oncologist from San Francisco?" Lauren laughed. "Why, he and Lucrezia were friends long before I was born. Why, she told me he's a good artist—took lessons from her for years. I think she said he started painting when he was just ten years old."

"Of course. You just said it all. She taught him so well that he does a bang-up job imitating her. I remember the day he first called to find out about my services. He said that he was so good with her brush strokes, he might as well go all the way and copy her work. He wanted to know if there was big money in art forgery. And *is* there money!" He took a big swallow of his drink and wiped his chin with his hand. "The old doctor didn't want to lose Lucrezia's friendship. How's that for chutzpah! Don't get me wrong, I've had my share of the profits. I have the expertise, so I placed the canvases in galleries and museums all over the world.

Why am I telling you all this? Like you didn't know. Not to worry, you can trust me. Hell, I'm the one who told him you were over here. But I sure admire you for being so cautious and acting so innocent."

Lauren shifted her legs to make sure her skirt was covering her knees. Felix's gaze was now fixed on her legs. "Dr. Carnot copies paintings from photographs?"

"Damn, but you must think I'm some kind of fool. I told you I could be trusted, so you can let down your guard. Can you imagine a forger able to keep an original masterpiece long enough to copy it? You of all people should know that's how all forgers work, since you're the one taking the photos. But I bet he didn't tell you that he can only copy Lucrezia's work. He doesn't tell that little tidbit. That's because he studied with her, and she's the only artist he imitates well enough to sell. Does a bang-up job, I'll say that for him." Felix flagged the waiter again for another double whiskey.

Lauren stopped the waiter. "Wait a minute." Her head was already spinning anyway. "Bring me a Scotch and water, please, with ice." She turned to Felix. "Where do you fit into this picture?" She still had trouble believing him. But it all had to be true. It made sense. All the pieces came together. Plain, innocent Diane Roberts was on her way to Chicago to help Dr. Carnot steal from Lucrezia. So that was why she had twenty-five thousand dollars cash in her purse, the very purse Lauren carried with her everywhere. It was too bizarre! And she had felt so guilty spending that money to buy some new clothes. It was payoff money! Stolen money! That made Diane as bad as Carnot and Felix.

"Oh, I'm just kind of a broker for anyone in any part of the world who wants to sell anything from a painting to a shipment of armaments. And now I have a private deal for us."

"Mr. Barrendo, uh, Felix, I don't think you

understand. I work for Lucrezia."

"Sure, that's what's so slick about this particular operation. Get Lucrezia to trust you, and you turn up with just peanuts and the doc has all the gravy. That was a stroke of genius on his part, bringing you right on the scene, as a detective working on finding the forger, no less." Felix glanced sideways at her. "If you really don't know all this, maybe I've got the wrong bird after all. It's just like that bloody bastard to screw up on all the information he gave me. He was plenty nervous about the first deal two years ago, but he sure liked counting the money it brought him and that tarantula wife of his. He spends money like my mother always wanted me to—on her."

Lauren decided she'd better play along with Felix or she'd probably have an angry underworld entrepreneur anxious to see the end of her. "I wasn't working for Dr. Carnot back then, so I didn't know too much about that first deal." Lauren took a long sip of her drink, thinking how slick Carnot had been to put his own gal in Lucrezia's employ as an investigator, no less. The nerve of that man! "You can tell him that I'm not taking any more pictures. In fact, thank him for me and tell him I quit. He doesn't even have to pay me. I'm working as a companion to Lucrezia. I like this job and I want to keep it. Tell him, I swear I won't give him away. I just want out."

She was actually telling the truth. She wouldn't tell anyone because whom could she tell what was being said at this table? No one in his right mind would believe her. Lauren's courage might be coming from the Scotch, but the more she thought about Dr. Carnot, the angrier she became. Why, he made Felix the sleazeball look like a saint! Imagine the gall of Georges Carnot! He was a trusted friend of one of the most prominent women in the world, and he'd been

160

ripping her off for at least two years. Calling him a bastard was too good for him.

"Well then," Felix said, "if you're not working for him, how about doing a little job for me? That is, if you know how to keep your mouth shut. This is no two-bit job even though it only involves two people." He smiled for the first time at his little joke. It wasn't a pleasant sight.

The menacing look Felix gave her would have been enough to close Lauren's mouth, but she had her own reasons for keeping quiet. If she were to tell anyone, she would have to explain that she wasn't Diane Roberts at all, but really Lauren Compton. She couldn't do that. The terrible truth was, she couldn't expose Dr. Carnot. Period. "I told you, I like the job I have and intend to keep it, so I'm not interested in anything you have to offer."

"Just wait one goddamned minute! What I have in mind has nothing to do with your quitting what you're doing. In fact, if it works like I think it will, just staying where you are will be perfect for us. Screw Carnot. We'll write him out of this one." Felix's eyes kept shifting from Lauren to a table near the back. He was as wary as he was crafty. "You sure no one knows you came here to meet me?"

"I didn't tell anyone. Why?"

"Got a funny feeling that someone is watching us. I'm generally right about these gut feelings of mine." Felix looked toward the back of the bar again, then turned to her. His dark eyes seemed ready to pop out of his head with what he was about to say. "I just want you to put a few little packages of sugar into the packings of canvases being shipped to certain foreign destinations. It's a piece of cake."

"You're asking me to move drugs?"

"Oh, come off it. Don't be so shocked. You put on a

161

real good show, but I don't buy your innocence. Dr. Carnot told me all about your financial arrangements, and I see where you've benefited big." Felix was sure of himself, and of her, or he would never have mentioned his plan to move drugs. He sat up straighter, and there was not the slightest sign that he had been drinking. He was a businessman waiting for an answer.

Lauren had trouble placing Diane Roberts in the sinister role of taking the photographs and being paid big money for them. She had felt so sorry and guilty about her death. She also had a feeling that Felix was a person who could assume many faces, a man who had been on the wrong side of the law for so long that his reflexes were automatic. She knew she had to tread carefully. "What can I tell you but the truth? I want to make a new life for myself. You look like an understanding man, and I might as well level with you. How about forgetting we ever met? I've fallen in love, and I don't want him to know I'm not on the up and up." Lauren lifted Felix's hand off her knee, smiling sweetly as she placed it on the table. If he touched her once more, she'd either scream or throw up.

Felix rose. "My dear, I'm a sucker for beautiful women, and you more than meet my qualifications, believe me. You may have noticed I've been taking pretty good inventory while we've been talking. I'm prepared to offer you the deal of your life. Better yet, I'm ready to give you the moon. Hell, I can afford it! Why, you only think you're in love. Love. What did it ever get anyone but a stretch in the tank? I can give you everything you've ever dreamed of. Wait until you see my yacht—swimming pool and all. It's got three bedrooms and four johns. How about that?" He looked down at Lauren, who was still seated. She hadn't answered. "You know, you're real class, baby. I'm making you a genuine offer."

Lauren stood, too. Once she saw how far she towered over Felix, she quickly sat down again. He'd paid her the supreme compliment by his offer, and there was no point in rubbing his nose in her refusal by humiliating him. She still needed his cooperation. "It all sounds wonderful and glamorous, Felix, but I've already committed myself, and like I said, I'm in love. I may turn out to be the world's biggest sucker, but I have to do what I think is best for me." She hoped that didn't sound too corny.

"Believe me, you'll never reach the heights of where I'm prepared to take you with anyone else." Lauren held her breath. She saw that he was thinking what his options were. "Okay," he said finally. It looked like he was through wheeling and dealing. "It seems that you've bought yourself a deal."

"Thanks, Felix. Bought? What do you mean, 'bought'?"

His bug eyes were dark with suppressed fury. "I mean I'll take your cut off the profits from this last deal. That includes all monies you were due from the sale of three 'Interludes' and two 'Beginnings.'" His voice was menacing. The offer sounded final.

"Did Georges copy only those five?"

"Yeah, plus the three in the beginning. But you've got to realize that you'll get no more money from them. Understood?"

"Understood," she whispered. She rose and walked out of the bar without once looking back. With every step, she expected to feel the hot pain of a bullet ripping through her back.

Once back in her room, Lauren locked and bolted the door, then ran to the bathroom to make sure that door was also secured. She turned on every light and drew all the blinds. She could still taste the fear she had felt as she turned her back on Felix Barrendo. Where were people like that bred? She couldn't imagine his ever having been a child. She shuddered. The memory of his touch made her cringe.

Imagine the nerve of Diane Roberts! Lauren's one consolation was that whatever she had done herself had not hurt anyone. She was merely trying to stay alive.

And what of Georges Carnot? There weren't words to describe how despicable a person he was. She had always thought of doctors as being above reproach. It just went to show how naive she was. Well, she had solved the mystery, found the criminal, but couldn't expose him for the simple reason that no one would believe her. She could see it all now—accusing one of Lucrezia's best friends of this preposterous crime. The first thing Carnot would do, of course, would be to expose her as an impostor. It didn't take much figuring out which one of them Lucrezia would believe. It was a no-win situation, and the worst part of all was that Lucrezia would wind up the loser.

She felt dirty. She stripped off her clothes and stepped into the shower. The warm water brought back memories of Cole's sudden appearance last night. If he tried to walk in on her tonight, he'd certainly think she had locked the door because of him. It didn't matter. She had shown him how she felt with such abandon that it had shocked her even as it had pleased him. She never dreamed she was capable of such raw emotion. Remembering the details of their discoveries of each other brought instant color to her cheeks. She would see Cole again soon. He was everything that Alex was not.

As she dressed, Lauren wondered how long she

could keep all she had learned about Georges Carnot secret. Somehow, very soon, she had to find a solution. But for the time being, she had to keep everything to herself.

She heard a soft knock. Ah, there was Cole. Tonight they were going to Simpson's on the Strand, and she was wearing a lovely dress of flowing white chiffon. Even though it wasn't green, she hoped it would please him. Lauren quickly glanced into the mirror one last time. Satisfied, she rushed to let him in.

Felix Barrendo didn't wait to get back to his own flat. He was in too much of a hurry to place a transatlantic call to San Francisco. He headed for a booth in the lobby of the hotel. What the hell time could it be there? What did he care! If he woke the bastard out of a sound sleep, so much the better. The more he thought about Diane Roberts, the more he realized he'd been had. She was some kind of a setup. Hell, she hadn't even known what he was talking about half the time. If he hadn't had so much to drink, he would have realized it right away.

After six rings, he heard a sleepy Georges Carnot answer the phone.

"Yeah, hello, you double-crossing sonovabitch!"

"Felix? What do you want? I told you not to call me here. Do you know what time it is? I have patients to see in a few hours."

"I don't give a damn about the time. You screwed me and I want to know why." He was still smarting over the snooty Miss Roberts turning him down. *If* she was Diane Roberts—and he was sure she wasn't.

"What are you talking about?" Felix could hear Carnot's muffled voice telling his wife to go back to sleep, that it was only a patient.

"You know frigging well what I'm talking about. That Roberts dame is not the Diane Roberts you told me about. She's never heard of your paintings, and I don't think she's ever used a camera even to take a picture of her grandmother. What're you trying to pull?"

"I don't get it." From the sound of Carnot's voice, he was nervous. "Do you think they're on to us and sent in the police? Or an undercover agent?"

"What do you mean 'on to us'? I'm not in on your scheme. It's your ball game, not mine. Besides, I don't think she's going to talk to anyone. She looked scared as hell."

The operator came on the line, wanting more money. Felix scratched his bald head. Shit, he should have reversed the charges. He couldn't even use his calling card and leave a record of any connection to this bastard. He dropped in more quarters. "You mean you don't know from nothing?"

"I swear! Diane Roberts has to have the answers."

"So find out what gives and let me know. Got it?"

"I most certainly will. I'll go to Chicago as soon as I can get away. I'd call her there, but I can't take the risk of questioning her over the phone—too risky. If there's an impostor, she probably won't leave London right away. I'll cancel some appointments and be on Lucrezia's doorstep in a week at the latest. Hold tight, Felix."

Felix hung up the phone. It wasn't his ass that was in a sling. No one could trace him to any transaction he'd ever made. He was just pissed off because the girl had turned him down.

Chapter Fourteen

Lauren arrived at Lucrezia's International just before nine the next morning. The gallery didn't open until ten, but she was eager to see if anyone would answer their ad. Knowing that Georges Carnot was the forger took a lot of the mystery out of what might happen today. She wished she could talk to someone about what she had learned from Felix. Keeping it all to herself was almost more than she could stand.

Phoebe hurried to unlock the door for her. "Good morning. I see you *did* get here bright and early."

"Oh, yes. I'm ready for all those creeps."

"Creeps?"

Lauren smiled. "Sorry, just a little American slang. Not a very flattering term, to put it mildly. You know, we're assuming our forger is here in London and that he can read. Even if he can, what would make him turn to the want ads? Don't you think we're pinning our hopes on a farfetched idea?"

"Maybe, but it's worth a try. Let's just wait and see. Would you excuse me while I get ready for the day? Mr. Merriweather should be here any minute."

"Sure. I didn't know he was coming in today. Did you call him to identify, or rather, *authenticate* any

Lucrezia's that might come in?"

"Yes and no," Phoebe said. "He works with me three days a week, and this happens to be one of his days."

"What does he do ordinarily?"

Phoebe laughed. "Wait until you meet him. You'll wonder why he works at all. Our Mr. Merriweather is eighty-eight years old." Still smiling, she turned and went into her office.

Lauren wandered around the gallery knowing she was headed for "Beginnings." As she stood before the painting that she and Alex had both loved so long ago, she couldn't help but think how much her life had changed since she had run away from her Oyster Bay home. She shuddered to think what she would have missed if she'd stayed there like the dumb little wife Alex expected her to be. From the start, he had only wanted someone young and attractive to wear on his arm.

She would never have known what it was like to be loved, really loved, and made love to. She'd have never known her own capacity for arousal. Lauren blushed as she thought of last night—Cole and last night. They had such a wonderful time. When she was with him, she felt more like a woman than she had ever dreamed possible. While they ate, they spoke to each other with only their eyes; when they danced, they blended together as if they were only one person; and when they made love, the whole world trembled, then stood still for just the two of them.

There was a mirror hanging in the gallery foyer. Lauren caught a glimpse of herself as she passed through, and she stopped to stare at her own reflection. She didn't recognize the glowing woman whose luminous face she saw before her. This was not the same person she was used to seeing. The white linen skirt, teamed with a yellow cotton sweater, and the

168

black-and-white spectators were smart, simple, and familiar, but the woman in the clothes had changed completely. In spite of all her problems, she was filled with a new vibrancy, a shining happiness, and it showed in her face. She didn't know this person who felt such an urgency to be with the man she loved every moment. There was no room for guilt anymore. If this were all wrong, then she wouldn't be so happy.

It was a relief to see a small, stooped, but bouncing elderly man carrying an umbrella come through the front door.

"You must be Mr. Merriweather," Lauren said as she took his hand in hers.

"Ah, the investigator. Phoebe's description of you hardly did you justice. I'm pleased to make your acquaintance. Won't you come into my office?"

Lauren followed as Mr. Merriweather placed his umbrella in a stand near the door, just inside his office. He looked at his watch, then went to a wall clock and adjusted the time, which was off a mere fraction of a second. Next he checked for messages on his desk, then looked at her over the top of his glasses. "Sit down, sit down." His voice was mellow and his inflections very British. Lauren loved the way he sounded and already liked the man.

"I understand you're a whiz at spotting bogus Lucrezias," she said.

"Well, my child, if you had lived around her paintings as long as I have, you'd be able to tell the real from the copies, too. Lucrezia and I go back a long way. I used to work for her husband's father—Brewster's father. I was his valet until I went to Rome with Brewster and Lucrezia. I was their houseman until Brewster died, then Lucrezia elevated me to this gallery back in my own London. She said no one other than Gia understood her work like I do." Mr. Merriweather looked flustered. "There I go again, telling my life story to anyone who will listen."

"It helps me to know you, and I'm grateful for the information." Lauren smiled and looked at the clock Mr. Merriweather had set. It was five after ten. No sellers yet. "Do you think our ad will bring in any forgers?" Lauren was no longer interested in forgers, although she felt she probably should be, just in case there were some other fake Lucrezias floating around in the world.

"It's difficult to predict. We shall just have to wait and see."

Soon Phoebe came to join them. They could see the front door from Merriweather's office. "I just heard about the murder of Lydia Patterson," she said to Lauren. "Do you know about it?"

"Well, yes, I do. As a matter of fact, Cole and I might have been the last ones to speak to her before she was killed. We stopped by there on our way to the airport."

"I remember her grandfather," Merriweather said. "He opened that Michigan Avenue gallery back in the twenties. Named it after the magnificent mile of Chicago's Gold Coast, even though they're inclined to call that area Streeterville. Let me think now, it seems the true magnificent mile really starts north of the Drake Hotel." He looked sheepishly at both women as though aware that he had gotten off the issue. "What was it you were speaking of, Phoebe?"

"Lydia Patterson. She was murdered in her studio." Lauren could tell by Phoebe's patience that she was used to talking to Mr. Merriweather.

"Murdered? Who did it?"

"The police are trying to find out—" Lauren stopped suddenly. "Oh, look! Here comes someone carrying something."

"I'll take care of him," Phoebe said.

Lauren and Mr. Merriweather watched as Phoebe spoke to a young man with long, blond, stringy hair. He was wearing jeans and carrying a rolled-up canvas. They saw her spread the painting out, but noticed that she didn't bother to secure the corner to study it at length. For a while, it looked as though the man might turn mean as Phoebe shook her head and tried to walk him to the door, but she evidently knew how to handle starving, would-be artists. He was soon on the sidewalk outside the gallery, and she was on her way to report to them.

They spent the whole day in much the same way. A few people had bought paintings for a nominal amount, either at a sidewalk show in the park or at an auction house and wanted to know their worth without having to pay fees. They could not be accommodated at this gallery. There were people who specialized in just that, but it was a costly process which more than likely was more expensive than the painting in question.

By five, Lauren had had enough disappointments for one day. She went back to the Dorchester and put in a call to Lucrezia. Speaking to the artist never failed to give her a lift. They managed to talk at some point each day to discuss Lauren's progress at the gallery. She knew how serious Lucrezia's condition was, yet Lauren never thought of her as ill or old, primarily because Lucrezia rarely discussed herself and made a point of being cheerful at all times.

"How's the mural coming along?" Lauren, too, tried very hard not to let her own troubles affect her mood.

"I spent most of the day there. It was the most exciting thing I've done in years. I found some sloppy work way up at the top, and no one seemed to know what to do about it, so I climbed that ladder and—"

"Lucrezia, you didn't!"

"My dear, you know the old saying, if you don't venture, you're not going to gain a damned thing. Well, I sailed forth, and by God, I fixed it! I took my trusty little brush, mixed my colors while practically standing on a cloud, and in no time at all, my masterpiece was saved. Even got a standing ovation from all my artists who were staring up from the atrium, holding their breaths, no doubt."

"I'm surprised there wasn't at least one heart attack. I'd have had one, seeing you up so high." Lauren didn't dare mention Lucrezia's age.

"Nonsense. Of course, Mario had to come along just as everyone was applauding, and he did everything but put a net under me as I climbed down. I've never seen him quite so furious. He spoiled all the fun and even rushed me into the clinic for a blood pressure check."

"Was it all right?"

"You're talking to me, aren't you? Really, if I can't tell you about my day without your worrying, don't bother to call me anymore."

By now, Lauren knew Lucrezia's caustic nature well enough to know that she didn't mean half of what she said. She was probably secretly pleased at having worried so many people by her daring feat. "Okay, I'm glad you got to fix the mural. How close is it to being finished?"

"That's what Dr. Hudson keeps asking. His clinic has been open to patients for almost three months, and the building has yet to be dedicated. His wife has planned a big reception, but they can't send out invitations until the mural is finished."

"And when do you expect that to be?"

"If you promise not to repeat it, I'll tell you a secret." Lucrezia didn't wait for Lauren's guarantee. "The mural *is* finished."

172

"How wonderful! But why haven't you told Dr. Hudson?"

"Because everyone would wonder why I'm still in Chicago. Mario would never stay on here without me. He doesn't trust anyone else with my medical needs, and I absolutely refuse to have him leave early on account of me."

"But if you told them now, they could mail the invitations and give their guests two or three weeks notice, which would be perfect. By that time, summer will be practically over, and we'd all be ready to go home. They would certainly want you to stay for the big dedication so they could show you off. It isn't everyone who can afford to have an original Lucrezia painted right on their wall." Lauren didn't realize that she felt so much a part of Lucrezia's family that she had said, "we," which included herself, when speaking of going home.

There was a pause on the other end of the transatlantic wire. "By God, you're right! You make me feel so much better about the whole thing. To tell you the truth, I've been feeling guilty about having my artists hang around the clinic, just dabbing at this corner and that line. They don't even know that I consider the mural finished. There comes a time when the artist just has to say, 'Sign it.' Tomorrow, I'll do just that. I've already finished the painting I've been working on here in the hotel. I think it's rather good."

"Wonderful, what are you calling it?"

"'Remembrance.' Do you like it?"

"From what I've seen of it, the title sounds perfect."

"Good. Oh, by the way, did the ad bring out the forgers?"

"Not yet. Phoebe and Mr. Merriweather are hoping for a better response tomorrow."

"Good luck, my dear. Kiss that nephew of mine on the front tooth for me. I'll speak to you tomorrow."

When Lucrezia hung up, Lauren thought about the expression she had used about kissing Cole. It was just a figure of speech, but Lucrezia had to suspect something or she'd never have said that much. She wondered if Cole had mentioned his feelings for her when talking to his aunt. Maybe. At any rate, Lucrezia had sounded pleased.

It was time to get ready for another evening with Cole. Lauren's pulses quickened in anticipation, but the guilt would not leave her. She should never have let their affair get this far. It was all her fault, and she couldn't blame Cole at all. If only her life could begin today. If only there were not all those skeletons from her past, all those stories she had invented hanging over her head. The day would come when the truth would have to be told. But she couldn't bring herself to think about that now, not while, in spite of everything, her heart was singing.

Cole spent the latter part of the afternoon at the Garrick Club. He'd been a member for years, as was his father before he died. They had met here for lunch as often as possible, sometimes to discuss a case, other times, just to chat. He would always be grateful for the special bond that had existed between them.

He hadn't seen some of his old friends in a long time, and it was good to see them again and be brought up to date on the local gossip. None of it was of much interest to him, though, since his mind was so completely filled with Diane these days, but he was glad he had left his office early enough to spend some time here.

Cole enjoyed planning the evening ahead of time. He would have loved taking Diane to the Royal Opera

House, but it was summer, and there was no opera in town. There wasn't much of interest in the theaters, either, but he did find one play that he thought Diane might enjoy. No one could be in London without attending the theater.

He would take Diane to the play, then to Mirabelle's for a late supper. If it were up to him, he'd spend all his time with her in the sack! God, she was lovely. She was truly an unusual woman, sexy as all hell, with a build on her that didn't stop. But still, she had brains and a certain sensitivity that made his heart do constant somersaults. He had already spoken of his love. Sometimes it made him feel like a bloody fool to be so openly happy just being around her, but that was the way she affected him. He couldn't help it any more than he could keep from breathing.

So many times he had told himself to slow down, take it easy. He'd been burned before, but Diane was so completely different from Iris. But he realized how little he knew about her. She always steered the conversation away from her past. It was as though she had been born the day he first laid eyes on her in that Evanston hospital. Well, that was all right with him. He didn't need to know any more than she wanted to tell him. He just knew that she loved him. Sometimes he felt as if this could be a new experience for her, a revelation. He understood her feelings; he felt the same way. He not only loved her, he liked her.

The hours didn't go quickly enough for Cole when Diane was out of his sight. He finally left the Garrick and went to his apartment to shower and change. He had told his valet to take the evening off after making sure that everything was in order. He looked around the apartment, wondering how Diane would like it. He had bought it shortly after his divorce, not wanting to stay in the large house he had occupied with Iris. It was in an older building and had large, airy rooms, high ceilings, hand-carved moldings, and a butler's pantry off the large kitchen. It was furnished in the Regency style, with a touch of Oriental added for contrast.

He felt satisfied that Diane would approve. The evening should be entertaining, and afterward . . .

The afterward seemed to be something they both looked forward to with equal pleasure. Lauren had buried all her feelings of guilt about being a married woman and not telling Cole. She couldn't justify her actions at all. She just felt that anything this wonderful had to be right. A whole new world had opened up to her, and she couldn't bring herself to throw any of it away. Not yet.

She was no longer shy about her body. Cole had done that for her, made her feel aware and proud of herself. She had never felt anything with Alex, and there had been no one before him. She believed this was really a first for her, that she had been a virgin before being with Cole. Her movements were fluid as she walked naked across Cole's bedroom to the built-in bar, her dark hair hanging in a fluffy cloud on her shoulders, her hips swinging seductively with each step. For the first time in her life, Lauren was aware of every movement she made, aware that she looked as desirable as she felt. She held the refilled glasses high over her head and smiled on her trip back to the bed.

"God, but you're beautiful!" Cole leaped forward, caught the brandy snifters just in time, put them on the bedside table, and pulled Lauren onto the bed once more. "You're going to kill me, my love, but hell, is there a better way to die?"

*   *   *

"You haven't even asked me what kind of characters answered our ad at the gallery," Lauren said, much later.

"Gallery? Characters? Who has time to think of work? I'm already exhausted." Cole ducked the pillow that Lauren threw at him. "Okay, okay, don't tell me, let me guess. You caught the forger today!"

It was a good opening. She knew she couldn't tell Cole about Felix or Dr. Carnot, but she had to let him know something so it wouldn't all be a complete surprise or London a waste of time and money. Later she would tell the truth, much later, when she could bring herself to say good-bye to this life and everything here that had made her happy. "No, do you think I'd wait this long if I had that kind of information?"

"Well, then, what went on at the gallery today?" His tone of voice was deliberately placatory.

Lauren wanted to keep the conversation light, but a serious note crept into her voice. "Nothing special, it's just that I think I've got a clue about where the forgery is being done. It could be California."

Cole sat up, immediately interested. "Clue? What kind of clue? Why California? What happened?"

Lauren was sorry she'd said anything so soon, and had no idea how she would handle this. She should have known Cole would have all sorts of questions. What should she tell him? More lies? "I don't have proof, but someone said something that led me to believe he knew of our forger and that his information came from California." That wasn't too far from the truth.

"Where is this person? I need to question him." Cole was already pulling on his clothes. "Why haven't you told me sooner?"

"For God's sake, it's three in the morning! Where do you think you're going?"

"If there's a chance of catching this guy, I don't give a damn what time it is. He's kept all of us up too many nights to count in the past two years." He was practically out the door.

"Darling, come back. I have no idea where to find this man."

"But who is he?" Cole looked distraught in his disappointment, and it was because of her. She had already said more than she intended.

"You have to remember that I'm a reporter and I can't reveal my source. You can understand that, can't you?" She hated herself for lying to him.

"Hell, no, I want the bastard! He's been costing Lucrezia a fortune and driving us all crazy, making us traipse all over the world looking for him."

"You'll get him, I promise, just as soon as I have all the facts. That's the way I work, and I intend doing it."

"If you don't think you can trust me—"

"Of course I trust you, but I've committed myself, and I just can't say any more now or I might blow the whole thing." Lauren began dressing.

"You're not spending the night?"

"I don't think you want me to, do you?" Lauren felt terrible that she had ruined their evening. She knew he was angry and she couldn't blame him. They had never gotten this close to the forger before.

"Don't go. I'm hungry. Let's go rustle up something to eat. My housekeeper promised to leave a glazed ham and some cheese in the fridge. You'll tell me what you know as soon as you can?"

Lauren's green eyes sparkled. "I promise. Damn, I love you! Come on, I'll race you to the kitchen. I'm starving, too."

Two days later, a forged "Interlude" was brought

into the studio by a legitimate owner who was in need of money. He had no idea that his prized Lucrezia was a fake. They gave him the full price of an original.

Meanwhile, Lauren had gotten up the nerve to tell Mr. Merriweather that she thought she had seen a "Beginnings" somewhere in the States and asked him if he would check out the one on the wall of the gallery. Sure enough, he said it lacked any semblance of Lucrezia's secret thumbprint. All this time they had had a forgery hanging right there. The forger was a master at copying Lucrezia's work.

That same day, another bogus "Beginnings" showed up.

Lauren couldn't help but wonder if Felix suspected her and was locating and dumping the fakes as fast as possible. If she could believe what he had said about the number of copies Dr. Carnot had painted, it meant that there was only one copy of each canvas out there somewhere. Cole had found the first three a long time ago.

Late in the day, Phoebe came running out of her office, almost too excited to speak. "You'll never believe this! I just got a call from Lucrezia's gallery in Buenos Aires and they've bought a fake 'Beginnings.' Some man said he gets the London papers, saw the ad, and decided to sell. I know this is all costing Lucrezia a fortune, but it's what she wanted. The forgers are really coming around."

"Your idea of running the ad was a real brainstorm. What would I have done without you?" Lauren put her arm around a glowing Phoebe. *Four down and one to go,* she thought.

Just before they closed, a call came in from Madrid. A woman wanted to sell her "Interlude." She hated to part with it, but she'd just gotten a divorce and needed the money. As soon as she got on her feet financially,

179

she was surely going to purchase another Lucrezia, since this one had given her so much pleasure.

Bingo! Lauren couldn't tell anyone how many copies had been made of each painting, but she knew, and that was enough—that is, unless Felix had lied. But she couldn't see why he would have, at that point in their conversation. All the fakes were in, and if she could figure out how to expose Carnot and keep him from painting more the case would be solved.

She called Lucrezia from the gallery and reported on how many bogus paintings had been found. She didn't mention that her job was finished, but once she hung up and saw that she was alone, she couldn't help but swing around, merrily whispering to the four walls, "Chicago, here we come!"

Chapter Fifteen

Lucrezia appeared to be dozing in her chair while the dialysis machine did its work. Dr. Rossi and Dr. Hudson stood a few feet away and spoke in low tones.

"Then we agree, no more dialysis?" Mario had trouble controlling his voice.

"There's no point in continuing to stick her and have her go through this procedure when it's not helping anymore."

"And you think we should give up on the idea of a transplant?"

"Yes, considering her age, it doesn't make much sense. The risks outweigh the possible benefits."

The two doctors moved toward the elevators.

Lucrezia opened one eye to make sure no one was watching. She was fully awake and had heard her negative prognosis. They weren't going to tell her yet, she was sure. Mario would wait until the evening before her next appointment, then break it to her as gently as possible. She had heard the catch in his voice and knew that he was suffering for her. Well, she had led a good life and was fortunate that she had always been surrounded by an abundance of love. It was her turn to repay some kindnesses by handling what little

181

time she had left with dignity.

Thanks to Diane's suggestion, she had informed the Hudsons that her mural was finished and signed. The invitations were already out, and the dedication was set for a week from next Sunday. Surely she would last that long. It didn't matter anymore if she went home to Monte Carlo without Mario. There was nothing more he could do for her. Dear Mario would be mentally banging his head against the wall for being a doctor yet being unable to cure her. She would have to show everyone how brave she could be. But damn, she wasn't ready to die!

The next evening, as Gia combed her hair, Lucrezia studied her face in the mirror. She looked the same, she thought. Each dialysis treatment left her feeling stronger for a day or two. She would get through the party just fine. Mario had tried to talk her out of having people in for cocktails tonight, but she had won the argument. It was comical to find him giving in to her so easily. He usually put up a big fuss when her health was involved. She could just imagine his thinking, *Oh, what the hell, let her have her fun!*

"Are you sure Angelo made enough of those tiny pizzas?" The hotel was catering the hors d'oeuvres as usual, but Angelo always made a few dinstinctly different foods that gave the party a more personal touch.

"Yeah, I'm sure. He even had me in the kitchen cutting out those round little pieces of dough. That boy sure knows how to cook good Italian food. He's already passing out trays to the people who've come on time." Gia was always in a good mood when speaking of her grandson. "You'd better not eat any. They're pretty damn strong and they'll burn up your kidneys

182

for sure."

Oh, now you're telling me what not to eat? Lucrezia wanted to shout, *It doesn't matter anymore!* She knew she had to have more control if she were going to follow through and be as noble as she planned. "Do you think the floral print is as becoming as the white silk?" She fully intended to wear the white but wanted Gia to know she still valued her opinion.

"With your black hair and beautiful skin, and because that silk flows around your body just right, I think the white." Gia grinned as Lucrezia motioned for her to help her into a full-length, sari-style gown of jacquard-woven silk that was especially flattering to her figure. She took a deep breath, put a smile on her face, and floated down the spiral stairs in her usual regal manner, making a fashion statement for those congregated below.

Mario waited for her at the foot of the steps. "My dear, you never fail to amaze me. You look smashing!" He handed her a drink that looked like a martini, but only the two of them knew that the glass contained clear water poured over an olive.

Everyone began speaking at once, bubbling over the finished mural and looking forward to the dedication of the Lincoln J. Hudson Dialysis Clinic. The doorbell rang time and again, guests greeted by Angelo's friendly grin. There were extra waiters passing food and drinks to people in the huge living room, and great bouquets and arrangements of fresh flowers were everywhere. Guests crowded into the room, talking, laughing, drinking, and eating, all of them having an unusually good time. Lucrezia's parties were never dull.

The door was opened once more, this time with a key. Lucrezia cried out in pleasure. She couldn't be more pleased. Cole and Diane stood in the foyer and looked radiant. "My dears, I didn't expect you back so soon, but I'm so happy!" She kissed them both warmly, then pulled them over to the bar for drinks and waved a waiter over with whatever food he was serving. "This is a lovely surprise." She linked her arm through Cole's, beaming up at him. "What made you decide to come back so soon without telling me?"

"We like surprises," Cole said with a broad smile. "You look especially great tonight, Auntie." He handed a glass of wine to Lauren and waited for the bartender to fix a whiskey for him. "I see you're still swilling your martinis. Never could figure out how you could hold them so well. They're powerful!"

Lucrezia winked at Diane. The young woman knew her little secret. "Clean living, darling, clean living. Come on. I want you to meet some of these people. The mayor is over there, by the piano, see . . . the one in the navy suit."

For the rest of the evening, Cole and Lauren met some guests and renewed acquaintances with others. They all ate so much of the finger food that once the guests left, none of them felt like going out for dinner.

Mario sat down, seeming glad for the chance. Lucrezia always said that anyone who sat down at a cocktail party was asking not to be included again. They were either bored or boring. If they sat because they were tired, they should have stayed at home and gone to bed. A guest had an obligation to help enliven the party. That was her hard and fast rule, and she lived by it even if no one else did. Before long, the four of them had their shoes off and their feet up on the cocktail table.

"Is everyone comfortable? I have an announcement to make." Lucrezia's voice was calm and casual.

"This is going to be good," Mario said. "Your

announcements always wind up being surprises. Just don't tell us you're planning another party anytime soon, Lu. It will take me a while to get over this one."

"No, no party—more like This Is Your Life, only it's my death instead of my life."

Three pairs of feet hit the carpeting at the same time when everyone but Lucrezia sat bolt upright.

"What are you talking about?" Cole looked shocked.

Mario's eyes looked sad, apologetic. "So you know. How?"

"Oh, Lucrezia, don't tell him like this," Lauren said.

"Hey, what's going on here?" Cole demanded. "What does everyone know that I don't? I don't like this kind of joke."

"It's no joke, darling." Lucrezia sat forward, too. "Diane is right. I've chosen the wrong time to tell you." She took Cole's hand, her eyes pleading with him to understand. "All I wanted was to spare you."

"To tell me *what?* To spare me from *what?*" Cole was on his feet, looking down at the little group, angry and perplexed. "For God's sake, you started to say something, so say it."

Lucrezia took a deep breath, then looked at Mario. "I was awake yesterday when you and Dr. Hudson came to check on me. I heard everything. I'm glad I found out that way. It was easier and saved you the pain of telling me." She rose and went to Cole. "Maybe I made a mistake in not speaking to you sooner, but I didn't want you to worry."

Cole looked down into his aunt's pained eyes. "Then tell me now, please. I have a right to know. If this has something to do with your health, we know some of the finest doctors in the world."

"I've either been to them or they've been consulted. I have nephritis. Everything possible has already been

185

done, so now it's just a question of time. Cole, wait—"
She put her fingers to his lips to keep him from
speaking. "Please listen to me, all of you. I am going to
die soon. I don't know exactly when, so that's a
blessing. But I want you to know that I'm not afraid,
not in the least. I'm quite resigned to the fact that
nothing more can be done to prolong my life. I feel so
fortunate that I've not really suffered, and as Mario
explained ages ago, I'll most likely become weaker and
weaker, but there will be little or no pain in the end."

"Oh, my God, how can you talk like this?" Cole said.
"Why didn't you tell me? Do you think I'm incapable of
coping or being a comfort to you?" Cole was obviously
distraught.

"My waiting spared you extra months of worry and
unhappiness. Even if it's not true, tell me I did the right
thing. I've worried so about this."

Cole put both arms around his aunt and hugged her
to him. "You can stop worrying. We're going to be
together from now on, and we'll have a hell of a time."
He looked over at Mario. "You could have told me
something. She looks so great. I can't believe it."

Very quietly, Mario said, "It's true. I wish it weren't,
but I'm afraid Lucrezia has had her last dialysis
treatment. They just aren't doing the job anymore.
Nothing is."

He sounded so forlorn that Lucrezia went to sit
beside him again and took his hand in hers, holding it
up to her cheek. "You've been my mainstay since
Brewster died. I couldn't have gone on without you. Or
you," she said, including Cole. "Just please don't feel
guilty. You've both brought nothing but happiness into
my life, and I'd have been lost without either of you."

*   *   *

Lauren wanted to remove herself from these wonderful people who were not afraid to show their love for each other. She was not a part of their inner circle, but she felt their pain. She, too, had come to love Lucrezia, but they couldn't know that. She was afraid to move, fearful of breaking the loving spell that held them together at this moment. Never had she witnessed such honest devotion. It was something she had never known. She felt privileged to have been accepted enough to have this scene take place in her presence. Lucrezia could very well have waited until she had the men alone.

Lauren looked at Cole. He was trying valiantly to control his emotions by putting on a smile for Lucrezia. But she knew him well enough by now to see the pain that registered behind his eyes. The bare fact of his aunt's imminent death was too shocking. Lucrezia should have told him sooner. Lauren wanted to go right to him, comfort him. She had no right. She didn't have the right to be here at all.

Tears of compassion rolled down her cheeks, unheeded. Lauren hardly knew if she were crying for Lucrezia, for Cole, for Mario Rossi, or for herself. No one noticed when she left the living room and let herself out the front door.

She took the elevator down two floors, thankful that she had it to herself. She ran to her room, unlocked the door, and, once inside, leaned against it in the dark and sobbed. She cried for Cole, Lucrezia, Mario, all the loveless years of her childhood after she lost her dad, and the misery of her marriage. She didn't know how long she stood there with her back against the door. She wasn't crying any longer, but she didn't have the will to move, to turn on the lights, to go to bed. She had complicated her life beyond repair, with no way to

187

untangle the web she had woven without causing Cole and everyone else further pain.

Lauren jumped when she heard a knock at the door. It had to be Cole. She looked out the peephole, then opened the door. Cole immediately pulled her into his arms, and as she sank against him, he folded his arms around her and held her tight. They didn't speak. There was no need for words.

"I want to stay here tonight, just be with you. All right?" Cole looked ten years older, his suntanned face ashen, his eyes rimmed with red.

"Yes, of course."

"You knew and you didn't tell me." It was a statement, not a question. He seemed to understand why.

Lauren led him to the bedroom.

The next few days hurried by. Lucrezia finished the second of the two paintings she had been working on since coming to Chicago. Signing the last canvas gave a finality to her work. She no longer had the energy to hold her beloved brushes. But Mario, Cole, and Lauren kept her so busy that she didn't have time to think. Knowing how much she loved people, they had friends in every night and sometimes during the day. She and Lauren decided what to serve, and Gia and Angelo carried on from there, along with the kitchen staff of the Ritz-Carlton.

Since Lauren had apprised Lucrezia of the status of the forged paintings in their daily conversations from London, they were anxiously awaiting the arrival of the last "Interlude" that was being shipped from Madrid. Lucrezia said she would be interested in comparing its brush strokes with the bogus "Interlude" that Lauren and Cole had brought back with them from London.

Lauren hoped that Felix Barrendo hadn't doubted her identity. Surely he had been in touch with Dr. Carnot by now. Carnot had to know that she hadn't given him away to Lucrezia, even though she no longer worked for him. There had been no word from him so far. Maybe that was a good sign.

Chapter Sixteen

At six-thirty on Tuesday evening, Cole opened Lucrezia's door. He had arrived half an hour early for dinner but decided to wait in Lucrezia's suite rather than his own. It seemed that he spent much of his time lately waiting—waiting for the day to come when the forger was caught so Lucrezia could have peace of mind, but most of all, waiting for a signal from Diane that she was ready for some sort of commitment. He realized that she occupied most of his thoughts these days. It was impossible to figure out the enigma that was Diane, this beautiful young woman who radiated caring and warmth, yet whose eyes told him that deep within her soul lay a part of her life that she could not bring herself to share.

Mario looked up and smiled when Cole walked into the living room. "Good, you're early. I could use the company. Diane is here, too, and she's upstairs with Lucrezia. I wonder sometimes what they do to themselves that takes so long."

Cole laughed. "Maybe that's why they always look so much better than we do."

"Come in and sit down. I was just glancing through the evening paper, trying to catch up on the news."

"Go right ahead, don't mind me. I think I'll watch TV." Cole stepped over to the credenza at the end of the room, opened the double doors, and clicked on the set concealed inside. "I haven't kept up with what's going on in the world all week." He flipped through the channels until he came to a network news program, then settled himself in a comfortable chair to watch.

Mario sat opposite him, engrossed in the newspaper, and Cole's mind wandered as the anchorman droned on. It seemed that nothing new or earth-shattering had happened in the last few days—a replay of the same old world problems—hunger in Ethiopia, crime in the city streets, changes in South Africa and Eastern Europe. Cole was about to turn off the set when a picture suddenly caught his attention, alerting him and causing the hairs on the back of his neck to stand on end. He tuned in immediately to the reporter's words: "The investigation into the alleged criminal activities of Alexander Compton, well-known international financier, has been put on hold, due to lack of evidence. The Senate hearing set for early September has been postponed indefinitely. Shown here are Compton and his late wife, Lauren, who was killed in last June's plane crash in Illinois. In other news, the stock market took a . . ."

"Did you see—?" Cole caught himself just before blurting out that the woman in the picture was the image of Diane. He suddenly felt sick all over.

Mario looked up briefly, apparently oblivious to the news program. "Did you say something?"

"Nothing; it's not important." Cole's mind raced. He would swear that the young woman in the quickly flashed picture was Diane. Oh, God, it couldn't be. How could two women who looked so much alike have been passengers on the same plane? But how could Diane—or Lauren Compton—have managed the

192

switch? It was all too incredible. Identifications in such matters were carefully checked, and even someone as powerful as Alexander Compton couldn't pull off a hoax like this, especially in a situation as chaotic as a plane crash. Besides, accidents could not be planned. Maybe Compton's wife had impersonated Diane before the plane even left California and managed to survive. No, that couldn't be. Back then, no one on the outside except Dr. Carnot knew about Lucrezia's new employee, and Carnot had the utmost integrity. Compton wouldn't have had any way of knowing about Diane Roberts. And what could Compton hope to accomplish by doing such a thing anyway?

His breathing was ragged as he pondered the possibilities for a moment, thinking back to his brief meeting with Alexander Compton a few years ago. At the time Cole had practiced law with his father and had handled the case for a prominent artist accused of having a part in smuggling a large amount of cocaine within the wrappings of a shipment of paintings. Cole remembered that Compton's name had cropped up in the investigation, and he had interviewed the powerful man, hoping to gather some information. The charges against the artist were eventually dropped, but the case had prompted Cole to devote most of his time to his aunt's multinational affairs.

It seemed absurd to imagine that someone as rich and powerful as Compton would plant his own wife right in the middle of Lucrezia's life, unless Lauren Compton was directly involved in her husband's dealings. What better way could he find to learn the ins and outs of shipments that spanned the globe? It was all too coincidental to believe. He had let his imagination run wild. Besides, by now the image of the woman on TV had already begun to fade from his memory. He would put the whole thing out of his mind.

But the picture became clear again all too soon when moments later, Lucrezia and Lauren entered the room. The resemblance of Diane Roberts to Lauren Compton was uncanny. For a moment, Cole stared at her, unable to move. She was wearing a pale-pink dress that fell in folds over her softly rounded hips and long, willowy frame. Her hair looked even darker and more luxurious than usual against the pink silk.

He blinked away his thoughts and stood, hurrying over to greet his aunt with a kiss. He took Diane's hand and caught the sweet fragrance that seemed to live on her skin. Here was the woman he loved, close enough to touch, close enough so that if he bent his head just a little, he could kiss the soft curve of her neck. Only seconds ago, he had placed her in a far different role— one of possible deceit and fraud. He must have been out of his mind. But somehow, he couldn't shake the lingering image of Lauren Compton.

Lucrezia walked over to the bar. "Anyone care for a drink before dinner? I see that Mario has made up a pitcher of martinis."

"I think I could use one," Cole said. "Here, let me do that." He proceeded to fill the glasses and noticed a look pass between his aunt and Mario. For months he had been puzzled by the fact that Lucrezia never touched a drop of alcohol. He had seen her pretend to drink martinis and wondered why. Now he understood. He couldn't bring himself to face the fact that his aunt was dying. She looked so vibrant and alive, so youthful in the floral print dress.

Drinks in hand, they seated themselves in the spacious living room, with Lucrezia and Mario on the sofa and Cole and Lauren in upholstered chairs, facing each other.

Cole could not take his eyes off this woman he knew as Diane. It was so hard pretending that they were mere

194

working acquaintances. He wanted to tell her about the news broadcast, hear her laugh at the absurdity and say that the resemblance was nothing more than coincidence. Somehow he had to know now, and he couldn't figure out just how to approach it. He decided to move cautiously. "Remember the trouble in the art world a few years back when the scandal broke about cocaine smuggling?"

"Of course, but why do you ask?" Lucrezia said.

"I hadn't thought about it for a long time until earlier tonight when I saw Alexander Compton on a news program. Did you know his wife was killed in the same plane crash that Diane lived through?" He directed his question to Lucrezia, but his eyes were on Diane. Her smile faded as her expression changed. Her whole face seemed to tighten as a crimson flush rose in her cheeks. The change in her expression was obvious, and Cole felt immediately sorry that he had made her feel uncomfortable, regardless of the reason. He longed to hold her close, whisper that it was all right, that they would work out whatever was troubling her. Surely she had a logical explanation. And besides, that brief, fleeting image of Lauren Compton was no proof that the two women were the same. He looked at her again, and her composure was intact, the smile back on her face. Hopefully he had imagined the momentary change in her.

"Why, I had no idea," Lucrezia said. "Oh, my dear, how truly fortunate you are!"

"Indeed I am. I remind myself every day . . . Tell me, how are the reception plans coming along?" Lauren asked, and Cole noticed how abruptly she changed the subject.

"Fairly well, I guess, but I have nothing to do with it," Lucrezia said. "Actually, Mrs. Hudson is taking care of everything. Thank God my part is over now that the mural is finished." She stood and began walking toward the door. "If everyone's ready, why don't we go to the restaurant? I'm getting very hungry for Chinese food."

Angelo was waiting outside the hotel in the white limousine. The ride to the Tang Dynasty on Walton took less than five minutes, and when Angelo stopped the car, he hurried around to open the door for them.

As they descended the short flight of stairs, they entered an elegant room, decorated with marble imported from Taiwan, with pieces of jade tastefully displayed in tall glass cases. Charles, the owner, personally escorted them to their table, and every waiter made them feel especially welcome. Dinner music provided a soft background for their conversation, which was unusually casual this evening.

Cole stared at Diane throughout the meal. She seemed preoccupied tonight and a little tense. He wondered if his remark about Alex Compton had anything to do with her mood. He kept telling himself that he had read too much in her reaction to the mention of Compton's name and the fact that his wife had been killed. He was relieved when dinner was finally over and the four of them sat in the limousine once more, this time outside the hotel, drawing the evening to a close.

"I must be getting old," Lucrezia said. "I feel very tired tonight."

"Old—you? Never!" Cole teased. "I think you just worked too hard finishing that new painting."

Lauren nodded. "I agree, she never seems to stop."

"Well, I'm putting Lucrezia to bed right away," Mario said. "Rest is the best medicine."

"Doctor's orders?" asked Lucrezia.

"I suppose so," Mario said with a laugh, "but since when did you ever listen to doctors?"

Lauren took the older woman's arm as they walked into the hotel lobby and approached the elevators. "I'll be in to help." She deliberately avoided any close contact with Cole in public. Lucrezia still had no idea that they had become lovers, and they guarded themselves against giving their affair away. Her reaction was impossible to predict.

"That won't be necessary, dear. Gia is still on duty, and we'll manage fine. Just relax and enjoy the rest of the evening."

Jason Lawrence climbed out of his rented car parked a few spaces behind the white limousine. In a way, he'd be sorry when this case finally came to a close. Hell, he was beginning to enjoy living the good life—eating in the finest restaurants, living in a plush hotel. Compton had made it clear that expenses were no object as long as he monitored Lauren Compton's every move.

During the past few weeks, he had managed to get a few pictures of her with his telescopic lens to prove to Compton that he had his wife under his thumb. He couldn't figure out why the man refused to let him nab her or put a bullet in her and be done with it. "Just make sure you know where she goes and what she's up to," Compton insisted. "We'll let the matter ride along as it is for now."

Jason entered the hotel lobby and parked himself as usual in a chair with a clear view of the door. He would hang out here a couple of hours just to make sure Lauren Compton had settled herself in for the night.

Lauren slipped out of her dress and donned a blue satin robe. Her flesh still crawled from the mention of Alex's name. This new life she had stumbled into

197

seemed a world away from Alex Compton and all the misery he had dealt her. Until tonight, it was as though her past had been miraculously erased, but now reality had set in once more. The guilt that had plagued her these past few days had begun to fade, and now she felt it all over again. She thought about how Cole looked at her when he mentioned Alex and his dead wife. Surely he had no reason to suspect that she was a fraud. But she couldn't get those questions in his eyes out of her mind.

She wondered if Cole would stop by later. He had made no mention of it when they said good night outside Lucrezia's suite. In fact, he had seemed unusually formal the whole evening. Maybe her own guilty feelings were causing her to read too much into this. In a way, she wanted to be alone and have a chance to sort out her feelings. Yet these few hours after Lucrezia retired were all they had together, and oh, how she longed to see him.

How strange life was. For the first time, she was truly in love and could not admit it to anyone. The worst part of all was the fact that she was already married to a man she loathed and feared. Maybe it would be better if she left Cole and Lucrezia and started still another life far away from here. Alex believed she was dead, so he would no longer present a problem and she could live in peace. But she wondered if she could bring herself to leave Cole, who was all she ever wanted in a man, and Lucrezia, who had been so good to her and needed her so much right now.

She began to pace nervously about her room, and at five minutes to ten, she heard Cole's knock. She opened the door and found him standing there, holding an ice bucket and a bottle of champagne in one hand and two glasses in the other. He smiled the same smile she had grown to love, but there was a different look in his eyes.

"Care for a little company?"

"I thought you weren't coming." Her heart sank as her eyes searched his, realizing the questions were still there. "Come in."

He stepped into the room and reached for the DO NOT DISTURB sign and slipped it on the knob outside the door. "At last I've got you alone," he said as he set the ice bucket and glasses on a table and strode toward her, taking her into his arms. "I've waited all day for this," he said as he touched his lips to hers. It was a lingering, gentle kiss, and she felt little shivers run up her spine. She looked into his eyes again and saw only tenderness there. Maybe her fears were all in her mind.

When he lifted his mouth, she said, "You're so late. I'd about given up."

"I had a talk with Mario about Lucrezia. She's looking weaker every day, and I've been so worried."

Lauren felt relieved. Maybe the fact that Cole knew of Lucrezia's illness explained his preoccupation and had nothing to do with her. "And what did he tell you?"

"Nothing new, just that she'll get progressively worse."

"She's still remarkable," Lauren said. "And so brave."

Cole moved to the table in the entryway and picked up the bottle. "How about a glass of champagne?"

"What's the occasion?"

"Since when did we need a reason? Just being together is enough."

She took the glass from him and settled herself on the sofa in the small sitting area off the bedroom. Cole downed his drink in one gulp and quickly poured another, as though bracing himself for what he had to say before sitting down beside her.

"You know," he said, "it's still hard for me to believe

that someone with a face that belongs on a magazine cover chose to be an investigative reporter."

"Oh, really? Just what is your idea of how reporters are supposed to look?"

He laughed. "Well, I'll put it this way—if I ever need something else investigated, I hope someone just like you will be on my side." He hesitated a moment, then said unexpectedly, "Where did you study journalism?"

"I went to college for four years."

"And how long have you been a reporter?"

She gave him a nervous little laugh. "What is this, Cole, the third degree? Am I on the witness stand? I'm sorry I don't have a copy of my résumé here, but Lucrezia probably does, and I'm sure she'd be glad to let you have a look. Just for the record, I've been a reporter for a long time, and a darned good one at that."

He instantly regretted his questions when the same tension he'd noticed earlier came back into her face and the flush returned to her cheeks. It was amazing how she didn't answer either one of his questions and turned the tables on him at the same time, putting him on the defensive. "Just forget I asked. I'm sorry if you thought this was a cross-examination, but I want to know everything about you. I guess that's just natural when you love someone."

He pulled her close and lowered his mouth gently onto hers. For an instant, he felt her stiffen, but his arms held her so firmly she could not pull away, and moments later, she lifted her arms around him and clung to him as if they were the last two people left on earth. His body began to pulse with the same passion he had known every time they made love. And then she pulled away from him and he saw tears shining in her eyes as she bent her head, turning away.

200

"No, darling, I'm sorry, but I think I need to be alone tonight."

"Diane . . ."

She turned slowly to face him, her green eyes huge and troubled. Her arms went around him once more, her lips hungrily reaching for his. He slipped the blue satin robe from her shoulders and pushed it away from her arms. Here was the woman he loved, the woman he needed, and somehow, some way, he would prove to himself that she was truly Diane Roberts. Not another word was spoken as she snuggled into him, glad for the warmth of his body, glad for the gentle stroking of his hands, glad to forget the awful guilt for just a little while. He stood and swept her into his arms and walked into the bedroom and placed her gently on the bed, slipped off his clothes, and lay beside her.

He kissed her hungrily, his mouth exploring the warmth of hers, savoring the sweet taste. His pulse sang wildly in his ears as he crushed her to him, aware of nothing in this world but Diane—her body that curved so perfectly into his, her long, silky hair, the scent of her perfume. His hands gently sought the soft secrets of her body, and she pressed against him in utter surrender. He felt himself drowning in desire, his senses spinning around a single vortex—Diane. His body reached deep inside her, their mouths holding tight in a kiss that seemed endless until the moment that their pleasure reached a peak and together they soared.

She lay in his arms in the dark room, and Cole felt suddenly frightened when the picture of Lauren Compton flashed again and again in his mind. How could he bear it if Diane turned out to be another man's wife, or, even worse, a fraud?

The night had grown old and the moon shone high above the city when he kissed her sleeping face and

201

moved away from her. He slipped on his clothes and left the room, sure that sleep for him would not come.

The next morning, Cole sat in the projection room of KTIL Television, an affiliate of CBS. He had wrestled with indecision all night, still haunted by the picture of Lauren Compton. He finally decided he had to put his doubts to rest once and for all, sickened by the prospect that the woman he loved had made fools of them all.

Last night he had not had the guts to confront Diane with his confusion, but he couldn't bear the thought of hurting her in any way. He had come up with the solution this morning. Byron Wagener, an old friend of his father, owned TV stations, including KTIL, in several U.S. cities. A call to Wagener in New York had given him easy access to the Chicago station and old tapes of Alexander Compton and his wife.

"We'll start with this one," the station manager said. "It's an excerpt from *Playgrounds of the Rich,* a program that aired on the network. It was filmed off the coast of Martinique two years ago, but it's the most recent one. All of Wagener's stations have a copy to use as a summer filler." He began to load the tape into the machine. "I've found two others from old newscasts but can dig deeper if you don't find what you're looking for."

"Do all of them include Mrs. Compton?"

"Don't think so. Must have misunderstood—thought you were interested in Compton himself. He's the one who's made the news, but we can check if you'd like." He flipped off the lights and turned on the machine, putting it on fast-forward until he came to the Comptons.

Cole felt his heart stop at the first sight of Lauren

Compton, the beautiful, pampered wife of one of the wealthiest men in the world. Lounging on the deck of Compton's yacht, with the blue-green water of the Caribbean in the background, she looked like a young goddess with all the world at her feet. She also was a carbon copy of Diane Roberts. Cole sat transfixed for a moment, his head a jumble of regret and anger.

"Hold it right there," he finally said when the woman turned her head to look full-face into the camera.

The picture froze on the screen at the flick of a switch, and Cole studied every detail, desperately trying to find some difference between Lauren Compton and Diane. But there was none. Same clear green eyes, same dark, thick hair that hung like a satin curtain to her shoulders, same heart-shaped face, same short, straight nose, same full, firm lips, same prominent cheekbones. She was slender and fine-boned, just like Diane, with alabaster skin that was almost translucent. Just last night, he had held this woman in his arms, made love to her, and clung to the hope that none of his suspicions could possibly be true.

Cole stared at her, hardly able to breathe, a sick, stunned feeling hitting him like a physical blow. He remembered the first time he had set eyes on Diane, how he thought such a face was not possible outside a painting that Lucrezia had created. And now he was seeing it again on another woman known by another name, a woman who was reportedly dead.

"Okay," he said at last. "Let's see more."

He had lost all heart in searching for the truth. He had it now with no idea of what to do with it. As the tape moved forward, he watched Lauren Compton smile at her husband and swing her head now and then to toss the wind-blown hair back from her face. She was wearing a sweater that matched her eyes and white shorts that allowed a clear view of her long, slender legs, the same legs he loved to stroke when they lay together in bed. He felt bile rise in his throat, remembering all the times they had made love, the night he had asked her to be his wife.

The tape ran on for several minutes, but the words of the narrator describing the idyllic life of the Comptons had no meaning for Cole, his head was so full of thoughts that darted in and out of his mind like the flicking tongues of angry snakes.

"That's about it for this one," the station manager told him. "Now, if you'd like, we can check the other two, but I doubt if we'll see Mrs. Compton."

Cole stood and held out his hand. "That won't be necessary. I have all I need." As the two men shook hands, he added, "This is confidential, you understand."

"Of course."

Cole felt numb all over when he left the station. His worst fears had come true, and he had no idea what to do. Over and over he wondered why Diane—or Lauren—had come into their lives, what her presence was all about, and where it would all end. Somehow he had to get to the bottom of it, and perhaps the best place to start was with Alexander Compton himself. But where did he begin? He thought about it a long time and finally hit on an idea. Howard Kingsley had been in the news lately concerning the Compton investigation. He had known Kingsley for years, way back to their college days at Cambridge. Kingsley had gone far in politics for a man his age, elected to the Senate at age thirty-two and already a prominent member of the Judiciary Committee. He would give Kingsley a call and hopefully be able to meet with him tomorrow.

Chapter Seventeen

Senator Howard Kingsley, an attractive, personable young man with the build of an athlete, stepped from behind his desk to greet his visitor when the secretary ushered Cole into his office on the sixth floor of the Senate Office Building in Washington. He had dark hair, a strong chin, and intelligent blue eyes behind horn-rimmed glasses.

"Good to see you again, Saunders." The senator extended his hand to Cole. "How long has it been?"

"Too long," Cole said as he shook Kingsley's hand. His friend had changed somewhat since their college years, His glasses were something new, and he was clean-shaven now, no longer sporting the mustache that he'd been so proud of back then. "I'm glad you could see me on such short notice."

"I'll have to admit I was a little surprised when you called. What brings you to Washington?"

Cole decided to get right to the point. He was taking up Kingsley's valuable time. "The Compton investigation. How's it going?"

Kingsley shook his head and motioned toward a sitting area at the end of the room. "Come sit down and let's talk. I'll have to admit, your call piqued my curiosity."

Cole took a seat in a plush, overstuffed chair facing the senator. "I understand the hearing has been postponed."

Kingsley's blue eyes dimmed. "We've had the F.B.I. and the Justice Department on this case for three years, but so far we don't have enough concrete evidence to nail him. Dammit, we know the man's running a multi-billion-dollar operation—illegal arms shipments, stock frauds, you name it, but so far we can't prove it. The bastard has a way of covering it all up with laundered money and legitimate businesses."

"What about drug shipments?"

"That, too, but the trail always stops just short of Compton. Damn, what we need is one good solid witness."

"What about his wife? Is she involved?"

"Well, unfortunately, she's dead. I seriously doubt that she had a part in it, but then, with a man like Compton, anything is possible. He'd use his own mother if there was a buck in it for him. Why do you ask?"

Cole hesitated before answering. He hated himself for his thoughts, and it was hard to bring Lauren Compton's name into this. But he had to know, had to find out why she had invaded their lives and what she was after. "Just curious. I was wondering if her body was positively identified."

"We had no reason to doubt the airport authorities. They're very careful about these things."

"Were dental records checked?"

"We assumed that every precaution was taken to make the identification. Tell me, why are you so interested?"

Cole knew he had to be careful. One slip could bring the F.B.I. and the Justice Department zooming in on

Lauren in a matter of hours. "I was wondering how Compton would benefit if his wife were alive."

Howard Kingsley leaned forward, his eyes wide. "Then you have reason to believe she is?"

"No, nothing definite. I'd rather not say any more."

"Hell, man, we need every piece of evidence we can get, whether it's relevant or not. We sift through everything."

"If my suspicions are right, you'll be the first to know."

"Then why are you here?"

"My first priority is to protect my aunt's interests. Is Compton involved in any shipments of paintings?"

"Not that we know of at this point, but Compton has his finger in pies all over the world. He owns controlling interest in everything from a toy factory in Taiwan to a diamond mine in Africa, not to mention all his U.S. holdings."

"But no connection with the art world?"

"I'm sure you recall the incident five or six years ago."

Cole nodded. "I represented the artist."

"Of course; I'd forgotten. Interpol found no evidence to connect Compton, but they ran into the same steel wall. The man has himself so well insulated that no one can touch him."

"Suppose his wife is still alive. How could Compton use her?"

"The possibilities are endless." Kingsley stood and walked over to the bar. "Care for a drink?"

"Scotch on the rocks will be fine."

Kingsley eyed Cole as he handed him a glass. "My curiosity is definitely aroused now. What makes you think she wasn't killed?"

"I may have seen someone who looks like her."

"My God, man, where?"

"Give me a chance to find out for sure. I just don't feel free to say anything else right now."

"But you don't understand how important this is. She could be a valuable help to us." He took a sip of his drink and placed his glass on the table. "In fact, a month or so before she was reportedly killed, I had a call from her. Said something about a tape she had made of Compton and sounded scared as hell. She disappeared after that, and we never heard another word from her. Next thing we knew, she was on that plane that crashed."

Cole's feelings immediately brightened. "She had a tape?"

"That's what she said."

"Could she have been running away from Compton?"

Kingsley shook his head. "We don't know why she dropped out of sight, but that's the assumption we made and we had no idea where to find her."

Cole downed the last of his drink and stood. "I won't take up any more of your time. Thanks for seeing me. You've been a big help."

"I don't know how much help I've been because I still don't know what you needed to know. You say you've seen someone who looks like Lauren Compton?"

"Possibly, but I'll be back in touch as soon as I'm sure." Cole shook the senator's hand and made his way out of the office.

As he stepped into the elevator, Cole realized how much better he felt. Until Kingsley mentioned the tape, he had felt like a mechanical man, going through the motions of living. Now he was beginning to get a picture of why Lauren might jump at the chance to change her identity. It made sense. If she were trying to get away from Alex Compton, she would naturally do anything to save her own life. Thank God Compton thought she was dead . . . Then a terrible thought hit him. It was possible, with Compton's reputation and connections, that he knew otherwise. If that were true and Lauren still had the tape, her life could be in danger. He was letting his imagination get the best of him. He had read Lauren Compton's obituary in the newspapers, even heard about a memorial service. For the life of him, he couldn't see any reason why Compton would go along with the belief that she had been killed if he knew she was still alive. At least he felt now that Lauren had nothing to do with her husband's criminal activities. Somehow he would get to the bottom of this. But for now he would bide his time, go along with her, and hope that one day soon they could get this whole thing straightened out.

Chapter Eighteen

Cole got his wish as soon as he returned from Washington on Thursday and found a message in his office asking him to return a call from Georges Carnot. Of course! He was the only one he knew who could positively identify Diane Roberts. He immediately dialed Georges's number in San Francisco and was elated to hear that the doctor was planning a trip to Chicago tomorrow. Georges had asked that he not mention his upcoming trip to Lucrezia or Diane. He wanted to surprise them.

Dr. Georges Carnot's plane landed at O'Hare Airport at 4:55 P.M. Cole waited outside the gate, anxious to see the good doctor again and hopefully solve the mystery surrounding Diane once and for all. He scanned the passengers filing through the door, and after waiting several minutes, he spotted Georges. He looked quietly elegant in a dark-blue suit with a faint pinstripe. He was a tall, slender man in his late fifties, with a head full of salt-and-pepper hair and a thin mustache. His gray eyes lit up at the sight of Cole.

The two men greeted each other warmly, and after a

short wait for the doctor's luggage, they were soon in Cole's car on their way to the hotel.

"How is Lucrezia doing these days?" Georges asked. "Working hard?" It was obvious that Dr. Carnot's English had improved since Cole last saw him nine years ago, but the French accent was definitely still there.

"She's not well," Cole said. "In fact, we're very worried about her, but I'll let her tell you about it."

Georges asked no more questions about Lucrezia. Instead, he seemed more interested in Diane. "How's your investigator coming along? Is she working out all right?"

"So far, so good."

"No bad effects from the plane crash, I hope. I was shocked when I heard she was a passenger."

"Just a few bruises and a mild concussion—nothing lasting, thank God. She's fully recovered and doing well."

"What's happened in the investigation?" Carnot asked.

"She obviously had a bit of luck in London not long ago, but she's not giving out any details yet." Cole shook his head and smiled.

"Oh? What sort of luck?"

"I'm not sure. She's not ready to give us any details, but I have the impression that she'd found a good lead. All I know is that the evidence seems to point to California."

Dr. Carnot's eyes widened. "So soon? That's incredible. California, you say? Any idea what it is?"

"Not at all."

"It seems to me that you're entitled to any information she might have."

Cole looked at him and smiled. "Well, thanks to you, we've hired a very good investigator, and we're leaving the whole thing up to her. I guess it's the reporter in her that makes her so secretive. She wants to have the whole story before she gives out any part of it. By the way," he added, "you didn't warn me in advance to expect such a beautiful woman."

"Diane *is* rather attractive, I suppose, but I never thought of her as beautiful. In any case, I'm anxious to see her again."

Not as anxious as I am, Cole thought as he maneuvered the car through the rush-hour city traffic and pulled into the Ritz-Carlton parking garage. He wanted to get this over with now, bring everything out into the open, and hopefully hear a perfectly logical and reasonable explanation from Lauren Compton. It would all be settled one way or the other in a matter of minutes.

When Cole entered the suite, Lauren and Lucrezia turned together, smiling at him with the special tenderness women reserve for the most important men in their lives. Cole had not been around much during the past few days, and when he did appear, he seemed remote and preoccupied. Now he was noticeably apprehensive.

"I've a surprise for you," he said. "Someone you both know. He's waiting outside the door."

An alarm went off inside Lauren's head. *Someone you both know. Oh, my God! Dr. Carnot!* It can't be anyone else. She found it hard to breathe. "I have a lot of work to do at the gallery. I really must be going."

"Not until you see my mystery guest," Cole said. He opened the door. "Come in, Georges."

Lauren felt her heart stop beating for an instant. It was all over. What would Lucrezia think of her when she found out she was a fraud? And Cole. The only man

213

she had ever loved would feel nothing for her but contempt. It was bound to happen. She had been a fool to think she could pull this off. She folded her arms across her waist to try to control her shaking as she watched the middle-aged man enter the room.

Lucrezia rushed over to him. "Georges! How wonderful to see you again. What brings you to Chicago?"

"I wanted to see you again before you left for Europe," he said. His words were meant for Lucrezia, but his eyes were on Lauren, and there was no sign of recognition.

"You already know Diane," Cole said.

"It's good to see you again." Lauren desperately tried to hide the tremor in her voice.

A shadow momentarily dimmed the doctor's gray eyes, but he smiled and held out his hand. "Miss Roberts, I heard about your ordeal, of course. Thank God you're alive and still healthy. How's your work coming along?"

Lauren couldn't believe she had heard him correctly. Dr. Carnot obviously had no intention of exposing her identity, at least not at the moment. She wondered what he had up his sleeve and if his cautiousness confirmed what Felix Barrendo had told her. She took a deep breath before answering. "Very well, thank you. I think I'm on the right trail, and it won't be long until we can get to the bottom of this." She kept right on talking, her voice low and controlled, only the way she bit off each word showing her nervousness. "In fact, we came close to finding the culprit when we were in London."

"We?" Dr. Carnot turned to Cole. "Then you know more than you let on. Now you've incited my curiosity, and I must know what you've learned."

"Sorry, old chap," Cole said. "Just as I told you,

214

she's keeping all this to herself and deserves all the credit. I'm as much in the dark as anyone."

"Well, then," the doctor said. "We'll all be waiting for your final report."

"You'll be one of the first to know, believe me," Lauren said. She had to get out of here. She needed a chance to be alone, calm down, and figure out what to do. "It's been lovely seeing you again, but I really must get back to the gallery before it closes. If you'll excuse me, I'll be on my way." She gave Lucrezia a peck on the cheek and Cole a wave. "I'll see you in about an hour."

Lauren hurried out the door. Her insides were still screaming from meeting the one person who could expose her. The fact that he hadn't made her more certain than ever that he was behind the art scam. What a pair she and Carnot were, both intent on defrauding a loving, generous woman, and neither in a position to expose the other. At least her deception was an effort to save her own life. Carnot's was obviously money. Still, there was no justification in letting this man get by with his scheme, one that could possibly ruin Lucrezia's reputation. Even if it meant her own skin, she had to find a way to tell Lucrezia and Cole the truth. She would wait for the right moment. Getting through these next few days would not be easy.

Later, when Lucrezia had excused herself to lie down before dinner, Cole sat in the living room having a drink with Georges. He felt relieved, yet still in shock that the doctor had not declared that the woman who called herself Diane Roberts was indeed an impostor. He had been so sure, and now he questioned his suspicions. Carnot had no reason to go along with the deception. Still, he couldn't shake a gnawing feeling inside him, and he couldn't quite bring himself to let go of his doubts.

"How well did you know Diane Roberts before you recommended her to Lucrezia?" Cole asked.

"Well enough. Her father was a bed patient for several weeks before he died, and Diane seldom left the hospital. I saw her daily and was very impressed when she got to the bottom of the drug thefts—caught an orderly red-handed, and that landed her quite a story in the newspapers." Carnot took a sip of his whiskey and water. "You're sure you're satisfied with her work?"

"Perfectly, but it's hard to imagine how someone so lovely could be this good at investigating."

Carnot's eyes narrowed. "Sometimes looks can be deceiving."

How true, Cole thought. He remembered the TV pictures of Lauren Compton and wondered again how two unrelated women could look exactly alike, let alone wind up on the same plane. It was much too coincidental. All he could do at this point was to keep his ears and eyes open and hope for the best.

Lauren paced the floor in her room. She had feigned a headache as an excuse not to have dinner with the others, choosing instead to eat alone in her room. Her dinner still sat uncovered and untouched on the table in the sitting area.

For the past few hours she had gone over her options again and again and still had come up with no solution. She lacked enough concrete proof that Dr. Carnot had indeed copied and sold Lucrezia's paintings, though Felix's disclosure, coupled with the fact that he had gone along with her deception, was proof enough for her. Still, she couldn't point her finger at him without indisputable evidence. If Carnot exposed her as a fraud, at least she owed it to herself to try to bring him down with her.

She was still walking the floor when the phone rang. Thinking it was probably Cole, she hurried to answer it.

"Who are you and what are you up to?" The smooth voice with its French accent sent a shiver through Lauren.

"I don't know what you mean."

"I don't care to play games. I'd like to come to your room and have a talk."

Lauren's hand shook, and she could barely hold the receiver. "No, that's not a good idea." Her voice was little more than a whisper.

"But you'll have to agree that we need to talk. I can't keep quiet about you forever."

"Not tonight. Please give me a little more time." Lauren felt tears fill her eyes and throat.

"Sorry, but I insist. I'll be up in a few minutes."

"Please—not here. We can meet somewhere."

"All right. What about the bar off the lobby?"

"That's better. Give me fifteen minutes."

Lauren hung up the phone and stood motionless for a long time. She suddenly felt afraid of this man, not the fact that he knew she was an impostor . . . there was something more. There was a menacing sound to his soft-spoken voice. It occurred to her that Georges Carnot had much more to lose by exposure than she did. She had done nothing criminal. At least she had the good sense not to see him alone. The bar offered privacy, yet there would be people around. She had no choice but to meet him, hear him out, and get it over with. Her nerves couldn't take much more.

Jason Lawrence glanced up from his newspaper, suddenly alert. He was seated in his usual chair in the

Ritz-Carlton lobby. An elevator door opened, and Lauren Compton stepped out, alone this time. It was getting late—half past ten, an unlikely time to see her in the lobby by herself. He watched her cross the room and walk into the bar. His interest was definitely aroused. This little venture called for close scrutiny.

He stood and ambled toward the bar and paused just outside. Lauren was seating herself at a table opposite a man he'd never before laid eyes on. So, maybe the little bitch had a new boyfriend. Nah, he wasn't her type, and from the looks they gave each other, there was no love lost between them. He walked over to a table behind them and sat down with his back to Lauren. Something told him this was a conversation he didn't want to miss.

"We might as well get right down to business," Carnot said. "First of all, you didn't answer my questions. Who are you and what are you up to?"

"I don't know where to begin. It just happened and I—" A waitress came by just then to take orders for drinks, interrupting the conversation. Lauren shook her head. "Nothing for me."

"I'll have whiskey and water," Georges Carnot said, "and make it a double." His voice was no longer smooth and gentle but filled instead with the gruffness of irritation. As soon as the waitress was out of earshot, he said, "Go on. I'm waiting."

"As you know . . ." Lauren began, "I was involved in a plane crash . . . and so was Diane Roberts."

"Yes, I'm perfectly aware of that."

"When I woke up in the hospital, I realized our identities had been mixed up."

"Those things happen, but that doesn't explain why you went along with it. It could have easily been straightened out, unless you wanted it that way—and obviously you did." Georges paused as the waitress delivered his drink. He took a sip and eyed Lauren curiously. "What happened to Diane Roberts?"

"She was killed in the crash."

"Did you know her?"

"We were seatmates for a while, and I'm sure she's dead. I was listed as dead, but I had her identification and she had mine."

"That doesn't explain why you went along with the mix-up. Are you in trouble with the law?"

"No."

"Then what are you hiding from?"

"I can't tell you, it's very personal."

"But I insist—demand—to know the reason."

"That's too bad because I don't intend to tell you."

Georges Carnot was furious. He wasn't used to having his demands denied, especially by females. He had nurses running their legs off at the hospital trying to please him. The only woman who could push him around was Emily, his wife, and she had damned near bankrupted him with her extravagant lifestyle, the homes she had to own, and her expensive tastes. If it hadn't been for Emily and trying to keep her happy, there never would have been a need to get into this art scam. But it was hard to resist when the opportunity presented itself. He hadn't intended for it to go on this long and become so far-reaching. He had a good income, one that would make most any woman feel like a queen, but hell, he was no millionaire.

"All right," he said, "then tell me, what do you intend to accomplish?"

"I took Diane's place and also her job. I intend to try to help Lucrezia solve her problem, regardless of the outcome."

"What do you mean by that?"

219

"It's possible that when Lucrezia finds out the truth, she'll probably be hurt."

Georges's eyes narrowed. This woman was trying to bluff him. He'd about decided that Felix was trying to pull something and had never really spoken to her. "Go on."

"I'd rather not say any more."

"Then perhaps you wouldn't object to my letting Lucrezia and Cole in on your secret."

The young woman seemed unusually composed as she looked him in the eye. "Why didn't you expose me earlier when you had the chance?"

"I learned a long time ago to bide my time and consider all the angles. It could be to my advantage to tell them all about you the first thing tomorrow. Do you know any reason why I shouldn't?"

"Maybe so."

"Let me be the judge." He took a long sip of his drink, eyeing her over the rim of his glass.

"Do you know a man named Felix Barrendo?"

Carnot almost choked on his drink. He began to cough furiously, and several seconds went by before he could speak. "Never heard of him."

"That's strange," Lauren said. It was obvious to Georges that she now had the upper hand. "I met with Felix and he told me all about the art fraud, the fake paintings, your part in it—the whole thing."

"It's a lie! Why would he tell you such a thing?"

"You're forgetting something. Felix had no reason to doubt that I was actually Diane Roberts. He went right along with the original plan, thinking you had planted her here in the first place to make sure nothing concerning you was discovered." She laughed. "In fact, your partner even tried to entice me into a little action on the side—leaving you out."

"That double-crossing bastard! And did you take him up on it?"

"Of course not."

"All right," he said. "What do you plan to do with this information? You can't prove a thing, you know."

"Nothing for the time being. It all depends on you, I suppose. What are your plans for me?"

"It seems to me it might be to our mutual benefit to keep both our mouths shut for the time being."

"I agree." Lauren stood. "Now that we've had our talk, I think I'll turn in—that is, unless you have something else to discuss."

"No." Carnot's voice was cold and harsh.

"You know, you're a real asshole. It's hard for me to believe that someone could actually do this to a lifelong friend. It's more than I can stomach to look at you." With that, she turned and left the bar.

Jason watched Lauren leave and felt strangely sorry for her. Felix Barrendo was one of the dirtiest crooks in the business. If this character she just met had dealings with his kind, Lauren could get much more than she bargained for. The time had come to make another call to Alex Compton.

He left the bar, hurried across the lobby, and boarded the elevator to his room on the twenty-fifth floor. He wasted no time in placing his call to Alex's private number.

"I think your wife has really gotten her tail in a crack this time. She's crossways with a fellow in cahoots with the devil himself. Ever heard of Felix Barrendo?" Jason heard Compton utter an acknowledgment and went on into more detail explaining Lauren's situation. "What should I do, let this guy take care of her?"

"No! Don't let her out of your sight. Glue yourself to her if you have to. I have no way of knowing how much she's told this Saunders fellow or where the tape is. I want her to live long enough to answer these questions, and she'll answer to me alone. Understand?"

"Sure, Mr. Compton, sure. Anything you say."

Chapter Nineteen

On Saturday, the group gathered in Lucrezia's living room for drinks before an early light supper. Lucrezia, resplendent in a wonderful gown of flowing black chiffon, was dressed for a preseason presentation at the opera, as was Mario, dashing in his black tuxedo. Cole, who had a long-standing invitation for dinner at the home of a client, wore a dark business suit, and Lauren was wearing a simple sleeveless dress of buttercup-yellow linen. Tonight was a work night for her at an auction near the west side of the city. Many of Lucrezia's prints from the Mag Mile Gallery would be offered, as well as one of her paintings. Georges was there, too, in casual attire—slacks and a sports shirt. He had designated tonight as a time to catch up on paperwork and had declined Lucrezia's invitation to attend the opera. He stood by the fireplace with his arm propped up on the mantel, saying very little and taking in the conversation around him.

Everyone was going his separate way, it seemed, and Cole had an eerie feeling. The weather had turned foul early in the afternoon, and a stiff wind off Lake Michigan had blown in heavy sheets of rain for hours. Now a light mist hovered over the city, and darkness had come early. He had begged Diane to forget the auction, but she had insisted on going, and he finally had to agree it was the right thing for her to do. Tonight's offerings contained too many of Lucrezia's works not to bear watching. But it was dangerous for a woman to be out alone searching for a cab late at night, especially so near the west side of town. Too bad Angelo couldn't wait for her in the limousine, but tonight of all nights, Lucrezia and Mario had chosen to go to the opera.

He looked at Diane, and the sight of her, so lovely in the yellow dress, filled him with so much love it came close to pain. Everything about her was so vibrantly beautiful. Her eyes were so clear and green; her hair was so dark and abundant; her skin was so smooth, much like fine porcelain. The possibility that she could be Alex Compton's wife was still very real to him, and every time he thought of it, hurt gripped his insides like a hot metal band. It was still impossible to figure out. Georges would have reacted immediately if this had not been Diane Roberts. He had no reason to go along with an impostor. Maybe he had let his imagination overtake his common sense. He had to hope this was the case.

He made his way across the room to Diane. "Sure you won't change your mind?"

"I'm sure," she said. "Sometimes I think you forget that I'm an employee here and not one of Lucrezia's guests."

"I could cancel my dinner plans and go with you. I should have thought of that earlier, but it's not too late."

"Don't be silly. They're expecting you in less than two hours. I'll be fine. I'm a big girl and perfectly able to take care of myself."

She was right, of course. Here was his imagination

again taking hold of his judgment. But he wished the feeling in the pit of his stomach would go away.

Georges Carnot stood outside the auditorium waiting impatiently for the auction to end. He pulled up the collar of his raincoat to shield the back of his neck from the persistent mist that now bordered on light rain and moved the brim of his hat closer to his face. A chill ran up his spine as he slipped his hand into his pocket and felt the cold steel of a revolver. Never in all his life had he expected to find himself in this position—a cold-blooded killer waiting for the chance to murder a beautiful young woman. He was a healer, not a killer. He had never harmed another living creature, always abhorring tales of hunters who stalked defenseless animals. But now he felt trapped, and the woman masquerading as Diane Roberts had brought this on herself.

He thought of the young woman's words berating him for betraying Lucrezia, his lifelong friend. Her words had cut deep into his very soul. But still, in a way he felt justified in what he had done. Lucrezia was a woman with no college education able to command millions for nothing more than mere talent. He had worked and studied medicine half his life and still lacked the funds to support the lifestyle his wife expected. He should have known from the beginning what he'd be up against when, late in life, he married the daughter of one of the wealthiest families in France. Emily was young, beautiful, and easily disappointed when she didn't get what she wanted. Despite the fact that she was much too pampered and spoiled, he loved her more than life itself, and he couldn't run the risk of losing her. And so he had pretended to be wealthy until at last his debts had caught up with him, forcing him to seek a new, very lucrative extra source of income.

It all came about quite unexpectedly when he happened to read of the new rash of forgery in the art industry. He knew Lucrezia's work well, and all his life he had worked at imitating her skill. He had rented a small apartment in San Francisco to use as a studio and set out to perfect copies of Lucrezia's paintings that soon became so nearly perfect that the trained eyes of many experts could hardly detect a difference. At last his talent, not quite brilliant enough to make him a master, was bringing him financial rewards. And he so desperately needed those rewards.

At first the guilt and worry about the consequences were almost too much for him, but as time went by, the newfound source of wealth became the driving force of his life. He had been very careful to go underground with the forgeries, protecting himself well, and never once had to fear reprisals.

But now this young woman could ruin his life forever. He wondered who she was and why she was hiding behind a dead woman's identity. But it didn't matter. All that counted now was saving himself. He couldn't take the risk of losing his wife, his medical practice, his very existence. He would rather be dead than in prison.

He had toyed with the idea of hiring a killer. Last night he had lain awake until dawn going over and over the alternatives. A hired gun only meant that another human being had something to hold over his head. No, it was better this way. Like his mother always told him, "If you want something done right, do it yourself." And so, this morning he had gone to a sleazy pawn shop and found it surprisingly simple to give a false name, slip the clerk an extra hundred-dollar bill, and walk out of there with a loaded gun.

He pulled the coat collar tighter around his neck.

Damn, the rain was getting harder now, and the wind made the air chilly. He waited half an hour longer until finally, the doors opened and people began to file out of the auction. He swallowed hard and braced himself. Soon the nightmare would be over. He slipped his hand back into his pocket, his fingers tightening on the cold handle of the revolver.

Lauren was among the last to leave the auction. She had stayed behind to make a final tally of the prints that were sold and to check the painting one last time for Lucrezia's hidden mark before they released it to the new owner. She was relieved that nothing seemed amiss. Everything was legitimate and aboveboard. Slipping on her raincoat, she walked out the door, surprised at how cool the weather had become. *Wouldn't you know,* she thought, *not a cab in sight, and it's raining even harder.* She hurried down the walk to the curb, ready to hail the first cab.

"Hello, Diane, or whoever you are" came the familiar accent of Dr. Carnot. "Cole was right. You really shouldn't be out here alone."

Lauren felt suddenly afraid. "What are you doing here? Were you at the auction?"

"No, I came to take you home."

There was something about the tone of his voice that gave her heart a frenzied leap. "Thank you, but I'd rather take a cab."

"You're going with me." He reached for her and grasped her around the waist.

She struggled, but he tightened his grip, and she felt something hard digging into her back. She refused to move. "I won't go another step. Let go of me!" She felt a sharp pain as the object dug harder into her back. *Oh, my God, he's got a gun! He's going to kill me!* She looked around frantically for someone to help her, but she didn't dare call out. He had a gun and she had no doubt that he would use it. To passersby, they must look like any normal couple, the man holding the woman close to him to shield her from the rain. For a terrifying moment, she thought she might faint. "Please let me go," she begged. "You have nothing to fear from me. I'll never say anything to give you away. I'd only be hurting myself. Please—we made a bargain. You—"

"Keep quiet and move." He pushed the gun harder into her back and gave her a shove. "This time I have the upper hand, and I don't think you have much choice."

The world blurred around her as she allowed herself to be pushed down the walk. "Where are you taking me?" Tears streamed down her face, and she felt her heart pounding irregularly in her chest. Somehow she had to get away from him.

"I have a rented car parked at the end of the block. Just keep walking, we're almost there."

When they reached the car, he pushed her into the street and stopped at the driver's side. Lauren knew she would die if she ever got inside. He relaxed his hold on her long enough to open the door, and she broke free momentarily. But he caught her arm and pulled her back.

"You can't get away, so quit trying. Get inside."

"I won't." Her breaths came in gasps, and she struggled for air, suffocating with fear. "I won't!"

He didn't speak as he bent over the steering wheel and shoved her across the driver's seat to the opposite side. Suddenly she heard a muffled sound and felt the weight of his upper body fall across her lap. Her hand fell on his back, and she felt something wet and sticky. Panicky, she looked up and saw a man running across the street, and in the glow of the streetlight, she caught the glint of a gun in his hand. It all happened so suddenly that she couldn't comprehend the reality. Dr. Carnot lay lifeless across her lap, and some stranger had saved her life. She couldn't believe it.

She sat very still for several seconds, paralyzed with a mixture of horror and relief. She finally began to gather her wits and realized she had to get out of there. She couldn't be found with a dead man, especially Dr. Carnot. How on earth could she explain it? She had never touched a dead body in her life, and she winced as she pushed it away, the smell of blood and death making her physically ill. She eased away from the lifeless body, opened the car door, and made it to the sidewalk. She pulled a tissue from her purse and wiped the blood from her hands. And then she had the presence of mind to open the car door and clean her fingerprints from the handle. She hurried down the street and frantically waved at an approaching cab. "Thank God," she muttered as it stopped and she climbed into the backseat. Seconds later, the cab pulled away, and Lauren, safe inside, was on her way to the hotel.

Jason stood in the shadows across the street from Carnot's car and watched Lauren's cab until it was out of sight. He moved silently and quickly to the car, opened the door, and pushed the body to the floor. Reaching inside Carnot's pocket, he found the key and started the motor. It wouldn't do to leave it here and have Lauren eventually connected to his murder.

He drove the car on back streets until he reached a remote area on the outskirts of the city, then pulled off the road and stepped out. Shit, he'd have a long walk in this rain before he could locate a cab.

229

Chapter Twenty

Lauren's phone rang at eight-thirty the next morning. She had been asleep less than two hours, having lain awake all night. Last night's horror seemed like a bad dream, but as she pulled herself out of a fitful sleep, it all came rushing back into her consciousness. She reached for the phone and mumbled, "Hello."

"Diane, it's Cole. We've had terrible news and Lucrezia is very upset."

A great dread gripped Lauren. She knew what was coming next. "What happened?"

"Georges Carnot is dead."

"Oh, no." Lauren tried desperately to put the sound of shock in her voice. "When?"

"We got a call this morning from the Chicago police."

"Police?"

"He was murdered last night, and they found his body this morning in a rented car."

"How awful! I'll be right up."

She dragged herself out of bed, went into the bathroom, and turned on the shower. When the cold water hit her in the face, all the worries of the night before washed over her. She had no idea who had seen

231

her with Georges Carnot in front of the auction or who had seen her leave the car. Since his body was discovered within a block of the auction, she would be among the first people questioned, and oh, God, maybe even be a suspect. There were bound to be questions, and sooner or later, the truth would come out. And who on earth would believe that the doctor had forced her into the car with a gun in her back? No one, that's who. A more likely deduction would be that she had killed him because he had somehow learned her true identity. It was all so unfair. She had been a victim and could very well be charged with a crime.

She stepped out of the shower, toweled herself dry, and slipped on her clothes—beige slacks and a light summer sweater. She gave her damp hair a few swipes with a brush, slipped on a pair of sandals, and left the room, dreading what lay ahead of her.

Lauren found Lucrezia in bed, distraught over the death of her longtime friend. Cole was in the bedroom with her, trying his best to offer comfort.

"Who would do such a thing?" Lucrezia said to Lauren as she entered the room.

"I have no idea." And that was the truth. She was in the car right beside him one minute, with his head in her lap the next, and had no idea who killed him. And how in God's name would she ever make the police believe that?

"They said it wasn't robbery," Cole said. "His watch and wallet were still on his body and everything was intact."

"Then it must have been for some other reason." Lucrezia dabbed her eyes with a tissue. "But what could it have been?"

"Odd where they found him," Cole said, "way out in the middle of nowhere."

"But he was in front of—" Lauren caught herself just

232

in time, and she felt a flush rise in her cheeks.

"What was that, dear?" asked Lucrezia.

"I only asked where they found him."

"The police said near the city limits on a side street on the west end of town," Cole said. "I can't for the life of me imagine what he was doing out there."

"None of this makes sense," Lucrezia said.

Lauren felt faint with relief and sank into a chair beside Lucrezia's bed. Carnot's car was found miles away from the auction. Whoever killed him had not only saved her life but put him in a place that removed any suspicion from her. How bizarre! She wondered if she would ever know the reason behind all this. It was as though someone were watching over her, making sure she was safe and protecting her false identity. Alex? Not likely. His attempt to follow her had failed during the plane crash, and he, like everyone else, believed she was dead. And even if he didn't, protecting her was the last thing he'd want to do. No, not Alex. But who?

"How about a cup of coffee?" Cole asked.

"I'd love it," said Lauren.

"Lucrezia?"

"No thank you, dear. I'm afraid I couldn't swallow a drop." She wiped her eyes again.

Cole poured Lauren's coffee from the silver service on a small table near the bed and handed her a cup and saucer. "There's one more thing I learned from the police. They found a gun with Georges's fingerprints on it."

"That's hard to believe," Lucrezia said. "Poor Georges never owned a gun in his life. What on earth was he mixed up in?"

Lauren wanted so badly to tell them that the man they mourned would have killed her if he hadn't been killed himself. In fact, last night when she had relived the nightmare again and again in her desperate attempts to fall asleep, she had decided to tell them both that their trusted friend had been the forger all along. Now the thought was out of the question. Lucrezia was in no shape to bear two terrible blows at one time. The man was dead, and his despicable acts had died with him. But if she kept her job and stayed with Lucrezia, her work would be a lie, would mean still another deception. Her life had become more complicated by the minute since she left Alex. She had even fallen in love.

"I have to go down to police headquarters," Cole said. "Will you be all right for an hour or so, Lucrezia?"

"Of course I will."

"I'll stay with her," said Lauren.

Cole took one last sip of coffee and pulled on his suit jacket. He bent to give his aunt a kiss on the cheek. "I won't be long," he said. "I promised to fill them in on Georges's background." He gave Lauren a long, affectionate look just before he walked out the door.

"Is there anything I can do for you?" Lauren asked. "Any calls I can make?"

"Thank you, dear, but Mario has taken care of that. He's called all our friends who knew Georges. My only regret is that I can't fly to Paris for the funeral. Mario has strictly forbidden it."

"Can you think of anything else I can do?"

"No, I think I'll try to rest, maybe even doze for a few minutes. Mario gave me a mild sedative earlier, and I can feel its effects." Lucrezia closed her eyes.

Lauren looked at Lucrezia lying so still on the white silk sheets and suddenly realized how ill this lovely woman was. Her face was so white against the sheets that she watched her closely to make sure she was still breathing. Georges Carnot's death was taking its toll, and Lauren wondered if this dear woman would ever recover from it. What a bastard the good doctor turned out to be!

Her thoughts turned to Lydia, so brutally murdered just weeks ago, and suddenly she sat bolt upright. Could these two deaths have any connection? What if she herself was the common thread? It didn't seem possible, but if it were true, who could be behind it? Alex? It was all so farfetched, but then with Alex, anything was possible. But Alex must have believed she was dead. He had even put out a statement to that effect to the news media after the crash. Maybe that was what he wanted the world to believe. She had always been so gullible, trusting and believing everyone, but she was learning. These past months might have been worth something after all.

Chapter Twenty-One

The day of the dedication at the Hudson Clinic
turned out to be a beautiful one in Chicago. It was ideal
baseball weather. The Cubs were slugging it out in
Wrigley Field. There was standing room only, as usual.
It was wonderful sailing weather, and hardly a boat
was left in the marina. The sails of weekend boaters
swaying gracefully in the gentle breeze dotted Lake
Michigan, and sun worshipers crowded the Oak Street
beach and all the sandy shores reaching northward.
Temperatures ranged between seventy and seventy-five
degrees, not too hot, not too cool, just perfect.

The ceremony was scheduled for three in the
afternoon. When all the speeches were over, Lucrezia's
team would unveil her mural. She was then expected to
stand before the microphone to say a few words that
would be an explanation of her artistic interpretation
of the dreams that Dr. Hudson had for his work in the
new clinic. Many Chicago politicians would be on
hand, as would people in the medical field.

Florence Hudson had arranged everything with
great thought and in good taste. A temporary drop
cloth covered the mural on one wall of the air-
conditioned atrium, and toward the back she had

arranged for a small, temporary podium. A pianist would play a variety of popular tunes.

A long, narrow refreshment table, appointed in brass and copper and centered by an arrangement of gold and bronze chrysanthemums, stood along the wall opposite the mural. Brass and copper trays held miniature spiced rolls, a variety of finger sandwiches, and dainty fruit pies, and a tiered copper tray bore clusters of frosted green and purple grapes, chilled balls and slices of fresh fruit. There were also ice molds surrounded by pale yellow roses and fresh pineapple rings. Yes, Florence Hudson had gone all out for her husband's big day.

Everything would go exactly as planned if Lucrezia would summon the will to attend these services. Georges Carnot's unexplained murder had left her weak with grief. They had been friends for many years; she had taught him to paint when he was just a child. His funeral had taken place without her. It was all too much for her.

Though Lauren knew the truth about Carnot's forgery of Lucrezia's works, she could only guess at who his murderer might be. Felix Barrendo? He wouldn't have bothered to save her life and move the body so she wouldn't be implicated. Alex? If he had found her and had known she was alive he would have welcomed her death at someone else's hand. In fact, he'd probably think it a good joke. No, she didn't have a clue about the murderer. But night after night, the bad dreams had persisted, and she couldn't seem to get over the horror that surrounded Carnot's death.

She was determined to try to get Lucrezia out of bed and urge her to attend the dedication. She had spoken with Dr. Rossi, and he thought that attending the function might conceivably break this cycle of grief that had taken such a toll on her strength.

Lauren tapped on Lucrezia's bedroom door. Gia opened it a crack, saw Lauren, and silently motioned for her to enter the darkened room.

"For goodness' sakes," Lauren said, "why is it so dark in here? Let's let the sun in. It's a glorious day."

"No, no! Lucrezia does not want to see the sun." Gia was right behind Lauren, closing the blinds as fast as she opened them.

"You're acting as though she were on her death bed. Stop it right now!"

"But she's so weak. She can't stand noise or light." Gia sounded pathetic.

Lauren went ahead, opening the blinds. "I know you're worried, but you want to do what's best for her, don't you?"

"Is that you, Diane?" Lucrezia's usually resonant voice sounded thin and weak. "The light hurts my eyes."

"I'm not going to allow you to bury yourself before your time," Lauren said. "Mario says you can go to the dedication, so I'm here to see that you go."

"Oh, my dear," she whispered, "there's no way I can go. There's no strength left in me. I'll die right here in this bed."

Lauren knelt beside the bed and took Lucrezia's frail hand in hers. "You hired me to do a job. Most of it is done, except for positive proof. If I tell you that the forger has been stopped, that I'm almost sure we've bought all the forgeries that were floating around, then would you be able to get out of bed? Would you be able to forget about Georges Carnot just for today?"

Lucrezia sat up, leaning on one elbow. "Do you really think offering a bribe will make me well? You're no nearer to solving this case than you were when you returned from London."

"You're right, but I learned a lot in London, and

some of it I haven't been free to reveal."

"Not able to reveal it, even to me? Well, what does it matter anyway, compared to the murder of my dear friend? Oh, who would do such a thing to Georges, and why? I keep asking that question over and over. What a terrible loss to the world of medicine." She frowned at Lauren. "What can't you reveal? And why not?" She sank back into the pillows.

"I wasn't bribing you at all. It won't be long before I can tell you everything, but for now, I can only say that if I'm right, the paintings were copied somewhere in California."

"You can tell me that much, but no more? That's preposterous!" Lucrezia's antennae were at full alert.

"Because I have a responsibility to my source." She should have known better than to try to tell Lucrezia a half-truth, but she didn't dare say anything more.

"Just who do you think hired you—your source, or me?" Lucrezia's voice was sharp. "Your first allegiance should be to me."

"It is, of course, but I want all the facts first, everything neatly wrapped up. That's how I always operate." *Oh, Lord,* Lauren thought, *how am I going to get out of this one?*

"You have a lot to learn, my dear, if you think you can tell Lucrezia that much and no more." She was furious, and much stronger, Lauren noticed.

"Well, I can tell you one thing more. There will never be another copy made by that same forger!"

"You're positive?"

"I can guarantee it."

"What a relief! Just when will your source allow you to tell me the whole story?" Even though she was ill, Lucrezia could still be sarcastic.

"In a week or two, I hope."

Lauren knew she should never have kept anything

from Lucrezia, but if she told her about Georges Carnot, her job would be over, and she'd have to tell her everything to make her understand. There would be no need to go to Monte Carlo with her. What would become of her then? This was the only way. Lucrezia didn't want to go to her home in Italy. She had decided to live out her last days in her Monte Carlo villa, and Lauren was determined to be with her. She'd tell her about her friend, Dr. Carnot, after they were comfortably settled in the villa.

"Promise?"

"I promise."

"Gia, do you think my black linen coatdress with the white organdy collar would be appropriate for a dedication, since I'm more or less in mourning?" By now, Lucrezia was sitting up.

"You'll look like a queen."

"Then why are you standing there? Run my bath, will you? I'll be there in a moment. Hurry! And you get dressed, too, Gia. You're coming along to see my mural unveiled. My, it's a beautiful day! We should have had these blinds open all along."

Lauren watched Lucrezia all but bounce out of the bed. She could have been the toast of Broadway. What an actress! A party was a party, especially when she and her work were to be honored.

Lauren had a triumphant smile on her face when she left the bedroom and heard Lucrezia talking to Gia on her way to the bathroom. "Pearls, yes, I believe pearls will look just right with that dress."

Of those guests who partook of the refreshments in the atrium of the Hudson Clinic, no one had a better time than Lucrezia. She seemed to gain strength from each compliment she received, and there were many yet to come since the unveiling was about to take place. First there was a speech honoring Dr. Mario Rossi for bringing his expertise to Chicago for the summer.

While Dr. Hudson was lauding Mario, Cole finally caught up with Lauren long enough to press her arm in thanks, and his eyes silently asked how in the world she had done it. No one had been able to budge Lucrezia, yet here she was, looking radiant. Lauren lifted her eyebrows, signaling that there had been nothing to it. She turned toward the podium with a smug look on her face.

Lucrezia was on stage now. She had brought notes for her speech with her, but never once needed to refer to them. She had probably been rehearsing them in her mind while everyone was begging her to try to get up and attend this function. At one point when she spoke, she had to hold onto the lecturn suddenly, as though she were not too steady on her feet, but she rallied immediately, finally getting to the drum roll and the actual dropping of the cloth that covered the mural.

She beamed at the oohs and aahs, and gazed in admiration at her finished work. It was breathtaking. The entire concept of stained-glass windows filled with graphic representations of the various stages of humankind was exciting and overwhelming. Lucrezia's use of colors was pure genius. The applause semed to go on and on.

Finally, there was silence, and Lucrezia continued her speech, first thanking everyone, then speaking from her heart.

"Many of you have wondered why an Italian artist would be interested in doing a mural on the wall of a medical facility situated in the middle of America. I have operated in the dark long enough. It's time for everyone to know the importance of the work that Dr. Hudson is doing and how grateful I am for the time and attention he has given me during my stay in Chicago. You see, I have nephritis and have been getting dialysis treatments the entire time of my visit. It seems that everyone can't be helped indefinitely, and I am one of those people. But I'm not sad. I know I've had the finest nephrologists in the world as my doctors and my friends."

"Tomorrow I leave for my home in Monte Carlo. I'll never be able to return to your beautiful city, but the memories of this visit and this day will be with me until the end. Thank you for allowing my artwork to remain behind in your keeping."

The applause was deafening. Tears were hastily wiped away. The festivities continued, but Lucrezia and her party entered a white limousine and were quickly whisked out of sight.

One man who watched the disappearing car didn't return to the atrium of the Hudson Clinic. He had gotten all the information he'd come for. He guessed he'd better find a phone and let Alex Compton know where his precious wife was off to next. Why in the hell he was paying all this bread to have her followed, he couldn't figure out. Compton was going to ice her soon anyway, he'd bet on it. Probably wanted to do that job himself.

Well, Lauren Compton was sure moving around. What the shit, he'd be glad to follow her to Monte Carlo. If this traveling kept up, he could soon be one of the Beautiful People in one of those fancy magazines. Jason dropped his cigarette butt on the grass without bothering to step on it. He snickered. It would be a good joke if this whole place went up in smoke, and the old lady's picture got burned. Listening to all those damned speeches pissed him off anyway.

243

Chapter Twenty-Two

It was after midnight when Alex Compton returned home from an exhausting yet satisfactory trip from Washington. His chauffeur pulled up in the circular drive in front of his home in Oyster Bay. The thirty-room house sat in the middle of twelve beautifully tended acres. The limousine had hardly come to a complete stop when he stepped out of the backseat and gave his driver a brusque wave.

The car moved away at once, but Alex lingered outside for a moment, breathing in the late-summer air. It was always good to come home. The meetings all week in Washington had been brief and to the point, but the one today with Senator Murray had not. Alex smiled to himself. It had been a thoroughly satisfactory meeting, with much accomplished. The Senate was on the verge of dropping the hearing altogether. Not enough evidence. He had taken care over the years to keep himself well insulated. That was the key. And it hadn't hurt his case to have made healthy contributions over the years to certain political campaigns—the magic golden rule.

He picked up his heavy leather briefcase and let himself in with his key. By now the servants would all be asleep. No need to disturb the whole household to announce his premature homecoming.

He switched on a light in the drawing room, and his eyes scanned the golden-hued Francophile formality—inlaid marble floors, eighteenth-century furniture, and silk-covered walls. He had selected each exquisite piece himself, and he felt a sense of pride when he took the time to savor the beauty.

It was still impossible to understand why Lauren had given all this up. He had considered her the perfect wife: beautiful, even-keeled, undemanding, acquiescent the once or twice a month when he came to her bed. She always turned to face him when he lay down beside her, her body always positioned the way he preferred. He never had to ask or beg or say anything, and when he was finished, he gave her a kiss good night with no lingering mush or clinging. They were so perfectly matched in every way that at first he found it hard to believe that Lauren had fled. When he found the bugs in the library, she was the last one he suspected of having put them there. That wasn't Lauren's style. She had stayed out of his business, content to run his house and keep out of his way. Thank God for Trudy. At least she had gotten the truth out of Lauren, and after all this time, he felt sure the tape was lost forever in the wreckage of the plane.

Deep down he hadn't wanted to blow Lauren to bits on the flight to Chicago, and now he was rather glad that she was still alive. And she would stay alive until he was sure the tape was actually destroyed. Yet there was always the possibility that she still had it with her. Jason Lawrence was a good man to have on the job, but God knows, the whole thing was taking too damned long.

He walked into the library and poured himself a double Scotch, then settled himself in a comfortable leather chair. He smiled to himself. Lauren thought herself safe and rid of him while she masqueraded as a dead woman with Lucrezia Saunders in Chicago. His eyes drifted to the opposite wall and rested on Lucrezia's "Beginnings." Little did he know when he bought the painting that his own wife would one day be playing out this charade. He wondered how long Lauren could keep up this pretense. The waiting was unbearable. Patience. Always have patience and make sure you understand the opposition. That was a rule he never broke.

He was startled from his reverie by the sudden ringing of his private phone. Who could be calling at this hour?

"Yes?"

"It's John Murray."

"Senator, what's on your mind this time of night?"

"I'll get right to the point. I'm afraid I have bad news. Late today, after you left, something came up. It seems that some evidence has been uncovered in the debris of the plane crash that killed your wife."

Alex felt shock waves travel through his body. "And?"

"The authorities found a tape and turned it over to the Justice Department. I haven't had a chance to listen to it, but there have already been some leaks, and it's just a matter of hours before it hits the wire services. From what I can gather, it doesn't look good. It seems that there's incriminating evidence against you and some of your operatives. I can't imagine why it was on the plane unless your wife—"

"That's possible. She had my library bugged."

"Well, that explains it. There was also a leak last summer that your wife contacted Senator Kingsley, but nothing ever came of it."

"The goddamned bitch! What did she tell him?"

247

"I have no idea. My source was sketchy about it, but there's something else. My source tells me that Kingsley had a visitor recently, a man named Saunders, and somehow he's connected to you. And there's more. The F.B.I. has concluded that the crash was caused by a bomb, and there's talk of trying to link you to the whole thing."

"Damn! You'll have to stop it, and I mean now."

"I'm just one person. This thing is getting big, and the dam could break any minute."

"Stall it!"

"I'll do what I can."

"Hell, man, what do you think I'm paying you for? You get hold of that tape and fix it. No excuses, understand?"

"I'll do what I can."

"Keep in touch."

Alex hung up the phone, his insides churning, his face hot with fury. He sat for a long time trying to digest this information and considering his options. He should have had Lauren killed the minute she was found. It wasn't often he miscalculated, but this time he had screwed up royally. The tape alone wouldn't stand up in court or wouldn't even be admissible, for that matter. Without Lauren's testimony, the whole thing would eventually die down. And, too, there was no way he could be linked to the bombing. He was thousands of miles away from Los Angeles when the plane took off.

His main objective was to do away with Lauren and the Saunders bastard before it was too late. But he had to talk to the little bitch first and find out exactly what she knew and what she could have told Kingsley. Right now, Lauren was officially dead, so he wouldn't be suspected if the body of Diane Roberts were discovered. He had been patient with Lauren long enough. Her masquerading days were over. According to Jason Lawrence, she was now on her way to Monte Carlo. Perfect. His own hotel in Nice was just a few miles away.

He picked up the phone and dialed his secretary's number in New York.

"I want my plane ready for an early takeoff tomorrow morning and a flight plan filed for Nice. I'll be at the airport at nine."

Chapter Twenty-Three

The long black limousine sped along the winding coastal road that led to Monte Carlo. Angelo and Gia had left Chicago two days early to get the house ready for Lucrezia's homecoming, and Angelo was waiting for them at the airport in Nice.

Lauren had been over this road many times in the past with Alex, who liked to make unannounced visits once or twice a year to the Saint-Saëns, the hotel he owned in Nice. But never before had the view been so breathtaking. Clouds floated like pink-tinged puffs of cotton candy and cast shadows over the Alps that rose majestically on the left, as though standing guard over the sparkling waters of the Mediterranean Sea on the right. Lauren gazed at the tremendous stretch of blue water speckled with white sails gleaming in the warm sunshine. It was as though some huge, magical hand had scooped out a chunk of the Alps to produce a magnificent playground.

The journey from Nice to Monte Carlo ended all too soon when Angelo turned onto a steep drive on the left that led to the back of Lucrezia's villa. The white stucco house was nestled like a pearl in the middle of a terraced bluff overlooking the sea. The moment they stepped from the car, the air was filled with the tangy fragrance of oranges growing abundantly on trees that dotted the grounds. As they climbed the stone steps leading to the villa's entrance, Lauren realized that this was the front of the house. Like all the villas in the surrounding hills, it was built to face the spectacular view of the sea.

"This has to be the most beautiful place in the world," Lauren said. She took a deep breath of the warm sea air. Nothing seemed real. It was as though she were living in a fantasy world, completely safe, free of Alex and all the fears, free of the sickening terror she had felt in Chicago. But the guilt that had plagued her for weeks was still there. She had no right to be here, no right to pretend any longer to be searching for the source of the forgeries. Somehow, some way, she had to figure out how to tell them about Georges Carnot without giving her identity away.

They stepped into a sunlit foyer with a high, vaulted ceiling. In the center of the entryway, on a painted antique French table, sat a Louis XV vase filled with late-summer flowers from Lucrezia's own garden. The house, with its black and white marble floors and seventeenth-century French antiques, was much like a palace, yet there was a warm, comfortable look about it. The front wall of the main salon, solid glass from the floor to the high ceiling, offered an unobstructed view of the sparkling sea below. Lauren fell instantly in love with the house. It was what fairy tales were made of.

She spent the next hour getting herself settled in her room. She was enchanted by the Tuscan bed with its fringed, tapestry canopy and white silk spread edged with wide French lace. The room was light and airy, its windows covered with a filmy white silk. She finished unpacking, and parting the draperies, she gazed at the view. The ordeal with Georges Carnot had taken its toll. Haunted by the circumstances of his death, she was still waking up, night after night, from awful dreams, dripping with perspiration. She had gone over the whole thing time and again but couldn't figure out why someone had saved her life, killed Carnot, and made sure she wouldn't be blamed. She was startled by a sudden knock at the door. It was Cole.

"It's still early," he said, "how about a swim in the surf before dinner?" He was clad in a beach robe over a pair of white trunks and carried a blanket over his arm.

"But I don't have a swimsuit."

Cole looked at her with a playful gleam in his eyes. "That's even better. The beach is private, and we'll have our little edge of the sea all to ourselves."

"You're terrible, Cole Saunders, suggesting such a thing right under Lucrezia's nose."

He grinned. "It was worth a try, but if you insist, you can wear one of the suits in the poolhouse. Lucrezia keeps a supply on hand for guests."

"Then let's do it," she said. "That water has been trying to seduce me since we got here."

They left the house and went down a row of stone steps to the kidney-shaped pool, blanked by a poolhouse on one side and a cabana on the other. Lauren found a black French bathing suit that looked as though it had been made for her, molding her slender body to perfection. She found a matching beach robe, and within minutes, she joined Cole, who waited for her in a cushioned lawn chair beside the pool.

"Damn, but you're beautiful," he said. He slipped his arm around her waist, and they walked down still another row of steep steps that led to the edge of the sea.

Lauren was unusually quiet as they strolled hand in hand down the lip of sand that ran between the wall of jutting rocks and the crashing waves. If only she had someone to talk to. She didn't even feel free to confide in the man she loved. She was tired of lying and pretending, tired of taking advantage of Lucrezia, tired of the whole damned thing.

"What's wrong?" Cole said.

"Nothing."

"Come on, you haven't been yourself for weeks. You're not eating enough to keep a child alive, and half the time, your mind is way off somewhere. Tell me, what's bothering you?"

She paused and turned to look at the sea. "Nothing, really, I'm fine."

Cole put his hands on her shoulders and turned her around to face him. There was a seriousness in his eyes that she'd rarely seen before. "It's me—Cole, the guy who loves you, remember? You've had me worried for a long time, and I won't let you shrug this off. I want to marry you, have babies with you, grow old with you."

Her eyes filled with tears as she shook her head and touched his cheek with her fingertips. "Don't you know that I love you, too—how much I want all the things you want? But I can't. I just can't marry you. Not now."

"But I love you." Cole's voice was soft and pleading. "Can you tell me what's bothering you?"

"I can't talk about it now, but someday you'll understand. Just know that I love you." The look in her eyes begged him not to press her.

"When? A year from now? Two years? What's going on? Something is definitely wrong, and you've got to tell me." His eyes seemed to burn into hers.

Lauren knew that she couldn't put him off any longer. She couldn't give him an answer now, and when the whole story finally came out, he probably wouldn't want an answer. But she couldn't bear the guilt any longer. It was bad enough that she had lied about her identity, but pretending to do a job was another matter. Her work was finished here, and Lucrezia and Cole deserved to know the truth about the forgeries. The time had come to tell Cole about Carnot and what she knew about his murder. She couldn't bear the thought of telling him that she was another man's wife and had lied to them from the beginning. It would be better to get as far away from here as possible and never have to see the contempt on his face. But it would be so hard to leave him. She couldn't imagine life without him.

She looked at him, her eyes swimming with tears. "There *is* something wrong, and you have every right to know. My job is over here, and it's time for me to leave."

"Leave? Good Lord, what are you talking about?" He stared at her in bewilderment.

"I found out two weeks ago who was behind the art forgery."

A flicker of anger danced in his eyes. "Why didn't you tell me?"

"I had to wait until I was sure, and then when Dr. Carnot was killed, I didn't know what to do."

"I have no idea what you're talking about, but something tells me I need to hear this sitting down." He led her to the shelter of the rocks, spread the blanket over the sand, and pulled her down beside him. "Now start from the beginning."

"Remember when I told you in London that I thought I was getting close to solving this thing?"

Cole nodded. "Go on."

"I was approached by a man named Felix Barrendo who said he worked for Dr. Carnot." She noticed the shocked look on Cole's face and dreaded telling him the rest. "He assumed that I knew Georges Carnot, even approached me about taking pictures of Lucrezia's

255

work and he—"

"Hold it a minute. You're not telling me that Georges had something to do with the forgeries?" He shook his head. "That can't be true."

She nodded. "Oh, yes, it is. It had been going on a long time."

"You're saying that this man told you Georges was forging Lucrezia's paintings? That's absurd. You can't take some stranger's word on something like this. This is a terrible accusation, and there's bound to be a logical explanation. Why, Georges had been a close friend over forty years, and why would he want to do such a thing? It doesn't make sense."

"That's exactly what I thought at first, and I didn't tell you because I had to be sure."

"I feel like going back to London and having a talk with this Barrendo character. He can't get away with this and I'll—"

"Wait, there's more," Lauren said. "I felt the same way until Dr. Carnot came to Chicago and I confronted him."

"I'm sure he was furious."

"He denied it, of course, but when I mentioned Felix Barrendo, he backed down and admitted the whole thing."

Cole raked his fingers through his blond hair. "My God! It's true? Why didn't you tell me?"

"I wanted to, but he threatened me, and I was so afraid, and I—"

"Threatened you? Georges Carnot wouldn't have harmed his worst enemy."

"He was desperate. Remember the night I went to the auction—the night he was murdered?"

"Yes, of course."

"He was waiting for me outside and forced me into his car at gunpoint. I know he would have killed

256

me if—"

Cole's face turned stark white. "Oh, my God!" He pulled her into his arms and held her. "You went through all this and never said a word. How did you get away from him?"

She drew herself away from Cole, determined to get the whole thing out in the open. "Someone shot him."

"Who?"

"I have no idea."

"If I'd have been there, I'd have shot him myself. Did you get a good look at him?"

"No, it was dark and it all happened so fast and I was so scared—"

"Where were you?"

"In his car, outside the auditorium."

"But his body was found miles from there."

"I know, and I haven't been able to figure it out. Whoever killed him must have moved the car. I've gone over and over this whole thing, and I can't make any sense out of it."

"But I still don't understand why you've waited so long to tell me."

"I wanted to, believe me, but everyone was so upset and shocked about Carnot's death, and you were so worried about Lucrezia. I thought it might be best if none of you ever knew that there won't be any more forgeries—by him, anyway. Now all this time has gone by, and I realized I was having to fake doing my job. I just can't go on with it any longer. Oh, damn, I want to stay here with you, but I can't. It just isn't fair." Her eyes filled with tears, and she shook her head.

"But I want you to stay. If you leave, Lucrezia will want to know why, and we'll have to tell her. She's too ill to hear something like this. Let's give her some time to get settled here first. Besides, I can't bear the thought of your leaving." His voice was hoarse and powerful and kind. "Oh, to think I almost lost you—"

"But my work here is over."

"Please, if not for me, do it for Lucrezia. She's so fond of you and you can help her get through these next few weeks."

A small smile dawned in her eyes. "I hadn't thought of it that way. Oh, I've been so worried for so long."

He pulled her close to him. "Don't ever talk about leaving again." He held her so close and so tight that she could barely breathe. He found her lips with his own, and he kissed her again and again, gently at first, and then with an urgent need. He unclasped the top of her swimsuit and pushed it aside. When he had eased the bikini down her slender legs, he whispered, "I never want to be away from you, not for a long, long time—at least until I'm ninety years old." He quickly removed his swimming trunks and lay down beside her. She came to him and gave herself completely, the past and the future blending into a now that she couldn't deny. She knew without any doubt that she belonged to him. Somehow, some way, she would find a way to tell him everything. But not now.

Jason Lawrence sat crouched behind a rock overlooking the beach, his eyes glazed with arousal as he watched Cole Saunders writhing on the blanket with Compton's wife. The whore! Oh, shit, he'd like to have a piece of Alex Compton's wife himself. She was one sexy dame. Compton would kill him in a minute if he laid a hand on her, though.

But this would be his night off. He'd head back to Nice for a few hours. His wallet was fat with Compton's money, and he could spend a little to find a whore of his own.

Chapter Twenty-Four

Jason sat in his car outside Cole's law office in Nice. It was past five o'clock, and he kept his eye trained on the office door. The city street teemed with late-afternoon activity, cars and buses lining up at the lights, bumper to bumper, horns blaring, people hurrying home from work. He had followed Cole Saunders around since noon, even had lunch at the same restaurant, just waiting to catch him at the right moment.

He was tired of these cat-and-mouse games. Hell, if it had been up to him, he'd have taken out Lauren Compton and her boyfriend months ago. He didn't agree with Compton's strategy, just keeping track of his wife, making sure she was still playing the role of another woman. Shit, if someone's causing a problem, get rid of them and be done with it. That was his rule, and it had worked for him since he was seventeen years old.

It had all started back in high school when he was a quiet, skinny kid who wore thick glasses, a kid that no one knew, much less ever noticed. He had never had a

259

date in his life, but that didn't mean he never thought about girls, and one in particular—a girl who caused him to wake up soaking wet in the middle of long, lonesome nights. Her name was Marla Thompson, and he was obsessed with her. Fat chance of ever getting to take her out, though. Hell, she was so good-looking, with that curly red hair and those big blue eyes, and so well stacked that she could have any guy she wanted. He had heard all the talk about Marla, how easy she was to lay, and had heard the guys kid each other about whose turn was next. But he didn't care. He worshipped this girl. He doubted that she even knew his name, but that didn't keep him from hanging around her, just blending into the group.

There was something about Marla, kind of a scared, sad look that none of the other kids seemed to notice. Jason knew that somewhere deep inside her lay a secret that she was afraid to tell.

That haunted look got worse in the spring of their senior year. One day after school, Jason was standing around on the outside of a group of guys, with Marla in the middle, and she suddenly burst out crying.

"It's Luke," she said, "my stepfather. I can't stand it anymore." She buried her face in her hands, her shoulders shaking. "I'd kill him if I could."

Tom Fisk, a football jock, put his arm around her. "Good gosh, Marla, what did he do—beat you?"

"No, not that . . . He—" She lowered her head, embarrassed. "He just won't leave me alone."

"You mean he raped you?"

Marla wouldn't look at Tom or any of the other guys. She just kept staring at the ground. "I guess you could call it that."

"When?" Tom asked, his fists clenched, his jaw set.

Marla raised her head but still didn't look at anyone. "It—it started when I was thirteen years old, but lately it's getting worse. I hate to go home, dread going to bed, 'cause I know he'll be there sooner or later."

"But didn't you tell your mother?" one of the guys asked.

"Oh, sure, I tried, but she didn't believe me. She just got mad and said I was a sex-crazed kid trying to break up her marriage. I swear to God, I'd like to see him dead. All these years, he's threatened to kill me and my mother if I ever told. Somehow I'll get to him first, but I just haven't figured out how to do it."

"You're not going to kill anyone, Marla," Tom said. "That's crazy."

"Maybe not," she said, "but I'll sure as hell see him dead. I've saved over a hundred dollars, and I'll pay someone to do it if I have to. Anyone interested?"

As Jason watched and listened, he felt rage boil inside him from the tips of his toes to the top of his head, rage at what the sonovabitch had done to Marla, rage at those three bastards who wouldn't lift a hand to help her. He looked at their faces and knew right off that not one of them gave a big damn about her. All of their big-man jock talk was nothing more than a pile of crap.

He thought about Marla all that night, never once closing his eyes. When morning came, he knew what he had to do. Here was his chance, a perfect opportunity. Not only would Marla be out of her misery, but she would also find out how much he loved her and then she would love him, too. He'd kill that bastard before another night went by. His mind was made up.

Happiness poured over Jason the next afternoon as he pulled his old Ford out of the parking lot to follow Marla's school bus home. He turned onto the country road and finally stopped when the bus dropped Marla off in front of a white frame house about a mile from the main highway.

He hopped out of his car and hurried to meet her before she got too close to the house. "Hey, wait, Marla, I want to talk to you."

"What about?"

"Your stepdad."

She looked alarmed. "How did you know about that? Who told you?"

"I was standing right there."

"Oh . . ."

"Are you serious about killing him?"

"Well, yeah, sure I am."

"Okay then, let's talk about it." He pulled her into the trees beside the road, shielding them from any view of the house. "I'll do it."

"You will? You'll kill him? When?" For the first time in months, he noticed that her eyes were shining.

"Anytime you say—tonight if you say so."

"Tonight? Oh, wow!" She touched his arm, and Jason felt a sudden ache in his loins. "I'll pay you . . . I have some money."

"I don't want your money."

"Then why would you do it?"

Jason's face burned. "Because I . . . I care about you and can't stand the thought of that bastard forcing himself on you."

"You'd do that for me?"

"Sure."

"No one's ever done anything just for me without expecting something."

Jason beamed. It was all working out. She could see how much he loved her, and at least for now she liked him. Before long she'd tell those hotshots at school to go to hell, and she'd be his alone. It was beautiful. "I'll do anything for you, Marla."

"So you'll do it tonight?"

"Yeah, but I need to know about him, like what does

he look like? And where does he work?"

"His name is Luke Henderson, and he's a big guy, about six feet tall, midforties, and his hair is thick, sort of sandy colored. He works at Stemmons Tire Factory—he's the foreman."

"What shift?"

"Nights right now. He gets off at eleven."

"What does he drive?"

"A black Chevy pickup."

"Does he come straight home?"

"Usually, but sometimes he stops off for a beer." Marla sighed. "I always dread the nights he gets home late, 'cause my mom's usually asleep and he heads straight for me."

"I can't wait to kill that bastard," Jason hissed.

"Then you'll really do it tonight?"

"You can count on it."

Marla grabbed him and kissed his cheek. "I'll love you forever for it."

When Jason left her, he had never felt such a glow inside him. *She loves me! She told me so!* His head was still spinning when he stopped in the driveway beside his house.

That night he told his mother that he had a headache and was going to bed early. He knew that suited her just fine. Now he would be out of her way and out of her hair, leaving her free to hole up in her bedroom with her current boyfriend and a cheap bottle of whiskey. This had been his mother's pattern as long as he could remember. She always tried to hide it from him, but he knew what was going on, had always known. He couldn't blame her, though. She worked hard all day as a waitress in a busy little coffee shop, always managing to put clothes on their backs and a roof over their heads, all by herself. He didn't remember his dad, who had split shortly after Jason was born.

Now that his mother was occupied, Jason found it easy to slip out of the house about half past ten and drive his old car to the outskirts of town, down the country road to Marla's house. He parked his car in the shadows and waited beside the house for Luke's black pickup. Inside his jacket pocket, he had his mother's .38 revolver, the gun she had kept hidden for years inside her dresser drawer. He was a damned good shot if he said so himself. For years he had occupied himself on many weekends by taking the gun to the woods and shooting at cans or any other target he could find. He kept a supply of bullets hidden in a box under his bed, never having to worry about his mother's finding them. Hell, she did good to keep the top layer of litter picked up, and cleaning under furniture never entered her head. Now all that practice was about to pay off big. By tomorrow, Marla Thompson would be all his.

As the minutes ticked by, he was growing impatient. He was ready to get this thing over with. To Jason's relief, Luke skipped his visit to the bar that night and came straight home. Shortly after eleven, the headlights appeared at the top of the hill, and moments later, the truck ground to a halt in front of the house.

As soon as Luke climbed out of the truck, Jason walked up to him. "Mr. Henderson?"

"Yeah, what do you want?"

Jason grinned. It was amazing how no one thought of a tall, skinny kid like him as a threat. He stepped right up to the older man, and Luke just stood there with his hands in his pockets. "I have a present for you from Marla." Jason reached for his gun, aimed, and fired. The bullet hit Luke right between the eyes, and Jason jumped back instantly to dodge the blood that spurted from the wound. Luke fell to the ground, and Jason raced to his car, started the motor, and had already passed the house before the yard lights came on. He was down the road, halfway to the highway before anyone realized what had happened.

Jason was surprised at how he felt—not a bit scared, just excited, thrilled, in fact, at what he had done. He had killed a man. It felt good, real good, and it had been so easy.

He didn't lay eyes on Marla during the next three days. She wasn't in school, and Jason figured they were busy giving old Luke a decent funeral. He heard kids buzzing at school about Marla's asking around for a volunteer to help her kill the bastard. All the guys were eyeing each other, wondering which one was stupid enough to do it. No one eyed him, though, and Jason smiled to himself. For once it was good to be the one the other kids didn't notice.

On the fourth day, when Marla came back to school, he couldn't wait to see her alone. He followed her bus home again, knowing full well that when he walked up to her she would throw her arms around him. His girl. He was on the biggest high of his life.

"Jason," she said, "you shouldn't be here."

"Why not? I did what you wanted."

"That's just it." She wouldn't look at him. "You shouldn't come around me. People might see you and figure it out."

Jason felt a strange sense of panic. She looked like she couldn't stand the sight of him. "But when this blows over, then you and I can . . . I mean, we can get together and—"

"Are you kidding? Us?" She laughed. "Listen, Jason, I appreciate what you did and all that, but don't get any ideas. I mean, really."

"But I thought . . . you said—"

"I never said anything like that and you know it." Her eyes were blue ice. "If you know what's good for you, you'll stay away from me. The police have been nosing around and asking a bunch of questions. Someone's told them how I was offering to pay to have Luke killed. Now isn't that something? Imagine that— paying someone to kill my own stepfather! If the police keep pushing, I may have to tell them what I know. Now, you wouldn't want that to happen, would you?" With that, she turned her back on Jason and hurried up the walk to the house.

At that moment, something died inside Jason. There was no such thing as love and trust. It had all been an illusion. Marla was a bitch, just like his mother, just like all women. He should have taken Marla's hundred dollars when she offered it. Now he had nothing to show for what he had done.

He seethed inside all night and all the next day as he watched her smile and cozy up to the football jocks. Well, Marla Thompson's flirting days were over. He'd be damned if the little whore would put him in prison for the rest of his life.

He left school early that day, drove to Marla's house, and hid his car behind a grove of trees. He crouched behind some bushes across the street from the house and waited for the bus to drop her off. As soon as it pulled away, he called out to her, "Hey, Marla!"

Just as she turned, he fired. For an instant, she stared at him, her eyes wide, and her hands flew up to her chest just before she collapsed to the ground. Jason knew she was dead. He had aimed at her heart and he never missed his target.

Afterward, it was funny that no one ever suspected him of the murders. It gave him a strange sense of power. He realized how simple it all was, and that's when he made his rule. If someone's causing a problem, get rid of them and be done with it.

*　　　*　　　*

Now as he sat on the street in Nice, he wondered why Compton had told him to scare the hell out of Cole Saunders, not kill him yet. Maybe Compton was getting soft in the head in his old age, but he gave the orders. He was sick of waiting and wished he could get this over with.

Minutes later, his wait was over when Saunders walked out the door and headed for his car parked beside the curb. Jason turned on the ignition, gunned the motor, and watched Cole's low-slung white Porsche join the traffic. He pulled out behind Saunders and followed at a safe distance, but close enough to keep him in sight. The Porsche headed out of the city toward the coast road leading to Monte Carlo. Good. Saunders was going to the villa. It was just as he planned and he hoped that the traffic would taper off when they reached the outskirts of Nice. This little escapade wouldn't work if there were witnesses. By the time they reached the halfway mark of the short trip, they had the road to themselves except for an occasional car approaching from the opposite direction.

It amused Jason to see Saunders looking in his rearview mirror and speeding up. He had obviously begun to wonder about the car behind him. He stayed close to Saunders's tail all the way to Monte Carlo, and when Cole pulled onto the corniche that led to the villa, Jason smiled. The fun was about to begin.

By now it was clear that Saunders had figured out that he was being followed, and he literally flew along the steep, winding road, tires squealing with each curve. Jason was close enough to see how low Saunders was bent over the steering wheel, his shoulders stiff. This was more fun than Jason had imagined, and his smile grew wider as they approached the steepest curve so far. Now was his chance to give Cole Saunders the scare of his life. As they hit the middle of the turn, he

267

stepped on the accelerator and rammed Cole's car from behind. Jason laughed out loud at the sight of this rich bastard madly fighting the steering wheel to right the car and keep from sailing over the edge of the cliff. Hell, he hadn't had this much fun in years.

He watched the speedometer climb to eighty, eighty-five, ninety miles an hour around hair-raising curves, tires screaming, and now and then, he pulled up beside Saunders on the left-hand side of the road, forcing him to hug the edge of the cliff. The look on Saunders's face was worth the whole trip. Each time he had the man in a bind within inches of going over the edge, Jason pulled back, giving Cole just enough room to make the curve. He couldn't remember ever laughing so hard. This was priceless.

Jason decided to pull back and give Saunders a false sense of security. Then he would shock the hell out of him. Just as he thought, the Porsche slowed down to seventy, then sixty-five miles an hour, and Jason could see him glance backward to check his opponent. He lagged behind the Porsche for several minutes, then stomped the accelerator and gave Saunders another good smack. The Porsche spun in a semicircle, almost turning over on its side, then righted itself, and with a spin of rocks and gravel, it peeled out at high speed. Laughing out loud, Jason banged both hands on the steering wheel, gleeful at the sight. Damn, what a ride!

He stayed within inches of Saunders's bumper, giving it an occasional bump, then hit the accelerator again and pulled to the left, side by side with the Porsche. He grinned when Saunders mouthed, "You bastard!" and gave the side of the Porsche a hard nudge, almost pushing it over the steep embankment. He loved the look on Saunders's face—utter fear and anger mixed together. He had gotten a little carried away that time. Hell, Compton said to scare the poor bastard, not kill him. But Jesus, the Porsche sailing over the side of that cliff would have been quite a sight. Reluctantly, he pulled back to ride the bumper.

And then Saunders surprised him. What in God's name was he up to? He came to a screeching halt as the road widened at a lookout point and sat dead still.

The game was over. It was just as well, but hot damn, it had been fun while it lasted. He had scared the shit out of Cole Saunders, and that was all Compton had wanted. He backed up, made a U-turn, and headed in the opposite direction, cackling so hard he could hardly see the road. He couldn't wait to see Compton in Nice and tell him all about it.

Cole sat frozen in the driver's seat, his heart pounding, his hands shaking. Some maniac had tried to kill him and backed out at the last minute. But who? He had no enemies as far as he knew. He climbed out of the car and stood at the small stone wall bordering the lookout. He paid no attention to the breathtaking view below. He was desperately trying to get his nerves under control and try to figure out who the man could have been.

So many bizarre events had taken place since—when? Since Diane had entered their lives, that's when. He was more convinced than ever that the woman he loved was not Diane Roberts at all, but Lauren Compton. At least now he believed that his earlier suspicions were unfounded. She would never have told him about Georges Carnot and the forgeries if she were working for Compton. She was incensed about Carnot's defrauding Lucrezia and had almost lost her own life by insisting on attending the auction and protecting Lucrezia's interests. It still puzzled him why Carnot hadn't exposed her as a fraud. Maybe they each had something to hold over the other's head. That could be it. And it could also explain why she waited so long to tell him that Carnot was the forger. That was probably why Georges tried to kill her. It was all coming together.

Carnot's death, however, was another matter. Someone had killed him, obviously to save Diane's life, and then moved the body so she wouldn't be involved. He wondered if somehow all these strange events were somehow connected, even the wild chase just minutes ago.

Diane—or Lauren—was hiding from someone, probably Compton, according to what John Kingsley had told him. He found it hard to imagine this lovely young woman married to that excuse for a human being. So many times he had sensed fear in her. No doubt there was a good reason. Whoever had caused Lauren Compton to change her identity could very well be after *him*. He would have to stay more alert. He climbed back in his car and drove very slowly up the corniche the remaining mile to the villa.

As soon as Cole entered the main salon of the villa, Lauren noticed how pale his face looked and how shaken he seemed. She felt suddenly frightened. "Are you all right?" She quickly rose from her chair beside the sofa where Lucrezia was reclining.

"I think someone just tried to kill me." He pulled off his suit coat and loosened his tie.

Lauren felt chilled all over. "Tried to kill you? Oh, Cole! What happened?"

"Well, if you can imagine a ninety-mile-an-hour chase on the corniche, that's exactly what happened."

Lucrezia was alarmed. "But who would do such a thing? Oh, my poor Cole!" She reached out for him, and Cole bent to kiss her.

"Don't worry, it turned out all right. Whoever it was had the perfect opportunity and backed away and went in the opposite direction. It was the damnedest thing. Probably some creep high on something, getting his kicks. But high or sober, he had nerves of steel."

Lauren's heart raced. Oh, God, what if Alex were behind this? What if he had been behind everything that had happened? But if he had somehow learned that she was alive and where she was, he'd surely go after her, not Cole. It didn't add up. Maybe this was Alex's twisted way of letting her know that he had caught up with her. She had come so close to telling Cole everything when she explained about Carnot. The time to tell him the whole thing was drawing very close. It would be the end of everything between them, but if there was a chance that Alex was behind this attempt on Cole's life, she had no choice.

Chapter Twenty-Five

The next morning, Lauren rode with Cole to Nice to leave the car with the dealer for repairs. She had hated lying to Lucrezia, telling her that she planned to do some work at the gallery, but Cole still insisted that they keep everything about Georges Carnot from his aunt. Lucrezia was getting weaker by the day, and Mario, who flew in from Rome to check on her regularly, had warned Cole that she might not live longer than a few weeks. And then there was the matter of the incident last night. Lauren's fears for Cole's life were still very real. It was too farfetched to imagine Alex's involvement, but still, she felt an odd sense of responsibility. It was probable that this was an isolated incident, just as Cole said, some creep out for sick thrills, but she couldn't shake the terrible burden of dread.

"Did you see the driver?" she asked, thinking out loud.

"Just for an instant."

"Did you get a good look at him?"

Cole laughed. "Hell, no, I was fighting to stay on the road."

"But what did he look like—hair color, that kind

273

of thing?"

He looked at her curiously. "Dark, I think. Why do you ask?"

"I was just thinking, maybe you could identify him. Aren't you going to the police?" She felt a little relieved. At least it wasn't Alex. But then, car chases were hardly Alex's style. He left that kind of thing to his henchmen.

"I haven't thought much about it. What good would it do? I don't have a license number, and I'm not sure I'd recognize him in the first place." He reached for her hand and gave it a squeeze. "Let's forget about it for now. The only damage done was a little scraped paint and a few dents on the bumper. My nerves took a beating, of course, but I've recovered from that."

They drove into Nice, a bustling city great for shopping, with a multitude of stores and boutiques, great for boating, with a marina jammed with sailboats and luxurious yachts, and great for relaxing, with the warm white sands of the Riviera and the cool breeze from the sea. The streets were relatively quiet this time of day since most of the tourists were still asleep in their hotel rooms, recovering from a late night of drinking and gambling at the casinos in nearby Monte Carlo.

They went straight to the dealer, who furnished them with a car to drive, with the promise that Cole's Porsche would be in perfect condition by late afternoon.

"Let's have some breakfast," Cole said as they drove away. "I'm starving."

He stopped at a sidewalk cafe in the center of town, and soon they were seated at a small round table under a canopy that flapped in the breeze. Lauren's eyes widened when the waiter brought them plates laden with egg soufflé, thick slices of ham, croissants dripping with butter, and fresh strawberries. She looked more relaxed at this moment than she had in weeks, and there was a special glow about her and a sparkle in her eyes. Cole wondered if her burden had been lifted when she told him about Georges Carnot. Maybe talking about it had helped to ease the horror of that terrible night. It drove him nuts to think of what could have happened to her if the unknown assailant hadn't come to her aid.

"You know, I think I'm starving, too," Lauren said as she dove into the food.

"That's good news." He leaned over and kissed the tip of her nose.

"I feel like Cinderella, forgetting the clock will eventually strike midnight."

"Why does midnight ever have to come?"

"Sooner or later it always does."

"But why?" He searched her face for a clue. "All you have to do is say yes to my proposal and this could go on forever."

A look of sadness crept into her eyes. "Let's not go into that again."

"But we can work out whatever is holding you back."

"We will, very soon, I promise, but not now. We're both starving, remember?"

A shadow momentarily dimmed his blue eyes, but he smiled. "Okay, I won't press you, but you're not off the hook for long." And he meant it. He had waited too long to hear the truth. The time had come to bring it all out into the open. It tore at his heart to think the woman he loved didn't trust him completely. Of course, he didn't know for a fact that Diane Roberts was indeed Lauren Compton. All the evidence was mere speculation. But he had a plan to prove her identity one way or the other, and today he intended to carry it out. His patience was about gone.

They finished eating, and Cole suggested that they look around town and do a little window shopping.

275

They set out down the sidewalk, stopping now and then to admire the displays, and Cole was taken by an elegant boutique in the middle of the block.

"Let's go inside," he said. "I'm going to buy you a gift."

Lauren laughed. "A gift? What's the occasion?"

"Your birthday," he said, grinning.

"But this isn't my birthday. What gave you that idea?"

He opened the door and took her arm, ushering her inside. "That just shows how little I know about you. You've never told me. For all I know, it could have been yesterday and I didn't even know it."

"Just for the record," she said, smiling, "I was twenty-eight years old on the eighth of March, so you didn't miss a thing. In fact, we didn't even know each other then."

"Well, I intend to make up for lost time anyway. See anything you like?"

"Don't be ridiculous, you don't need to buy me anything."

"But I want to. Since it's not your birthday, let's just call it a 'welcome to Nice' present. Now tell me, what would you like?"

Lauren laughed. "Oh, no, this is all your doing. If you insist, then you pick it out."

She smiled as Cole studied the merchandise—the ropes of pearls, gold chains, ivory pins, perfume, and an endless array of earrings. He paused at the lingerie counter and gave Lauren a wicked little grin, then moved on, finally stopping at a glass case containing jewelry and evening accessories.

"Let me have a look at the gold minaudière on the end," he told the clerk. He opened the small, kidney-shaped case and ran his fingers over the black velvet lining. As far as he knew, she hadn't bought anything like this for herself since the crash and it would be perfect for dressy evenings. "I'll take it," he said, and handed it back to the clerk for wrapping.

Lauren shook her head. "Oh, no, that's much too expensive. I can't let you do that."

"It's already done, and I want you to have it."

The clerk accepted Cole's check, wrote him a receipt, and slid the minaudière into a padded silk bag.

Lauren gave him a kiss when they left the shop. "I'll always treasure it. It's a beautiful birthday present."

Cole pulled her close, not knowing whether to feel relieved or sad. At least he knew beyond any doubt that she was indeed an impostor. Yesterday, before he left his office, he had pulled Diane Roberts's résumé from the files and checked the date of her birth. Diane was born on July 18 and was thirty-two years old. He hated having to trick her this way, but he had to find out. Before this day was over, he would know the whole truth.

They rode out to the shore and spent the morning walking along the beach, kicking off their shoes and wading in the surf. By now, the beach was dotted with colorful umbrellas, and they found one of their own, joining the other sun worshipers.

"Too bad we didn't bring swimsuits," Cole said.

"It's just as well. I'm afraid I'd be out of style at this beach because I'd never have the nerve to go topless." She gave Cole a nudge. "By the way, you can put your eyes back in your head."

"You're more beautiful than any woman out here, and you're the only one with clothes on."

Lauren beamed. "If I am, it's because you make me feel that way."

He pulled her to him and kissed her. "We haven't had

much of a chance to be by ourselves since we left Chicago." He brushed her lips with his own and smoothed her windblown hair. "Hungry? It's past one."

"Not a bit. After that breakfast, I may never want to eat again."

Cole grinned. "I have a wonderful idea. What do you say we find a hotel and spend the rest of the day in bed? I think I'll go mad if I can't get you alone."

Lauren gave him a playful kiss. "I think you're reading my mind."

"The Saint-Saëns is just a mile or so from here," Cole said as they headed for the car.

Lauren felt suddenly unnerved. "The Saint-Saëns? Oh no, not there." Of all the hotels in the area, Cole had to pick the one that Alex owned. She couldn't bear the thought of setting foot in that place again. And besides, someone on the staff was sure to recognize her, and that would lead to disaster. Alex would be notified immediately, and then it would be all over. Somehow she had to talk Cole out of this, but she couldn't think of a plausible reason. She knew she sounded like a spoiled child, bent on having her way.

"Why not? It's right on the beach, and it's quiet and very private."

"Let's go to the Hotel de Paris in Monte Carlo. I've always wanted to go there, and it's not that far away."

"Yes, but it's usually booked. We wouldn't stand a chance of getting a room without a reservation." He gave a low growl. "Besides, woman, I don't want to wait to get my hands on you any longer than I have to." He tightened his arm around her and gave her a quick kiss.

"But not the Saint-Saëns." She thought of all the times she had been there with Alex, all the times he had embarrassed her, throwing his weight around with the staff, all the times he had humiliated her, putting her down in front of his friends.

"Come on, trust me. I hear it's elegant." He opened the car door for her and she climbed inside. "What do you have against the Saint-Saëns? Have you ever been there before?"

"No." She was out of arguments, short of telling him that she really didn't think it was such a good idea since her husband happened to own the hotel. She bit her lip to keep from saying more, pulled a scarf from her purse, tied it around her head, and slipped on her dark glasses, wondering what in hell she would do if someone called her by name.

"I know you'll love it." Cole turned the car around and headed down the coast road in the opposite direction.

Minutes later, a parking attendant was taking care of the car, and a doorman was ushering them inside the Saint-Saëns Hotel. Lauren's heart pounded as she ducked her head and stayed close to Cole's side while he registered at the desk. She had never seen the desk clerk before. Apparently he was new, and he showed no sign that he even noticed her. They followed the bellman to the elevator, and he punched the button for the fourth floor. She was silent all the way up, frozen with fear that when the door opened, someone would surely recognize her. When the bellman finally stopped at their room and opened the door, she felt limp with relief. So far, it was working out. Now if they could just get out of here this easily . . .

Cole tipped the bellman and closed the door. "Now, see, I was right. It's a great room."

And Lauren had to admit that it was. It was furnished with lovely English antiques, marble tables, tapestries, and a huge Victorian feather bed, topped with a filmy white canopy. This was the first time she had seen one of the guest rooms. Alex kept the whole top floor reserved at all times, the four-bedroom suite for his own use, and all the other rooms for his personal guests. She was glad that nothing looked familiar. She could wipe away all the bad memories and know that Alex had never touched any part of this room.

She flew into Cole's arms. "It's a lovely room, and I'm glad we came." She began to unbutton his shirt.

"Oh, I love you so much." His hunger mounted as his fingers found the zipper at the back of her slacks and the buttons on her blouse.

"And I love you." She said the words quietly and simply, but the love in her eyes spoke volumes. She belonged to him. No matter what happened, she was his for the rest of her life.

He kissed her gently as he finished undressing her. His eyes admired her soft, silky flesh, her face, her eyes, and her lips as his hands moved over her body. When he buried his lips in her neck, she kissed the side of his face, the lean curve of his cheekbone, and then met his sweet, hungry mouth with her own. She was surrounded by the clean scent of sun and skin as she closed her eyes, pulling him even closer to mold herself to him.

He was still kissing her when he picked her up in his arms and laid her gently on the bed. She watched as he finished removing his clothes, aching with hunger for him. He got into bed and reached out for her, and she came to him, giving herself freely and joyfully. She knew she had never loved anyone as much as she loved Cole. Lauren lost all sense of time and place, the memories of all that had happened in the past a blur. Nothing mattered except Cole, his body caressing her, arousing her, pounding her, becoming one with hers, and finally bringing her to a blessed sense of peace. They lay on the big feather bed, contented, her head nestled on his shoulder, his lips pressed to her temple.

"I love you, Lauren Compton," he whispered.

At first the full meaning of his words didn't register, and then an electric shock ran through every nerve of her body. "You know! Oh, my God, you know!" She sat upright and stared at him in disbelief.

He nodded, his eyes never leaving her face.

"But how? How long? Oh, I feel like such a fool." He reached out for her, but she shrank away. "No, you have to tell me how you found out."

"I wasn't sure until today when you told me your birthday, but I've suspected it for a long time. Why did you do it? Are you in some kind of trouble?" His voice was soft and gentle and kind, but his eyes were troubled, begging for answers. "Why did you want the world to believe you were dead?"

She felt so naked and vulnerable. Her hands shook as she reached for a blanket to cover herself. "You've suspected me for a long time? Why did you let me go on with this? You never said a word."

"Answer my questions first. Why did you pretend to be Diane Roberts? My God, I asked you to marry me, and still you didn't trust me."

"I was afraid of losing you. At first it didn't matter, I was only thinking of myself, but then I fell in love with you and I couldn't take the risk." Tears burned her eyes, and she turned her head away.

Cole reached out for her again and pulled her into his arms. "Please give me a chance." He brushed away the tears that trickled down her cheeks. "Just tell me how it happened."

"I was running away from my husband when the plane crashed, and then when I woke up, everyone was calling me Diane Roberts, and it seemed the perfect way out." The words came in a rush, and suddenly she wanted to tell him everything all at once. "I was so afraid of Alex—he would have killed me—

and then when he thought I died in the crash, I found a way to get away from him forever. Oh, Cole, I've felt so terrible all this time."

"When I was in Washington, Senator Kingsley told me you had called him, said you had evidence against Alex Compton."

She drew herself away from him. "You've known that long and let me go on with this charade? You could have asked me about it then. Can't you see how that makes me feel? All this time, you've known that I was a fraud and a liar and still you let me go on."

"I only suspected it, Lauren, you've got to believe me. But right now, I have to get to the bottom of this." He took her into his arms and gave her a gentle kiss. "If you were afraid for your life, then it's my problem, too. Did you have any kind of evidence against Compton?" His voice was soft, but she could see the worried look in his eyes.

"I had his library and his private phone bugged, and then I ran away when I listened to the tape. But he found me, and I was desperately trying to run away again. He's done some terrible things—arms shipments, extortion, even murder. And I found out names of powerful people all over the world who are involved with him." Her eyes were wide with fright, remembering how she felt the night she fled Oyster Bay.

Cole raked his fingers through his hair, his face grave. "Oh, my God—a tape! That's what it is!"

"What are you talking about?"

"I read an article in the newspaper just yesterday about new evidence found in sorting through the debris on the plane. Enough to reopen the investigation of Alex Compton's affairs. That must have been what they found. Did you have it with you?"

"Yes, in my purse. That is, Diane Roberts had it. Our bags got mixed up just before the crash, and I thought

282

the tape was destroyed." Her hands flew up to her mouth. "Oh, Cole, if Alex ever finds me, he'll kill me. What am I going to do?"

"Nothing now. You were right in doing exactly what you did, and no one could blame you. Let's give it some time, and we'll figure this out together. At least we have time on our side." He kissed her again and ran his hands up and down her back, soothing away the tension.

Lauren relaxed against him, a great sense of relief spreading all over her body. It was all finally out in the open, and everything would be all right. She was safe with Cole. He understood and he loved her, and now she would never have to face Alex alone again. She lay in his arms, more content and happy than she had been in her whole life. Cole made love to her again, and this time she knew that their lives were forever intertwined. All the barriers were finally gone. She curled up beside him and slept peacefully for the first time in years.

Shortly after five o'clock, Cole roused her with a kiss. "Wake up, Lauren." It felt so good to hear him say her name. "The car will be ready in about an hour and I'm starving. Let's go downstairs for a bite."

They quickly dressed and left the room, and Lauren drew back when the elevator door opened to take them down.

"What's wrong?" Cole asked, taking her arm.

"Remember when I tried to talk you out of coming here?"

"Well, I wondered what you had against this place."

"Alex owns the Saint-Saëns and I know most of the personnel. What if someone recognizes me?"

"Oh, damn, you're right. To think that I put you through all this and never even knew what you were going through." He kissed her and held her close. "When the door opens, keep your head down, walk

283

straight through the lobby, out the front door, and wait outside while I check out. It shouldn't take long at all, and I'll probably be there by the time they bring the car around." He kissed her again, just as the elevator door opened in the lobby.

Lauren did as Cole said, and moments later, she was standing outside, profoundly relieved. Incredibly, no one had seen her, and all her worries had been for nothing.

"Hold it right here just a moment," Alex Compton said to his driver. The limousine stopped abruptly in its approach to the entrance of the Saint-Saëns Hotel. He saw her, but he had to look twice to be sure it was Lauren. She looked different somehow. There was a softer look to her face, and her hair hung loosely just below her shoulders. She hadn't worn it so casually in years except late at night in her bedroom when she sat before her dressing table and brushed it until it shone. He was shocked that he would see her here of all places, standing right in front of his own hotel.

He stiffened with anger when the door opened and a young man walked out and hurried to stand very close to her. He watched, spellbound, as the man touched her face and she turned to look at him. He felt pain deep in his gut when he saw Lauren's face, his own wife's face, glow with yearning and adoration, a look he had never seen in all the years of their marriage. He knew beyond any doubt that the man was Cole Saunders. The bastard!

Tomorrow their love affair would come to an end.

Chapter Twenty-Six

Last night when Lauren and Cole got back to the villa, they were shocked to find Lucrezia alone in the house. While they were in Nice, Gia had received word that her daughter, Angelo's mother, had undergone emergency surgery and was in serious condition at a hospital in Rome. Lucrezia had shooed them off to the airport around noon, insisting that she could take care of herself for a few hours and that she would be in good hands with Cole and Lauren as soon as they returned.

The moment they arrived, Lauren pitched in and took over Gia's duties, glad to make herself useful. Lately, Lucrezia spent most of the time in her bedroom, and Lauren wondered how Gia, who was getting on in years, managed all she did, trotting up and down the stairs, making sure that all Lucrezia's needs were met. Fortunately, the cleaning was left to maids who came in daily, but still, managing Lucrezia's household was a full-time job.

Lauren was relieved that Gia and Angelo kept the freezer stocked with cooked food that only needed thawing or popping into the microwave. She had never learned to cook and shuddered to think how the meals would turn out if they were left entirely up to her. She had felt awkward last night preparing dinner for the first time, but everything had worked out surprisingly well. Now at four o'clock in the afternoon, she was in the kitchen again, arranging watercress finger sandwiches and little white cakes on a silver tray. Lucrezia never missed afternoon tea, having carried on the English tradition since her early days as Brewster Saunders's wife. Lauren checked to make sure she had remembered everything—sugar cubes, cream, spoons, and white linen napkins. Satisfied, she was about to carry the tray upstairs when she heard the kitchen phone. She answered on the first ring.

"Hello, Lauren, or should I say Diane?"

Lauren gripped the receiver with both hands, aching to hang up on the one person in the world she had hoped never to hear from again. Her knees buckled. There wasn't a chair within reach. She wondered if she could even speak, let alone keep him from hearing fear in her voice.

"Lauren?"

"Hello, Alex. When did you get here?" She prayed that he was calling from New York and was nowhere near the Riviera.

"Oh, so you were expecting me."

"You must be losing your touch. It took a little longer this time." She refused to allow him the upper hand. She wasn't the same woman who had stolen away in the night, afraid of her own shadow.

"Not as long as you think."

"Okay, Alex, why are you here?"

"To see you, of course. When can we meet?"

"The next time we meet will be in divorce court."

"But I was planning on taking you home."

"Go to hell!"

He chuckled. "Well, I see you've gotten a little feisty this summer. The least you can do is talk this over with me in person. You owe me that much."

"Owe you? I don't owe you a damn thing. Just what do you really want?"

"Just a little meeting."

"Forget it. I won't see you tonight or ever, except in court. Get the hell out of my life and leave me alone."

"I think you *will* see me when you hear what I have to say. You'll meet me tonight or watch Cole Saunders die."

"You bastard! Leave Cole out of this. Damn, I wish I'd thought to have this phone bugged, too, so I'd have a tape of all this. How dare you threaten Cole's life!"

"Did he tell you how close he came to dying on the coast road the other day? It would have been so easy."

"You! You were behind that! You sick fiend. I should have known." Her knees buckled again.

"I'm dead serious. Either you meet me tonight, or next time he'll be killed. Do you understand?"

Lauren felt limp with fear. She had no choice. She knew Alex didn't make idle threats. She would do anything to protect Cole, even move back into Alex's home if it came to that. It was all over—all she felt for Cole, all their plans . . . everything. She swallowed hard, determined not to let him know how frightened she felt. "All right, I'll see you. Where do you want to meet?"

"How about my suite at the Saint-Saëns, say around eight?"

"No, not there." She had to win this round. She had to stand her ground and refuse to meet him on his home turf.

"You mean after your little rendezvous yesterday, you're not ready to go back? From the look on your face, I assumed you enjoyed it."

"Why you dirty bastard!" She had been so worried that one of his employees would see her and report it

287

to Alex, and he was there all along. "So that's how you found me."

"Oh, I wouldn't say that exactly. In fact, I kept up with you pretty well in Chicago and London."

Lauren felt like a fool. Damn you, Alex! All this time, she had felt that she was finally rid of him, had carried on this stupid masquerade, kept it from Cole and Lucrezia, and Alex had been laughing at her every step of the way. "My, my, you seem to be everywhere."

"Well, you just never know when I might turn up . . . but enough of that. Let's get back to the subject at hand. What do you say, the Saint-Saëns at eight?"

"No, I won't go there, but maybe a bar or a restaurant."

"Absolutely not. It wouldn't do to be seen together in public until after we announce to the world that you've been in a hospital all this time suffering from amnesia or some other damn thing. We'll think of something. Right now, you're supposed to be dead. The hotel is the perfect place."

"I won't go there, and that's final."

He laughed. "I don't think you're in much of a position to negotiate."

Lauren knew she was walking on quicksand. It would be so like him to slam down the receiver and carry out his threat, just to prove his point that nobody defied him. But she had to take a chance. Meeting him at his hotel gave her no leeway. With his own people around, he would have her on board his plane, alive or dead, within an hour of her arrival. She searched her mind for a neutral place, one that he would agree to, and finally came up with an idea. "What about Lucrezia's International. You know, the gallery in Nice? It will be closed by then and completely private. I'll meet you there if you'll give me your word that you'll be alone." Her voice shook and she wondered if

Alex's word was worth anything at all.

He pondered her suggestion for a long time, and Lauren knew he was considering all the possibilities and trying to figure all the angles. Finally, to her surprise, he said, "All right, I'll agree to it on certain conditions. First, you, too, will be alone. Second, you'll come to Nice by cab, and, third, you won't notify the police. Understood?"

"Yes."

"Another thing, keep in mind that the place will be watched. You'll be followed, but once you're there, I'll get rid of my men. That's a promise. Don't be late." Lauren heard a click, followed by a dial tone.

For a long time, she stood with the dead receiver in her hand, too stunned to move. It was hard to comprehend the reality of the whole thing. Alex had not only found her; he had known her whereabouts all this time. He had waited this long, biding his time to find out what had happened to the tape. She felt cold all over and shook with fright. She had just signed her own death warrant. All his talk about wanting her to come home was just that. Talk. He had no more plans to resume their marriage than she did. He meant to kill her, and she had agreed to walk right into his trap. She had to figure out some way to keep from meeting him. But if she didn't go, the alternative was certain death for Cole. Alex was ingenious at putting his victims in a no-win situation. Dazed, she was unaware that Cole was standing in the doorway.

"Need some help?" he asked as he walked into the kitchen. "Why are you holding the receiver? Who's on the line?" He hurried over to her, alarmed when she didn't answer. "Lauren, what's wrong? Who called?"

She looked at the receiver, realized that it was still in her hand, and placed it back on the phone. "Alex." Her voice was low and flat.

"Oh, shit! What did he want?"

"Let's get these trays upstairs and I'll tell you and Lucrezia the whole thing together. It's time to be honest with her. I've waited far too long."

Cole's face was a mask of worry and concern. "Dammit, what did he say?"

"Just wait until we're all together. I can only go over it once."

"I don't like the sound of this at all." He picked up the heavy tray and held the door for Lauren to go ahead of him.

All the way up the stairs to Lucrezia's bedroom, Lauren prayed that she could make Lucrezia understand. How she dreaded telling this kind, generous woman that she had been deceiving her for months. But it had to be done. This could very well be her last chance.

She waited until she had poured the tea and served the sandwiches before she began. Her hands were moist with perspiration, and she began to pace the floor. "Lucrezia, there's something I need to tell you, and I don't know where to begin." She swallowed hard, bracing herself. "I'm not who you think I am. In fact, I've been lying to you all this time."

Lucrezia, who was regally clad in a rose-colored negligee bordered with ostrich feathers, reclined on a chaise longue. She glared at Lauren and set her cup on the saucer. "What do you mean, 'lying to me'?"

Lauren realized that this was going to be even harder than she had imagined, but she couldn't blame Lucrezia for any reaction she might have. She deserved her sharp tongue. "Well, to begin with, I'm not Diane Roberts."

Lucrezia pursed her lips in anger. "Not Diane? Then who the hell are you?"

"My name is Lauren Compton." She was still

walking back and forth, rubbing her palms together. "Diane was killed in the plane crash, and our identities were mixed up. It's a long story, but I'll spare you the details right now. I was running away from my husband because I knew he would kill me if he had the chance. You see, he was under a Congressional investigation, and I knew too much about him. In fact I . . ."

"Did you say your name was Compton? Alexander Compton's wife?" Lucrezia stared at her with cold, dark eyes.

Lauren nodded. "I'm sorry. I've been so unfair to you. I didn't want to go through with this, but at the time, I didn't think I had much choice. When I woke up in the hospital and realized everyone assumed that I was Diane, it seemed the perfect solution." She began to pace again.

Lucrezia turned to Cole and looked him in the eye. "How long have you known about this?"

"Just since yesterday, but I've suspected it since we got back from London. I saw Lauren's picture on television."

"Cole!" Lauren said. "And you never said a word!"

Cole stood and led Lauren to a chair beside the chaise longue. "Let's not get into that again. Sit down before you wear a hole in the carpet. I'm going crazy wanting to know what Compton had to say."

"I'll get to that in a minute, but first I've got to explain all this to Lucrezia. When I read in the newspaper that Alex had identified my body, I thought I was rid of him forever. I figured I could become Diane Roberts for a little while and then go far away and start all over and never have to be afraid of him again. I was so desperate." Lauren looked into Lucrezia's face for a sign of sympathy and support. There was none.

"There's something that doesn't add up," Lucrezia

said. "Georges knew Diane Roberts and even recommended her to me. Why didn't he expose you? He had no reason to go along with this."

Lauren looked at Cole, not knowing how to handle this, and he nodded for her to go ahead and get the whole thing out. "Remember when I told you that the person responsible for the forgeries was probably in California? Well, as it turned out . . ." She hesitated, hating to hurt Lucrezia more, and gave Cole a pleading look.

"It was Georges all along," Cole said.

Lucrezia's hands flew up to her mouth and she glared at Cole. "How could you? How absurd! This woman is married to Alexander Compton, and you'd take her word against a lifelong friend?" She shook her head. "I won't listen to this."

"Wait, Lucrezia, don't be so quick to judge Lauren until you know all the facts."

"It's true," Lauren said. "Somehow he found out that I was on to him, and he didn't dare give me away until he had a chance to threaten to expose me. It was a trade-off as far as he was concerned."

"Just what gave you the idea that Georges was involved in the first place?" Lucrezia asked. "This is preposterous." Her voice had a sharp, angry edge.

Lauren hated what they were doing to Lucrezia. She was too ill and frail to hear all of this, have her faith in a good friend destroyed. But now she had committed herself and she had gone too far not to continue. She took a deep breath and went on, "When we were in London, I was approached by a man named Felix Barrendo. He worked with Dr. Carnot, and I assume was his partner. He naturally thought I was Diane, who incidentally was part of this whole thing, too."

"My God, you're telling me that Georges sent someone to investigate the forgeries who was really

292

working against me?" Her face turned stark white. "That's not possible. Georges was only trying to help me, and if Diane Roberts had anything to do with the forgeries, I'm sure he wasn't aware of it."

"I know," Cole said, "I felt the same way, but I think you'd better hear Lauren out."

"This Felix Barrendo told me how many paintings Dr. Carnot had copied and gave me an assignment to take pictures of others," Lauren said. "Apparently, Diane . . ."

"Pictures!" Lucrezia said. "I hadn't thought of that. Of course! All this time I thought the forger had to be working with originals, but the right artist could do it with good photos."

"Barrendo took for granted that I'd be willing to make more photographs."

Lucrezia shook her head, her eyes suddenly bright with unshed tears. "Well, I'll be damned! It must have been Georges after all. I don't know of anyone who could have copied my brush strokes so well from a picture. He worked for years trying to perfect those strokes, and he came very close. Diane Roberts took the photos?"

"Apparently she had been working for him for some time. When I was in the hospital after the crash, I looked in her purse and found a brown envelope containing a huge sum of cash. I couldn't imagine why at the time, but then it all began to make sense after this meeting with Barrendo."

"It's true. It was Georges. How could my good friend be so cruel? Why did he do it? I should hate him for this, I suppose, but somehow I don't. He must have had a good reason." Lucrezia's face looked drawn and her hands were trembling. She stared at Lauren. "Why didn't you come to me with this when you first found out?"

"It all happened so fast, but I guess I was just trying to protect myself. He was the only one who could expose me as a fraud, and then, after he died, you were so upset and I didn't want to add to your grief."

"It was really my idea to keep it from you for a while," Cole said. "I was so worried about your health and thought it best at the time."

"You both forget I'm a tough old woman and able to take almost anything." Lucrezia's face softened. "Do you suppose these forgeries have anything to do with Georges's death?"

Cole shook his head. "We don't know, but I think you need to hear the rest of this. Georges was waiting for Lauren outside the auction and forced her into his car at gunpoint."

Lucrezia looked horrified. "Georges? Oh no . . ."

"Yes, he did," Cole said, "and I think he intended to kill her. He couldn't run the risk of getting caught. And then the strangest thing happened. Before he could drive away, someone came out of the shadows and shot him. Whoever it was drove his car miles from there and left his body inside."

By now, Lucrezia's face was full of compassion. She reached for Lauren's hand. "Oh, my dear, what you must have gone through. To think you might have been killed! I'm so relieved that you're the one who came to us instead of Diane Roberts. Georges could have completely ruined my reputation if you hadn't found out about him." She gave Lauren's hand a squeeze. "And I don't blame you at all for changing places with that woman. From what I've heard of Alexander Compton, you're very lucky you got away from him."

Lauren's eyes filled with tears of relief. Lucrezia not only didn't hate her, she understood. She leaned over and embraced the older woman. "I never meant for this to go on so long. I just didn't plan . . ."

"On falling in love?" Lucrezia looked at Cole and smiled. "You two must think I'm deaf and blind. I've wondered how long it would take you to get around to admitting that you adored each other."

"We just didn't know how you'd react." Lauren said.

Lucrezia smiled. "I might be seventy-two years old, but I'm not old enough to be mid-Victorian. In fact, I'm planning to live to see the two of you married."

"You'll probably live longer than I will," Lauren said. "Alex called me a few minutes ago. He's in Monte Carlo."

Lucrezia's smile turned to astonishment. "How in God's name did he find you? He thought you were dead."

"Never underestimate Alex Compton. The devil himself couldn't hide from him long. I don't know how he found me, but he did, and I've agreed to meet him tonight at the gallery in Nice."

Lauren watched a pallor steal over Cole's face, changing his suntan to a pale beige. "The hell you will! Why did you tell him that?"

"I had to." Lauren stood and began to pace again. "You need to understand that Alex always gets his own way. He didn't leave me any choice."

Cole jumped to his feet and put his arms around Lauren. "No choice? You damn well *do* have a choice. You won't go. There's no way I'd let you go near that bastard."

"But I have to go. Otherwise Alex will . . ."

"Did he threaten your life?" Cole's blue eyes blazed. "No."

"Then what threats did he make?"

"He threatened you, Cole. He'll kill you if I don't go."

295

Lucrezia's face turned stark white. "Oh, my God . . . Cole!"

"Well, to hell with that! I'll take my chances with the bastard."

"No, you don't understand. Do you realize who you're dealing with? Alex is one of the biggest crime bosses in the world."

Cole pulled her close to him. "Don't worry about me. I'm perfectly able to take care of myself."

Lauren shook her head. "Alex admitted that one of his men chased you the other night. Don't you see how easy it would be?"

"Well, I lived through that all right." He kissed her forehead and smoothed her hair away from her face. "I'm still here, so don't worry about me."

"Only because Alex just meant to scare you."

"Now why would he want to do that?"

"To prove a point, don't you see?"

"I think you should listen to Lauren," Lucrezia said. There was an edge of terror in her voice. "The man has hired killers, and all the bodyguards in the world couldn't save your life. When a person like that puts a contract out on you, you're as good as dead. Please, Cole . . . listen to her."

"She's right," Lauren said. "I'll meet with Alex and take my chances. That's all I can do."

"Then we'll go together. I won't let you face him alone."

"Oh, no. I have to go alone. If we show up together, we'll both be killed. He made that very clear. Please, Cole . . . don't insist on going. Please . . ." She would get down on her knees if she had to. Somehow she had to keep him away. But she could understand his reasoning. She felt the same way about him.

"I'll tell you what," Cole said. "I'll call the police in

296

Nice and fill them in."

Lauren clutched his arm. "No! Not the police. Alex said explicitly that the police were not to be notified."

"Well, to hell with Alex! I'm sure he doesn't want the police involved, but I'll be damned if we're going into this blind. Let's see what they come up with and go from there. That's all we can do. I'm calling them now." He jammed his clenched fists into his pockets and left the room.

For the next fifteen minutes, Lauren sat hunched up in a chair, her arms wrapped around her knees, her eyes staring at everything in the room, but seeing nothing. Lucrezia was silent, too, the pain in both women so intense, it gradually became numbness.

When Cole walked back into the bedroom, he looked somewhat relieved. "I think we've come up with something. Lucrezia, isn't there an entrance to the gallery from the store next door?"

"Yes," she said, "at the back. All the businesses in the building are connected that way."

He turned to Lauren. "Then I'll go early and enter from another building. I'll be in a back room of the gallery, but he'll never know I'm there unless I see that you're in danger."

"What about the police? He was very emphatic about that. They can't be involved."

"Here's the plan. I'll drop you off at La Fleur, a dress shop in Nice, and someone from the department will be there to wire you so they can record every word. The police will have the recorder in the store next door, so if there's trouble, they can be there in seconds. What do you think?"

"It just might work, except for one thing. Alex insisted that I go by cab, and he made it clear that I'd be followed."

"Then we'll call a cab. That's no big problem. In fact, we can probably arrange to have a policeman driving it."

Lauren threw her arms around Cole. "I think we have a solution." She couldn't help but remember the last time she had Alex recorded and all that had happened as a result. Maybe this time things would be different.

Chapter Twenty-Seven

Jason propped his foot on the bumper of his rented car and lit a cigarette. He had parked the car on the side of the road about two hundred feet from the steep drive leading to Lucrezia's villa and had been hanging around for nearly an hour. Shit, he hated these long, boring jobs. But Compton had said that his wife's cab could arrive anytime between six and eight, and it was almost seven. He could very well have another hour's wait. He had come early, a feeling in his gut telling him that Lauren Compton might have a trick up her sleeve.

Another quarter hour dragged by, and twilight was beginning to settle over the mountains. Good. It was always better to work in the darkness. He came alert suddenly, the reflection of headlights on the curve ahead bringing his senses alive. He kept his eyes trained on the road as the vehicle rounded the curve. Hot damn, it was a cab! Now maybe things would pick up.

He jumped into his car, quickly started the motor, and moved it to block the drive diagonally, then stepped out and hid himself among a clump of low evergreens a few feet away. Seconds later, the cab made its approach to the driveway and abruptly stopped. Jason grinned as the driver climbed out of his cab to inspect the offending car. He waited to make his move until the man bent to look inside the window on the driver's side. Then, with the silent movements of a mountain cat, he crept toward the driver, raised his arm, and cracked him on the back of the head with the butt of his gun. The bastard never knew what hit him as he crumpled to the ground. Jason prided himself on his efficiency, and this was one damned clean hit.

Jason quickly rolled him over. The man was alive, but definitely in never-never land. He went through his pockets and pulled out a wallet, some loose change and keys, and a small black case. He smiled as he opened it. So this was Lauren Compton's trick. The bastard was a goddamned cop. This put some spice in a job that could have been no more than routine. Hell, it was downright rewarding.

He wasted no time in dragging the limp, heavy man across the road to the edge of the steep cliff, the waves of the Mediterranean Sea crashing against the rocks far below. He pulled the man to his feet, balancing him with his arms to teeter on the edge, and then let go. The cop sailed like a silent bird and finally landed on the jagged rocks. It was a beautiful sight. Jason could have stood there another hour enjoying his latest achievement. There was nothing quite as exhilarating as killing a cop. But time was growing short.

He ran back to his car and drove it off the road, up the side of the hill, hidden from view behind a growth of low bushes and trees. Then he made his way back to the cab and positioned himself behind the wheel. Hell, he never knew from one day to the next what his job with Compton would bring. Now he was a goddamned cabbie.

Jason pulled up the drive, stopped in front of the main house, and honked the horn. He was impatient to bring this job to a close, move on to something new.

This game Compton was playing with his wife was getting old. It had gone on too damned long. He waited a few more minutes and honked the horn again. Shit! What could be keeping the bitch?

The door opened and Lauren Compton appeared just before Jason sounded the horn again. She hurried to the cab and climbed into the backseat. Goddamn, she was a good-looking dame. He picked up the tension in her as soon as she sat down. Too bad she was Compton's wife. All this time he had tailed her, his loins had ached for a chance to give her just one good screwing, and tonight she would be dead. Damned shame.

"Where to, ma'am?"

"Oh good, you speak English," she said. "You don't have to pretend with me. I've been told you're a policeman, and I can't tell you how relieved I am that you're here. I suppose you know to take me to La Fleur."

Jason nodded and smiled. Stupid, gullible people like this Compton dame were no challenge at all. It took some of the fun out of it. He turned the cab around, down the steep drive to the coast road. He didn't have the vaguest idea where the hell La Fleur was, or what it was, for that matter. This could present a problem. He naturally assumed that he'd take her to the gallery downtown. Those were his instructions. But what the hell, he'd figure out something.

He was sorry that Lauren Compton was in no mood to talk. He could probably get some information out of her. He couldn't blame her, though. She was obviously nervous. The perfume she wore almost drove him out of his mind. Damn! He couldn't pass up a chance like this. If things went according to plan, she'd be back in the cab a little after eight, and from then on, she was all his. He would have himself a juicy little piece of Lauren

Compton before he killed her. Compton would never know. Just thinking about it filled him with so much pleasure he felt real pain.

The drive to the outskirts of Nice took only ten minutes, and Jason didn't have a clue as to which direction to take. Maybe Lauren Compton was too preoccupied to notice. Shit, he had no choice but to ask.

"You'll have to direct me to this La Fleur place. Can't say I've ever been there."

"I can understand that since it's a dress shop," she said. "It's in the center of town, and you'll need to turn left at the first traffic light."

Jason did as he was told, followed her directions, and finally stopped at the curb in front of a fancy, expensive-looking store.

"I don't think this will take too long, if you don't mind waiting." She opened the car door and rushed inside the shop.

Jason sat in the cab, his eyes intent on the store windows. The shop was well lighted, and he could see Lauren looking through the racks, pulling out garments. "Well, I'll be damned," he muttered. The stupid bitch was shopping for clothes. Women! Here she was, minutes away from a premature death, and she was picking out new outfits. He didn't take his eyes off the window for a second, and the next thing he knew, she was headed toward the back, carrying the dresses. It was the damnedest thing he'd ever seen. She was going into a dressing room to try on some goddamned clothes. This one topped them all.

Cole reached inside the desk drawer, pulled out a small revolver, and filled the chamber with bullets. He had bought the gun five years ago, feeling at the time that Lucrezia needed some protection in the isolated villa. It had remained in the drawer all this time, and as far as he knew, it had never been fired. He slipped the gun into the breast pocket of his jacket and hoped that it would not be needed.

Watching Lauren leave in the cab had been the hardest thing he had ever done. At least she wouldn't have to face Alex Compton all by herself. He had done the best he could to cover all the angles, but a feeling that something could go wrong kept gnawing deep in the pit of his stomach. A man with Compton's reputation and his vast network of resources was not so easily duped. He felt sure that Compton had figured every possible scenario. He realized he was hanging all his hopes on Compton's not knowing that the buildings on the block were connected on the inside.

It was seven-fifteen now, and Cole figured that Lauren was in the process of getting rigged to record the meeting. They should be finished well before eight. If he left now, he would have plenty of time to get himself positioned at the back of the gallery before she arrived.

He left the house through the back door and made his way to the garage. As soon as he pulled out the key to unlock the side door, he knew something was wrong. It was already open. He felt the hairs on the back of his neck stand on end. He had locked the door himself as he always did. Lucrezia insisted on it, and he agreed. The property was too remote not to take precautions. He stepped inside, his hand touching the revolver, his eyes scanning every square foot of the four-car garage. Nothing seemed amiss. Whoever had been here earlier was gone. He pressed the button to raise the main door automatically and sat down in his Porsche and inserted the key to start the car. There was only a click, no sign that the motor would even turn over. "Damn!" He hopped out and ran to open the hood. "You sonovabitch!" Every wire had been severed. He knew even before he looked that the same was true of the other two cars—the limousine and Lucrezia's black Mercedes. Compton had figured all the angles all right, the first being to leave him stranded without transportation, miles from Nice. At least there was still time to call a cab.

He ran back to the house and picked up the phone in the kitchen. No dial tone. "Shit!" Frantically, he clicked the receiver, knowing full well that the line had been cut. Beads of perspiration popped out on his upper lip. Compton had gone to extremes to keep him away from the gallery. No doubt he assumed that the police were in on this, too, and had taken measures to prevent their intervention. It was possible that Lauren had no protection at all. He should never have let her go. Damn, they were no better than babes going up against a master of crime. He felt sick all over. Lauren's life was in jeopardy.

His only hope of making it to Nice in time was to find a motorist on the coast road willing to stop and give him a ride. He quickly left the house and was halfway down the long drive when he abruptly stopped. He was playing right into Compton's hands and leading himself right into a trap. Flagging down a car was the natural thing to do in a situation like this. No doubt Compton had a car lying in wait for him. He had to think of something else. And quick. It was already seven-thirty. The closest house was about a quarter of a mile away, through rugged terrain, if he went the back way. He could be there in ten minutes if he hurried. The house was owned by a family named Donatti, who lived in Milan. They used the villa for a vacation place. He had to hope that they were home.

He ran in the opposite direction, turned left at the

top of the drive, and cut through the wild growth of trees and vines. There was no trail on the side of the mountain, and Cole fought desperately to keep his bearings and head in the right direction. By now, darkness was settling over the area, and the ground was covered with jutting rocks. He felt that an eternity had gone by before he caught sight of the Donattis' villa in the shadows. The house was completely dark, and Cole's heart sank. He ran to the door and banged with his fists, knowing full well that the house was unoccupied, but hoping against hope that he was wrong.

Cole wracked his brain, frantically searching for another solution, and then it came to him. If the Donattis had left for Milan, they had probably set the burglar alarm. That was it! It was worth a try. He stepped back, picked up a large stone, and hurled it through a front window. Instantly, the sound of the alarm echoed all around him. He sat down on the stone steps and waited. The police would arrive within minutes and help him get to Nice. But time was running out. There was no hope now of getting to the gallery by eight.

The minutes dragged by as Jason waited, his eyes still on the store windows, his patience gone. The dame had been in there forty-five minutes, and it was already a quarter to eight. Just at that moment, he caught sight of her walking through the store and heading for the door, empty-handed. Damn, if it wasn't about time. And to top it off, she hadn't bought a frigging thing. Women!

Lauren opened the back door of the cab and climbed inside. "Thanks for waiting. I had no idea it would take so long. I guess it's about time to go to Lucrezia's

305

International and get this over with. Know where that is?"

"You bet I do," he said, and within minutes, he delivered her to the door of the gallery. "I'll be right here waiting," he said, grinning.

"Thanks. I can't tell you how much better I feel knowing you're so close."

Jason watched her backside as she unlocked the door of the gallery. Hot damn! She had one pretty ass. And very soon it would be his for the taking.

As soon as Lauren opened the door and walked inside the dark gallery, she knew that Alex was already there, waiting for her. The scent of his pipe was sickeningly familiar. Everything seemed to be happening in slow motion, as though a replay of an earlier event were taking place. She realized that this was the final closing of a full circle in her life. After months of being on the other side of the mirror, she had stepped back through and was no longer Diane Roberts, but Lauren again, in the same room with Alex Compton once more. Her fear of meeting him grew so strong that she ached to turn and run. But Cole's life was at stake. She had no choice. Every muscle in her body tensed as she took a deep breath and switched on the lights.

There Alex sat in an upholstered chair just inside the reception area. The fact that he didn't bother to rise warned Lauren of the degree of his rage. He looked as distinguished as ever, dressed in a dark, conservative business suit, every silver hair on his head immaculately in place. The sensual mouth that had attracted her years ago looked cruel and merciless, yet he managed the semblance of a smile. Everything about him frightened her, but she was determined not to let him know she was afraid.

306

"Well, hello again, Lauren." There was a challenge even in his greeting, giving her notice that he still had the upper hand, that nothing had changed.

"Hello, Alex. Doing your own lock-picking these days?"

He gave her a humorless smile. "You should know by now that there's no lock that can keep me from what I want." He motioned toward a chair. "Sit down and let's talk. It's been a long time, but then, you've been dead all summer, I keep forgetting."

"You've never forgotten a thing in your whole miserable life." Lauren passed up the chair he suggested and took a seat facing him, glad to relieve her shaking legs.

"Well, I see you've developed a little spunk these past months. It becomes you." Before she could answer, he added, "This getting laid regularly by your new British boyfriend seems to agree with you." His voice was cold and harsh. "How about showing me some of your new moves in our bed?"

Lauren's green eyes flashed. How does he know all this? Who's been keeping him informed? Her skin crawled, just thinking of what he was capable of doing to her. She had been such a fool to think she had gotten away from him. *"Our* bed? Don't flatter yourself. Your bed will be behind steel bars very soon, and I have no intention of joining you there." Her voice never quavered, but her heart pounded so loudly that she was afraid it would affect the wires under her jacket. The wires! She had to get him to admit guilt at every chance. "How long have you been here?" she asked, hoping to change the subject.

"Long enough."

His words could very well have a double meaning, and she felt suddenly frantic. Cole! Of course, Alex would have his men search the gallery, check everything out before she arrived. Oh, Lord, they could have found Cole and killed him! They had thought they were so clever with all their plans to get the best of Alex, and he had been giant steps ahead of them all the way. Maybe they hadn't found him. The police were right next door. Surely they would have heard any sort of search and commotion and intervened. She had to believe this. *Cole can't be dead. I won't let him be dead.*

"So tell me, how have you been?" he asked. "You look even more beautiful than ever."

"Believe me, every moment away from you was sheer pleasure." She stood and turned her back to him. She couldn't stand to look at his face. "Okay, I didn't agree to meet with you to trade barbs. What do you want?"

"What I want," he said, "is to take my wife home with me."

Lauren swung around to face him once more. "I'll see you in hell first."

His laughter sent a chill through her. It had that menacing, terrifying sound that she remembered so well, a sound that gave notice that he could eliminate anyone who dared to cross him. "Oh, come on, I could have had you picked up anytime in the past few months, and surely you know it."

Lauren thought about the wires fastened to her chest, the police next door, listening to and recording every word. She had nothing so far. Somehow she had to prod him into speaking of his business affairs. If she didn't get something out of him soon, they would consider her a fool. Alex was a respected member of this community. He had endowed the local hospital, was a property owner, and was instrumental in kicking off a drive to build a new library. She had to get some concrete proof, verbal admissions of his illegal dealings.

She looked him in the eye. "Surely you knew before I

308

came here that I'd never go back with you. Why did you want this meeting? I came because you threatened Cole Saunders's life. Did you really mean to kill him?"

"He'd already be dead if you hadn't come. I don't make idle threats."

Lauren felt relieved. Not only did the police hear his admission of a death threat, but it sounded like Cole was still alive. "Okay, spit it out. What do you want from me?" Her courage was mounting, and her voice was cold.

"You're in too big of a hurry, and I'm enjoying looking at you. I can't wait to get you home and—"

"Go to hell! You can stop all that right now, or I'm leaving. This conversation is turning my stomach."

Alex's attitude changed immediately. Lauren knew he wasn't used to this lack of respect. "All right, down to business, if that's how you want it. Tell me, what exactly is on the tape you made—the one in government hands, thanks to your stupidity."

"You'll find out in court!" She started for the door. "If that's all you wanted, you've got your answer."

"Wait just a goddamned minute. Don't get fresh with me. Where the hell do you think you're going?"

Lauren faced him, her eyes green fire. "Or what?"

"Or you'll wind up the way you should have when your plane blew up." He was livid with anger.

She looked at him in horror. "You bastard! Do you mean you tried to kill me by putting a bomb on Flight 333?"

"Yes, goddamn it, I did! I couldn't let you live once Trudy found out you had that tape on the plane."

Lauren shook her head, suddenly sick all over. "You're more of a monster than I thought." Shivers of revulsion wracked her body. She forgot about the wires, forgot everything but the horrors before the crash . . . screams that still woke her in the middle of the night . . . screams that she'd tried to block out to go on. To go on by using a false identity that she thought would save her life, a life that shouldn't have survived the explosion after all. It was a joke on Alex that she was still alive.

"Yes, I killed all those people just to destroy you and that damned tape," he said between clenched teeth. "What did they mean to me, those people? They were only ants to be controlled by men with brains and power. The contents of that tape could have been the end of worldwide enterprises, stock-market manipulations . . ."

"You fiend! Alex, you're mad." She sank back down in her chair. "And I thought I knew all about you."

"Now you know why you're here. What do you think you found out on that tape?" Alex was still on his feet, glaring down at her.

Lauren felt there must be enough recorded already, but she felt a sense of doom. Alex wouldn't let her live beyond this meeting. He would win after all. Still, she had to go on, in spite of her imminent death, had to get proof for the authorities so he would be put away forever. "Okay, if you want some specifics, there's enough evidence to send you and your friends to jail for the rest of your lives."

"For instance?" His eyes had that hard, menacing glint, a sign of danger to anyone who dared to threaten him, a sign that violence could erupt in him any second. She knew that look so well and winced, reliving the pain his fists had caused her, remembering with renewed grief the end of the life of the child growing inside her.

"I know names, important names of people all over the world who are part of your operation." She felt defiant. If this were to be the end of her own life, it would not be in vain. She would take Alex with her.

"Operation? Just what kind of operation?"

"Aw, come on, do you really want me to spell it out? Illegal arms shipments to the Middle East, to name one, and Central America. And then there's the shipment of drugs out of Colombia, hijacking, loan sharking, extortion . . . even murder. Oh, Alex, believe me, I know plenty. I know that you order murders of people as casually as you'd order dinner."

He smiled. "And you think you can prove all this?"

"Yes."

"You're lying, you little bitch. You don't have an ounce of proof."

"Oh, no? It's all on the tape. It's funny isn't it? You're going to prison because you wouldn't give me a divorce. That's all I wanted. The dates are all there. One specifically cites the time when thousands of arms were stolen from the government and shipped to Third World revolutionaries."

Alex's eyes glinted as he reached out to grab her by the lapel of her jacket, and jerked her to her feet. He raised a clenched fist, and she could almost feel the stabbing pain of his blow. She jerked away from him, her eyes full of hatred. "Get your hands off me, you bastard! Don't even think about hitting me or there'll be another charge against you. I don't think you can afford any more trouble. Just wait until the committee hears all about your money laundering schemes and the phony businesses you and your friends hide behind."

"You'll never live to tell all this." He had a murderous look about him, a crazed look, as he ranted on, laughing. "You're the cause of more deaths than you know of. Once you bugged that library, the dominoes began tumbling down and down. First it was the airplane, but I couldn't stop there." He was gaining a strange kind of confidence, and his voice became more calm. "There was a nurse, too. Can't think of her name offhand . . . Isabel something or other."

"Isabel Scott? What did she have to do with this? My God, did you kill her, too?"

"She had to die," he said as lightly as though speaking of the weather. "She knew you were alive, and I wanted to keep you dead for a while. The same was true of that woman at the gallery in Chicago."

"Lydia Patterson!" Lauren was horrified, sick to think she had married him, lived with him, let him make love to her. She felt dirty all over. "You filthy bastard! You're even worse than I ever imagined."

He smiled. "In a way you owe my hit man a vote of thanks. He's not all bad, you know. He even saved your life once. Remember the doctor?"

She nodded, too stunned to answer, conditioned at this point to realize that Alex was capable of the worst things imaginable. Her only consolation was that Alex's every word, his every admission, was being captured on tape. How ironic this whole thing was. It had all started with a recording, and he was hanging himself with another one.

"So you see, Lauren, you can't blame me for any of this. You caused it all with your goddamned snooping."

"You're even sicker than I thought if you believe that. Prison would be too good for you. You belong in hell."

"Well, you see, you have no proof, and as far as I'm concerned, this conversation never took place. I have twenty witnesses who'll swear that I'm on board a yacht with them in the middle of the Mediterranean this very minute."

"I've got to get out of here, as far away from you as I possibly can. The very sight of you makes me feel contaminated."

"You're free to leave anytime," he said. "Your cab

is waiting."

Lauren could hardly believe what she was hearing. She grabbed her purse from the chair and headed straight for the door and stopped just before she opened it. "So help me God, Alex Compton, I hope I never have to lay eyes on you again."

"Go ahead, Lauren, get in the cab."

When she turned the knob, an alarm blared in her head. This was too easy. Alex would never willingly let her leave here alive after what he had told her. Something was wrong. Alex didn't do his own killing. He left that kind of dirty work to others and kept his own hands clean. And then it came to her. The cab! He was too eager to get her inside the cab. The driver could be one of his men, not a policeman at all. She was trapped. The police were in a back room in the building next door, and she stood between Alex and his own man. *Oh, God! Where is Cole?* Surely he wouldn't let her leave like this. Surely he could see the trap that Alex had set for her. She felt frantic. Suddenly she turned around, brushed past him, and ran with all her heart and soul toward the back of the gallery.

"Cole! Help me, Cole! Cole . . ."

At that moment, voices echoed from the back, and she could hear the rushing sounds of footsteps. Thank God.

"You bitch! You brought the police!" Alex raised his gun and fired, taking dead aim at Lauren's back.

She stopped, frozen for a second, and fell in a heap on the floor.

Alex took one look, realized she was dead, and rushed out the door to the waiting cab.

Chapter Twenty-Eight

Limousine after limousine stopped in front of New York's Plaza Hotel, delivering everyone who mattered in Alex Compton's eyes, from stars of the movies, stage, and TV, to politicians, bankers, and corporate giants. They had all turned out for what was sure to be remembered as the party of the year. Yes, the stars were shining brightly, not only in the sky, but in the ballroom of this hotel. Only klieg lights were missing.

Alex glowed, reveling in his importance, as he greeted his guests. The news that the Senate committee had canceled its investigation into his alleged criminal activities had sent him into a continuous high, and, by God, he intended to celebrate and serve notice that Alex Compton was still invincible.

All the monies he had spent over the years to buy powerful political figures had been well spent, Alex thought with a smile. John Murray had come through and had managed to get his hands on Lauren's tape of his library and erase key sections that the committee had been counting on. Yes, by God, he was truly invincible. No one could touch him, not even the United States Senate.

He thought of his wife and laughed out loud, then

greeted still another famous movie star. He kissed her hand as the media cameras clicked away. Last June when Lauren's death in the plane crash was announced, the news had flashed around the world. But Diane Roberts's recent murder in Nice, France, hadn't caused so much as a ripple in the Mediterranean Sea.

His extravagance tonight was deliberately prodigious. He intended to outspend the most self-indulgent wastrel. Guests served themselves from three bars and danced to two shifts of New York's most popular orchestras. Tuxedo-clad waiters carried huge trays of hors d'oeuvres in and out of chatting groups of the world's Beautiful People, and every conceivable delicacy burdened banquet tables, decorated with ice molds and exquisite tropical flowers.

"You said you'd do it, and you did, sweetie." Iris Saunders tossed her red head in admiration. "I agree with you, screw them all! Oh, my God, speaking of screwing, look at that general with my best model."

It pleased Alex no end that Cole Saunders's ex-wife had agreed to serve as his hostess for the evening and would be in his bed very soon. There was a kind of poetic justice involved here, he thought. After all, Cole had slept with Lauren all summer . . . that is, until her death. He couldn't keep from smiling. The world was still his.

"You look especially handsome when you smile. You should try it more often." Before Alex could reply, Iris was off, calling over her shoulder, "I'd better break up that little twosome. Can't have the general proposing to my chicklet before our next issue goes to press!"

As the evening wore on, the music blared louder and louder. Alex headed a table of the most prominent guests in the room. He gloated as important people proposed toast after toast in his honor.

Suddenly, complete silence filled the ballroom. Musicians stopped playing. People stopped talking. It was as though a plug had been pulled and everyone was too shocked to react.

Then came a rasping noise from unseen loudspeakers, followed by: YOU BASTARD! ARE YOU SAYING THAT YOU WERE RESPONSIBLE FOR THE CRASH OF FLIGHT 333? The voice belonged to Lauren Compton, and murmurs rippled through the room.

YES, GODDAMN IT I AM! I COULDN'T LET YOU LIVE ONCE TRUDY FOUND OUT YOU HAD THAT TAPE ON THE PLANE. Gasps went up, followed by silence, people too stunned to speak.

YOU'RE MORE OF A MONSTER THAN I THOUGHT.

YES, I KILLED ALL THOSE PEOPLE JUST TO DESTROY YOU AND THAT DAMNED TAPE. WHAT DID THEY MEAN TO ME, THOSE PEOPLE? THEY WERE ONLY ANTS TO BE CONTROLLED BY MEN WITH BRAINS AND POWER. THE CONTENTS OF THAT TAPE COULD HAVE BEEN THE END OF WORLD-WIDE ENTERPRISES, STOCK-MARKET MANIPULATIONS . . .

By now, Alex realized that by some insane hoax, he was hearing his own voice admitting horrors never meant to be told. He rose from his chair and flung it behind him in rage. "Turn that damned thing off! Where the hell is it coming from?" His guests, filled with fear and excitement, sat mesmerized, and no one else moved.

. . . THERE WAS A NURSE, TOO. CAN'T THINK OF HER NAME OFFHAND . . . ISABEL SOMETHING OR OTHER.

ISABEL SCOTT? MY GOD, DID YOU KILL

HER, TOO?

SHE HAD TO DIE.

Alex Compton was a man obsessed. He ran about the room like a crazed animal, pulling at his hair, searching, searching for the source of the voices on the loudspeakers. His own words were sending him to death row. How could this be? Who knew that he had admitted all this to Lauren? The goddamned bitch had tricked him! But she was dead, and no one could prove a thing. He would deny it all. He had an airtight alibi. Twenty people or more would swear that he was with them on a yacht in the middle of the Mediterranean. Dazed, he looked around the room for some kind of support.

THE SAME WAS TRUE OF THAT WOMAN IN THE GALLERY IN CHICAGO.

YOU KILLED LYDIA PATTERSON! YOU BASTARD! YOU'RE EVEN WORSE THAN I EVER IMAGINED. The voice was still unmistakably Lauren's.

Iris Saunders rose from her chair and shuddered as she gave Alex a contemptible look and quietly left the room. The mayor and his wife left by a side exit.

REMEMBER THE DOCTOR WHO TRIED TO KILL YOU?

"Enough! Enough!" Alex picked up a bottle of wine and crashed it against the wall. "Turn that thing off! I killed you, you bitch. Where are you? I'll do it again!" But the tape played over and over, continually repeating the admissions by his own voice.

The guests acted much like a group trained in filing out of a burning building. They gathered their belongings and left in stunned silence in an orderly fashion.

Police appeared from nowhere and surrounded the ballroom, while two plainclothes policemen quietly clamped handcuffs on a bewildered Alex Compton.

Standing in the doorway, observing the whole thing, Cole looked at Lauren and smiled. "More champagne, my love?"

"Why not? I can't think of a better reason to celebrate."

They raised their glasses in a toast to the end of a nightmare. Lauren's green silk gown didn't quite conceal the remains of bandages on her left shoulder. Around her neck she wore a magnificent emerald necklace, an engagement gift from Cole.

As the police ushered Alex past them, he screamed, "You? Alive? But I shot you. You were dead!"

Lauren barely glanced at him. "You always thought you were invincible, but you see, you never were."

Once he was gone, Lauren looked at Cole, her face glowing with happiness and satisfaction, and raised her glass once more. "To us, darling. That bastard is finally out of my life."

"Amen!" Cole leaned down and planted a kiss on the tip of her nose. "How's your shoulder holding up?"

"It's fine, just fine. You know, it was worth getting shot to have this revenge. Maybe my soul is a bit rusty—I loved every minute of Alex's agony!" Lauren's eyes shone with love for the man at her side. "I can't wait to get back to Lucrezia. What she wouldn't give to have been here! She'll eat up every last detail of this night. Her idea worked out perfectly."

"Yes, and she's promised to stay alive until we can get married. Want to bet that she makes it?"